DAIMON HIGH BOOK ONE

CLAIRE

DAIMON HIGH BOOK ONE

CLAIRE

L.K. BASTIAN

Large House Press

Cover Design by Novak Illustrations

Interior: Lange House Press

ISBN: 978-1-944137-19-9

CHAPTER ONE

"Watch it, Claire," Jax scowled at me.

I rubbed my knee, standing while Jax wiped his pant leg as if he thought I'd gotten it dirty. I looked at the freshman still on the floor.

"Trying to help a loser?" Jax shifted his foot and toppled the stack of books I'd just helped the kid with. "Oops." He grinned at his buddies. "You know, you shouldn't leave books in the middle of the hallway. It's rude."

My dad is gonna kill me for this. I grabbed all one hundred ninety-five pounds of the quarterback with all one hundred five pounds of me and slammed him into the locker with little effort. Only great restraint kept me from bringing my knee up to his groin. Instead, I slammed his back into the locker a second time, making sure the handle dug into the soft spot near his kidney.

Silence enveloped the hallway as news of my actions spread. The usual din of hundreds of students disappeared as surprised looks replaced conversation. I tried to loosen my fingers, but my body didn't want to let go. My mind battled between rational thought and a desire to hurt him.

"Don't ever do that again," I growled through clenched teeth, feeling an unfamiliar vibration deep in my throat.

The look on Jax's face was frightened. *Of me?* I looked around the circle of his buddies surrounding us. They were silent as they stared. I couldn't understand why they didn't give him a hard time about getting beaten up by a girl. I glanced at the freshman. He averted his eyes and gathered his books before disappearing into the crowd.

I loosened my hold on Jax's shirt and yanked my hands away in disgust. In truth, I was disgusted with myself.

I bent down to my bag and when I stood, blue eyes stared at me. Paul's shocked expression stabbed me in the heart. We hadn't spoken in months though we'd been best friends for years before that. I scooped up my bag and stormed off down the hall. The crowd parted in front of me as if wanting to avoid a disease. Or maybe they were worried I'd slam them into the walls too if they didn't move fast enough. It was possible, given my mood.

I ducked my head and picked up my pace. Kegan fell into step with me, but he didn't say a word as he adjusted his wire-frame glasses. His presence was calming. I smiled to let him know I appreciated it. He nodded and just kept pace with me.

From the corner of my eye, I could see the new principal watching. I clenched my teeth and looked directly at her. *No sense in postponing the inevitable. She'll call my parents and Dad will up the number of sessions with my shrink.*

She smiled briefly as if she were amused and turned away without a word. My heart thudded with unused adrenaline. The click of her high heels on the tile floor grew fainter as she walked away.

"Did you see that?" I asked.

Kegan shook his head. "See what?"

"Quinn just smiled at me. I'm sure she saw what happened. If it were still Mr. Beagly, I'd be in detention now."

"He sent you there a lot?" Kegan looked me up and down. "What kind of girl were you before I moved here?"

I winked at him. "The worst kind ever."

He raised his eyebrows. "Ooh, do tell."

"Let's just say I have a temper." I glanced back down the hallway, half expecting to see the crowd still there.

Kegan leaned over and whispered, "By the way, that was awesome."

I stared at him, surprised but pleased at his comment.

"Jax looked completely freaked. He needed to be brought down a peg or two. Maybe next time he'll be more careful who he messes with."

"Yeah, he'd better." I elbowed him playfully, thinking of how Jax always bullied anyone who didn't fit the popular mold. The squeaky shoes of an office aide approaching us made me turn. "Looks like I've gotten my summons to detention anyway."

Kegan shook his head in sympathy. "That sucks."

The aide handed me a slip of paper and then gave one to Kegan. I stared at it. "Why him?"

"I just deliver 'em," he said before turning away.

***

"Denise, what are you doing in here?" a short redhead asked the gorgeous blonde sitting across from her as Kegan and I walked into the detention room.

"No idea, Kat. This note told me to show up for the last ten minutes of class." Denise popped her gum as she looked around the room. When her eyes caught mine, she looked away quickly. They didn't stay on Kegan's much longer, but her cheeks flushed.

"Same here." Kat waved her paper like a fan. She looked at Kegan. "How about you?"

"Yeah," he said. "We both did."

Kat turned to the other girl in the room, who held her paper up. She wiggled it without looking at any of us, her eyes on a notebook full of doodles.

"She's got one, too," Denise announced.

"No kidding," I said, slipping into a desk.

"Get over yourself, Claire," Denise said.

The door opened, cutting off my response. Mrs. Jones entered, limping slightly and clutching a brown clipboard in her stubby hands. Scratching her hairy upper lip, she tossed the clipboard onto Denise's desk. "Sign the roll. Principal Quinn will be here in a moment, so don't give me any trouble."

She did a headcount, eyes widening when she saw me. "Hey, Claire," Mrs. Jones said. "Haven't seen you in here for a while. I thought you'd cleaned up your act. What'd you do now?"

"Ha." I rolled my eyes. "I'm surprised you haven't heard." I handed her the note and so did the others.

Mrs. Jones shuffled through them all. "You all have the same note, but it says nothing about the rule you violated." She limped to her desk at the back of the room and opened a worn paperback romance novel. She always had one of those while she endured her time as warden.

Denise wrapped her manicured fingers around the clipboard as she shook her long blonde hair back out of her face. She signed her name, slid gracefully out of her chair, and presented the roll to me like it was something important. I watched her smile at Kegan, who ignored her. Not many guys could.

I scratched my signature under her swirling cursive and then leaned back while Kegan signed it. I took it and lobbed it two aisles, to the quiet girl sitting there without ruffling the paper. She caught it, barely. Everyone looked at me, eyes wide. They were definitely new to detention.

Kat twisted her wild curls into a bun and shoved a pencil through to hold it tight. She leaned across the desk separating her from the quiet girl and took the clipboard. She signed her name, stood up, leaned over the desk between us, and handed the clipboard back to me, apparently trying to show me how I should have done it.

I set the clipboard on the floor and kicked it so it slid back to Mrs. Jones. She stopped it with her foot without even taking her eyes off her book. I smirked at Kat. She shook her head, but a faint smile pulled at the corner of her mouth.

Why is Kat in here? Maybe she'd gotten in trouble for freeing the mice from the science lab. She had started the recycling programs at school and run a petition for a vegetarian option at lunch. I'd even signed it though I loved meat. The redder the better.

"You're Emily, right?" Kat whispered to the quiet girl. "Don't we have a class together?"

Emily eyed Kat up and down. She nodded and mumbled, "Biology."

"Oh, that's right," Kat said. "I knew I'd seen you before."

Emily went back to her doodling. I looked at the clock, noting we'd been in here four minutes already. Where was Quinn and what would it take to keep her from telling my parents? They had enough ammunition against me.

"Do you think this is because of Jax?" Kegan whispered.

"Why are you all in here then? I've never seen them in here before."

Kegan shrugged and looked as clueless as I felt.

"So are you still with Blake?" Kat asked Denise.

"Yeah, he's great," Denise said with a lovesick sigh. "Kind of got tired of the jock type and figured I'd try a new flavor. He's in the drama club and loves to recite lines to me." Denise smiled and fiddled with her earring. "It's always nice to have a little conversation with a guy now and then."

"Nice to talk to someone intelligent, or nice to talk instead of just making out?" Kat asked.

Denise giggled. "A little of both, I guess." She licked her lips as if remembering something delicious.

"Ugh," I groaned. "Don't you have any class?" I glared at her as years of hatred flared up inside.

"What's the matter, Claire? Jealous?" Denise sneered.

Fighting the urge to growl at her, I smiled sweetly. "Not at all. You're not my type."

Emily snorted a laugh, surprising me since I'd almost forgotten she was here. Kat tried to hide a smile. Kegan bumped knuckles with me.

"You're jealous, I know it." Denise narrowed her eyes. "You wanted one of my boys, but he never fell for you. Which one was he?"

"Shut up," I snapped, trying not to think of Paul.

"I'm sure there has to be at least one who'd give you the time of day."

"I don't want your leftovers!" I lunged forward, wanting to rip out her hair, but I stopped myself just before making contact. I clenched my fists and tried to hide them under the desk, shocked I'd just done that.

Denise reared back at my response. Kegan's eyes looked huge when I peeked at him. Even Mrs. Jones glanced up from her book.

"Knock it off, Claire," Mrs. Jones said. "You know better than that." She returned to her imaginary love interest.

I ground my teeth together, not wanting her to know what she said was so close to the truth. She'd used my best friend for her dating pleasure and dumped him in less than three weeks. He'd tried to resume our friendship even though he knew how much I despised Denise. I hadn't spoken to him all summer. I wasn't ready to forgive him for his betrayal.

I closed my eyes and started the breathing exercises Dr. Lowe had taught me — in through the nose to the count of ten, out through the mouth. It took me about a minute and a half to get my heart rate back down. Eventually I was calm enough to look around the room again.

Kegan had his head on the desk, almost asleep. I smiled. The only way I'd survived the loneliness was because Kegan had moved to town. We immediately hit it off, though there was nothing romantic in our relationship. He was just the coolest guy ever: smart, charming, cute, funny, even though his obsession with Star Wars was a little annoying. The fact that he wouldn't give Denise the time of day made him all the more perfect.

Denise and Kat hadn't said a word during my breathing. I knew they'd been watching me the whole time. I rolled my eyes and glanced away, focusing instead on Emily.

It was kind of hard to get a feel for her. Thick, long, black bangs nearly covered her gray eyes. She leaned back in a relaxed position in the hard desk, with her flip-flops poking out. *I thought those were against the dress code?* Her figure was hard to be sure of, by the way she sat, but she looked healthy, if just a little plump.

She looked nothing like Denise sitting up in front of me. Tall and thin, she was co-captain of the cheer squad. She was also a straight-A student, popular with everyone, and most likely to be voted Homecoming Queen, even though she was only a junior like the rest of us. It was disgusting how she had so many guys after her. When she broke up with one, she had another lined up within minutes.

And no one complained about her. They all acted like it was such a privilege to have been one of her "guys." I'd talked it over with Kegan once and neither one of us could figure out her attraction. Even the girls in school worshiped her. Just having Denise smile at you apparently marked you as special.

Denise never smiled at me.

I'd known her since we were five. Our parents moved into houses on opposite ends of the same street around the same time and met at a park soon after. They thought it was fate. Their daughters, both without siblings, would grow up to be best friends. Good thing they finally stopped forcing us to play together during the summer between fourth and fifth grade. I'd have probably strangled her by now.

Kat shifted in her seat to face Mrs. Jones. "Why are we here? I didn't do anything detention worthy."

"You were called in here by Principal Quinn," Mrs. Jones said.

"Obviously, but where is she?" Denise asked.

"She'll be here when she's ready." Mrs. Jones didn't even look up from her book.

I fought the urge to grind my teeth and started my breathing again. Denise glared at me over her shoulder as if my breathing bothered her, so I breathed louder. Just looking at her made my hair stand on end and my lips tighten. She closed her eyes and mumbled something under her breath, too low for me to make out.

A soft thump in the back of the room made me look back in time to see Mrs. Jones slump forward awkwardly in her chair and start snoring softly.

I snorted, stood up shouldering my bag, and said, "I'm outta here." Just then the door swung open with a bang as it slammed against the bookshelf to the side. Principal Quinn had arrived.

CHAPTER TWO

Principal Quinn swept into the room wearing red and black. Her ebony hair was pulled back in a tight bun with red lacquered styling sticks, reminding me of chopsticks, poking out on either side. Her form-fitting suit and black stilettos were a bit extravagant for a high school principal.

"Sit down, Claire." Quinn smiled. It wasn't pleasant.

I looked over my shoulder at Mrs. Jones, still happily snoring away. The door slamming and the shouting hadn't fazed her at all. I dropped my bag on the floor and pushed the desk before slumping into it.

One corner of her mouth rose in the semblance of a smile. Quinn looked out the window and back at the door and took a deep breath. "You are in danger." The way she said it sent a shiver through me, making me almost believe her.

"From what?" Emily asked.

Quinn frowned. "What I'm going to tell you will be hard to believe, but it's true."

The hairs on the back of my neck rose. Something about her made me nervous. Not because she was an authority figure — that never bothered me before — but something more basic in her person. This was the first time I had any real interaction with her. I'd noticed her watching me many times, but she always kept her distance.

"The five of you will become a danger to each other and to those near you if you aren't trained." I looked around the room at the others, thinking she'd chosen an interesting group to joke with.

Apparently, Denise thought the same thing. "Yeah right. A cheerleader, an environmentalist, a wallflower, a geek, and a . . ." Denise paused as she tried to figure out how to refer to me.

I bared my teeth and nearly growled at her, shocking myself in the process. *Growling?*

"And her," Denise pointed at me, "will start killing each other."

"I'm not talking about your image in school. I'm talking about your true identities," Quinn said. "I want the help of a vampire, a witch, a shapeshifter, an elementalist, and a werewolf."

The room echoed with silence for a moment. Mrs. Jones' light snoring had even stopped. Quinn didn't move a muscle, just met my blank stare. The absurdity of it was too much. I burst out laughing. The others joined me, a little more hesitantly. I couldn't believe I'd thought she was serious when she said we were in danger.

"Silence!" Quinn boomed. "You will hear me out!"

We quieted down, but I fought a smile. This was too good. Quinn was playing us. I studied the bare walls and the bookshelf near the front of the room for a hidden camera. This would make for some great entertainment in the faculty room.

"Okay, sure, Principal Quinn. We'll let you train us in our magical powers." I bit my cheek to stop from laughing out loud. I grinned when Kat snorted just before she slapped a hand over her mouth.

"Of course you doubt me." Quinn's voice lowered and her eyes smoldered. "You are all supernaturals, brought together by fate because of your unique abilities. You have no clue what you really are."

I stopped smiling as her appearance became more menacing. Her angular features grew sharper and more narrowed. Her skinny shoulders stretched a little as she took a deep breath. Her bright red lacquered fingernails pressed into her skin as she placed them on her forehead to rub at it as if she were developing a huge headache.

Quinn grumbled. "We'll see how long you doubt me after I reveal things about each of you."

She moved to stand directly in front of Denise. Glaring down at her, she took a deep breath and wrinkled her nose as if she smelled something unpleasant. Denise squared her shoulders and cocked her head to the side, giving me the impression she didn't like Quinn's reaction.

"We have a Vampire, who requires the life force of others to gain strength and power. She sucks the essence of her boyfriends until she runs out, then moves on to another. She could drink their blood if she desired, but so far she prefers to just take their energy by proximity."

Denise took a shocked breath. She looked as if she wanted to say something. Quinn lifted one long finger, silencing her before she moved on. She stepped over to Kat, who stared at Denise with a look of speculation. When Quinn stopped in front of her, Kat dropped her feet to the floor and leaned her head back to see Quinn's face better.

"We have a witch who is close to nature and gathers her power from the earth itself. She treats the earth kindly and is rewarded."

Kat stared at Quinn. Her jaw muscles tightened as she shook her head. I couldn't tell if it was more denial, or unbelief. She didn't look amused.

Sliding between the desks, Quinn approached Emily. Without seeming to move, Emily sank lower into her chair. Quinn lifted one eyebrow and pursed her lips, smiling as if she found something funny.

"Our Shapeshifter can blend in with her surroundings, nearly making herself invisible when she doesn't want to be noticed. She can look older or younger depending on what she wants. She can alter her appearance to resemble someone else."

Emily's eyebrows rose as her eyes widened. A beautiful smile transformed her face.

Quinn crossed the aisle, putting her hands on Kegan's desk. She leaned down to lock on his eyes. "Our elementalist can manipulate the elements. He's able to see how things work and therefore can understand the complexities of nature and technology." Kegan adjusted his glasses and studied her more intently.

Quinn's hips swayed as she walked smoothly to stop in front of me. The gaze of the others bored into me. I knew what was coming.

"And a werewolf. Violent, angry, trying to deny who she is. The full moon is hard on her because she was born under a new moon. She misses school every month during the full moon since she's unable to control her temper and doesn't want to hurt anyone, although there are people at this school she'd really love to rip apart."

I cringed when she looked at Denise. I lowered my eyes, not wanting to see the others' reaction to me. I knew what she said was foolish, impossible even, but I hated to think she knew about my anger issues. She was trying to twist that into some demented story that I wanted to tear people apart and howl at the moon.

Quinn stopped talking and folded her long arms across her chest, smiling at all of us in turn. No one said a word. I'm sure they were as shocked by the information as I was.

Quinn walked to the front of the room again and sat down on the edge of a desk in front of Denise. After a few moments of silence, interrupted only by the soft snores of Mrs. Jones, Quinn frowned and asked, "What? No questions for me?"

"You have quite the imagination Principal Quinn, but seriously—" I said.

"I know what I'm talking about!" she shouted. She clenched her jaw as well as her fists and then took a long hissing breath before saying, "Believe me. I used to be just like you. I can spot a supernatural from the moment I lay eyes on one. You are the reason I came here."

I glanced around the room at the others, a little wary of what she may say next.

"You're a supernatural?" Kat asked. I couldn't tell if she was serious in her question or just playing along.

Quinn nodded briefly. "Yes. And so are you."

I shook my head, refusing to believe this nonsense. The principal narrowed her eyes. "You are different, though. A vampire that feasts on guys left and right, but never drinks their blood or drains them completely. An elementalist that is immune to her because his molecules work differently, and he finds friendship with the one girl everyone else is afraid of. A witch that uses her powers for good instead of grander reasons. A shapeshifter that goes anywhere she wants, unobserved, but never does anything improper. And then when I caused Jax to bump our werewolf as a test, she used self-control and stopped mid-attack. She walked away without taking a full revenge."

"That was you?" I gasped. What did she mean by self-control? I'd felt completely unhinged.

Quinn smiled the same way she had in the hallway. "I came here hoping to recruit you to my cause. I have noticed a change in the balance resulting from the effects of you five, and I want to tip the scales in my favor."

"And what do you expect us to do?" Denise asked, waving her hand at all of us as if it were ridiculous.

"I will teach you how to tap your powers and train you to assist me in my task," Quinn said, reaching forward and resting her hand on Denise's shoulder. The principal then walked around the room and placed her hands on the shoulders of each person casually as she passed. At first, they moved away slightly from her touch. When she let go and moved to the next person, they leaned toward her as if longing to maintain the contact.

"I'm in," Emily said before Quinn got to Kegan. Sitting straight, she looked taller and a little thinner. The desire to look away from her was gone. I was startled at her eagerness to join in this farce.

"I'll do what I can," Kat said.

"Me, too," Denise agreed.

I looked at Kegan as Quinn approached us. He shook his head like he couldn't believe the others were interested. Quinn squeezed Kegan's shoulder and he stiffened slightly. She tightened her grip until her fingernails pressed into his shirt. He relaxed suddenly and said, "I'm game."

I stared at her hand on his shoulder, and then I looked up at her. I knew right then I didn't want her to touch me. She had done something to them, I was sure of it. I no longer doubted she was a supernatural of some kind. She had them agreeing to join her with a single touch, but she never told us what we were supposed to do.

I kept my teeth clenched tight, not daring to say anything. I waited. They all looked at me expectantly, and finally I shrugged, "As long as my parents don't hear about this detention."

"That is wise of you. Without my instruction, you will not survive what's to come." Principal Quinn nodded, but she still looked at me like she didn't quite trust me. The feeling was mutual.

"So how will you teach us?" Denise asked.

"I will meet you each morning before school," Quinn said. "You will be here at five, every weekday morning."

"What, not on the weekends too?" I said, rolling my eyes. Everyone looked at me as if I were crazy. She had bewitched them and they were all ready to join her in whatever she was going to do. *I'm not the crazy one.*

"No," Quinn said. "I have other things to do." They all nodded as if this made perfect sense.

"This is absurd," I mumbled under my breath. The look from Quinn made me sure she'd heard it.

"I'll help you get started," Principal Quinn said. "I will open your understanding of yourselves and powers." She moved around the room, touching each person's face. "You should feel fortunate. Others are only able to access their powers after decades of study. Consider this your payment for assisting me."

Crap. There's no way out of this. She's gonna touch me and do some weird voodoo magic. When it was my turn, she paused for a fraction of a second as if trying to predict my reaction. I didn't blink as our eyes locked. Placing her hand on my head, she pressed her thumbs against the soft area between my eyes and the bridge of my nose. She spoke in a deep gravelly voice saying something under her breath in a language I didn't recognize. My head went from feeling fuzzy to incredibly clear in seconds. She dropped her hands to my shoulder and some of my misgivings left, but something about her still didn't seem right.

She breathed in deeply and took a moment to gather herself. "Now, get out of here and meet me in the gym tomorrow morning at five. Do not make me wait. I have no patience."

She slammed the door shut as she left.

I stared at it for a few seconds then looked at the others again. *What just happened?* Quinn had never told us why we were really in danger. She never told us what we'd be doing, yet we had all agreed to join her in the morning. Even me. A cold chill crept down my spine. The others shivered at the same time. The lights flickered and Mrs. Jones stirred on her chair but remained asleep. At a squeak of the door opening again, I turned around expectantly. It was another office aide with a note in her hand. She walked over to Mrs. Jones and cleared her throat.

When that didn't wake her up, she tapped Mrs. Jones' shoulder. "Excuse me, Mrs. Jones. This message is for you."

Mrs. Jones sat up quickly, wiping drool from her lips. She adjusted her glasses, tugged her shirt down over her big hips, and patted her hair before she took the paper from the messenger. She looked up. "Apparently, there has been some kind of mistake. You were not supposed to be sent here. Principal Quinn does not want to see you. Go back to class and then go home when school is released." She picked up her book and grabbed a tissue out of her pocket to clean up the puddle of drool on the desk.

We exchanged confused looks as we glanced at the clock on the wall. There were still ten minutes before the final bell. Did Quinn do something, or had I just imagined everything?

"Well, come on. Get going, or you'll be seeing Principal Quinn for skipping class," Mrs. Jones said when none of us moved.

"But we—" Emily began before being interrupted by a cough.

"Come on. Let's go," Denise said. "Don't wanna bring the wrath of the principal on us." She raised her eyebrows at Emily.

We got up slowly and walked out the door. Just outside the room, Kat said, "Did what I think just happened really happen?"

"Depends on what you think just happened." I put my hands on my hips and looked at Kat. We were about the same height standing face to face.

"Uh, I just saw the principal and now I plan to meet her tomorrow morning at five for some personal tutoring." Kat said it with just the hint of a question in her voice.

"Me too," Emily said, and Kegan nodded.

"Same for me," Denise said.

"Then yup," I said. At least it wasn't just in my head. I turned down the hallway, leaving the others behind. Kegan caught up quickly.

"Weird, huh?" he asked.

"Yeah, did you see what she did? Touching everyone like that?"

"I know. Now I can see strange things out of the corner of my eyes."

Crap. "Like what?" *Does he really have powers?* I hoped not. If he did, then that would mean what Quinn said about me being a werewolf was more likely to be true, and I didn't want to believe that.

"It's almost fuzzy, like when you haven't slept for a long time, or like when you see the heat rising off hot asphalt."

"Shhh." I put my hand on Kegan's arm, surprising him. I looked back at the others still standing next to the detention room, surprised I could hear them so clearly.

"Man, she's touchy. Working with her will suck," Denise said.

I led Kegan over to the water fountain, faking interest in the homecoming poster hanging above it. When I glanced back, I saw Emily reach up and pat Denise on the shoulder with a laugh. "Don't worry, even though you're mortal enemies, I think you can manage to work together nicely."

As Emily walked down the hallway in the other direction, I heard her say, "This'll be fun." My hearing had improved immensely. *Crap. Crap.* What had Quinn done?

"Can you hear them?" I looked at Kegan hopefully. He shook his head and stared at me like he was surprised I could. *Crap. Crap. Crap.*

He took a long, noisy drink from the fountain. I motioned for him to keep quiet. He just rolled his and walked away. I ignored him, listening for more.

"What did she mean by that?" Denise asked Kat, who still stood next to her.

"You're the vampire," Kat whispered. "Claire is the werewolf."

So Kat apparently thought this was possible.

"Werewolves and vampires are enemies in most mythology."

"I guess that explains why she's never liked me. Everyone else loves me," Denise said.

I clenched my teeth to prevent myself from saying something. Either they didn't know I was still within hearing distance, or they didn't care.

"Sorry. It's just that I haven't ever had any problem relating to other people," Denise said, sounding slightly embarrassed.

"Oh, I know," Kat said. "I was just surprised at how matter-of-fact you were about it."

"So you believe what Quinn just told us?" Denise asked.

"Yeah," Kat said, in almost a whisper that was still easy for me to hear. "I kinda do."

I refused to believe I'd turn into a werewolf. No way I'd become some hairy beast and start eating people. I wouldn't let myself.

Mrs. Jones came out of the detention room and saw the two girls talking. She shushed them and hurried them down the hall. "Get back to class. I know you've only got two minutes left, but at least pretend you're walking that way."

She shook her head as she watched them giggle down the hallway with their heads together. "Girls," she said as she shook her head and went back into the room, already opening up her paperback romance. She didn't even look my way.

CHAPTER THREE

I leaned back against my locker as Kegan approached. "Crazy meeting, huh."

I nodded. "She's nuts."

"Certifiable," Kegan said slowly. He jerked his thumb down the hallway. "Looks like our vampire's sucking energy."

Denise was making out with Blake. Three weeks — maybe four, tops — was the longest she stayed with any one particular guy. It seemed like the stronger they were, the longer they lasted. If what Quinn said were true, all these guys were merely food for her.

Blake kissed her but she just stood there, eyes open. I'd seen this before. "She's gonna dump him."

"What? How do you know?" Kegan looked at me, and then back to Denise.

"She's not responding like she normally does."

"Eww. You watch her enough to know how she looks when she kisses?" Kegan teased.

"Shut up. I can't help it if she's only ten feet away from me. Anyone in this school knows how she kisses."

"How do you know she's breaking up?" Kegan stared at the couple. "I'd say they look pretty happy right now."

"Keep watching. You'll see."

I'd never understood it. After a make-out session, the guys took a moment to recover, but they always seemed eager to do it again later. I closed my eyes trying to scrub my mind of the unwanted memories of her making out with Paul. They came at the most annoying times. I turned to my locker and did the combination, but glanced back at Denise and Blake.

Denise looked like she was ready to start glowing. I looked closer and saw an actual aura around her. I squeezed my eyes tight before opening them to the same image. Something freaky was going on. Quinn had done something to me. When Denise changed, Blake changed as well, intensifying his kiss.

That explained it. While she feasted on them, they felt her joy and euphoria. Denise was like a drug to them. My stomach clenched, then rolled. Lucky for the guys, Denise knew when to stop, otherwise they'd have loved every minute of their murder.

Denise stopped the kiss suddenly. Blake stepped back, looking surprised. She blinked hard. "I'm so sorry," she said, almost sobbing.

"What's wrong, babe?"

"I'm a terrible person. You'd be much better without me." Denise sniffed.

"No kidding," I whispered aside to Kegan. He shook his head but kept watching.

Blake smiled sadly. "I figured it'd be soon." He reached up, taking a loose strand of Denise's hair and tucked it behind her ear. "I'd hoped to set a new record." He took a deep breath and touched her lips with his fingertips. "I am definitely gonna miss these. You've got something special in your kiss, you know?"

Denise gasped. She started to cry, clearly shocking Blake — he probably didn't even know she could cry. *I'd* never seen her cry, especially over breaking up with a guy. I glanced at Kegan, but he never took his eyes off the two.

Blake looked around quickly at the students passing, smiling sheepishly. "See you around." He walked a few steps, paused, and then squared his shoulders as he walked forward.

Good for you, Blake, I silently cheered.

"No way." Kegan looked at me after finally tearing his eyes away from the break up. "You called it, but I still can't believe she dumped him."

I turned and yanked my locker open. I'd just watched a vampire sucking the energy from someone. I'd actually seen it. The idea that we were supernaturals wasn't as far-fetched as it seemed at first.

The hairs on the back of my neck rose as I thought about what I'd learned of myself, too. I knew I got more and more irritated every day. I always figured it was because of my hormones. That's what Mom claimed. They even put me on the pill to smooth them, but it didn't help. They'd made me even crazier. I was off them now, thank goodness.

When my parents sent me to see a therapist, I was livid. Now, hearing Quinn tell me that my anger and irritation weren't just in my head like my parents thought was a relief. Tears stung my eyes as a burst of laughter escaped me. Kegan looked at me like I was crazy. "What?"

I shook my head and dug through the junk in my locker. "Never mind."

It was fantasy, but it wasn't just in my head. I snorted at the thought I was a mythical creature. I wouldn't turn into a wolf. That was ridiculous. I'd probably just be extra mean or strong, or something, but Denise would definitely be the type to start drinking the blood of others. I looked over at her. She was talking with friends as if nothing had happened.

Blake strolled toward me down the hall with his bag over his shoulder. He didn't seem bothered that the most popular girl in school had just dumped him. He still had a foolish expression on his face, like he was on some kind of high. As he passed, a comforting embrace washed over me. I didn't feel things like that very often, but it oozed off Blake.

"Did you feel that?"

"What?" Kegan asked as he studied me. "Are you all right?"

"I don't know." I shivered when I realized I must have gotten a bit of the euphoria Denise gave Blake when she sucked his energy. I watched him for a moment as he continued down the hall. Had all the guys been the same? When I took my eyes off Blake's back, I saw Paul watching me. I turned back to look at Denise, laughing with those around her. She had ruined everything.

"I gotta go. I'll see you tomorrow." I didn't meet Kegan's eyes, just grabbed my books out of my locker, shoved them in my bag, and hefted it over my shoulder. It would be quicker to walk down the hallway out the front doors, but I didn't want to walk past Denise right now. I didn't trust myself. Turning to the left, I stormed to the side doors, twice as far as the other options, and kicked them open with a booted foot.

CHAPTER FOUR

The lights around the building gave off a hazy glow through the early morning mist. As I approached the gym, I wasn't even breathing hard, though I'd run to school instead of bringing my clunker. I pulled the door open and walked in. The odor of the stale sweat from the jocks was unpleasant but not overpowering. I lifted my arm and sniffed. Nothing, not even sweating.

I walked past the girl's locker rooms and got a whiff of a light floral scent, a strange combination of girl's perfume, deodorant, and shampoo. Passing the boys locker room, I could smell the sweaty socks, wet towels, the rubber from the basketballs, and some industrial strength cleaner and deodorizer that didn't quite cut it.

When I got into the gymnasium, I was alone. The scent of smoke caught my attention but it passed quickly. I climbed up three rows of benches and sat down. It felt strange to be here so early, but I was actually excited for my first lesson.

Last night, I'd pulled out the journal my shrink made me start. I compared dates with a lunar calendar, and saw the days of the month closest to the full moon were always the worst. I'd read over the entries of the last three months and, on each full moon, the pages were filled with rantings of how much I hated everything and how angry I was. The pages were almost ripped in places where I'd pressed so hard with my pen in my fury to get the words out on paper.

Somehow what Quinn said made more sense when I saw the proof of my behaviors in my own handwriting. There *was* something strange about me. Not that I believed I would really turn into a werewolf, but I was interested enough to want to find out more about myself.

Moments later, the door opened. I closed my eyes and listened. A quiet swishing made me think of a long skirt's motion as the legs they covered brushed against it. The slight click of beads bouncing against each other brought to mind a long strand of wooden beads wrapped twice around the neck of the wearer. The footsteps were slow, yet purposeful, with no hesitation.

That's Kat.

When Kat's head appeared by the handrail against the bleachers, I smiled. The beaded necklace had metal swirls interspersed between the large wooden beads, and the peasant skirt and blouse she wore were loose and flowing. The leather sandals hadn't made much sound as she walked. When she joined me on my bench, I wondered if picturing her so well was because of some supernatural ability that werewolves were supposed to have. No, if I were truthful with myself, I'd always been observant, but I never focused much on it before.

The door on the other side of the gym opened. Emily jogged toward us in a form fitting t-shirt and denim jeans and waved toward the entrance we'd come in. I turned to see Denise dressed in a short skirt and tight blouse. She seemed distracted as she pulled her hair into a ponytail. When she saw Emily, she flashed a smile before she looked toward Kat and me. Denise's smile disappeared when her eyes met mine. She joined Emily in the center of the gym and they sat on the floor together.

"Let's go join them," Kat said, standing up and pulling me by the arm.

I reluctantly let her lead me down the bleachers to the center of the gym, but only because Kegan entered the gym and headed to the center of the ball court. I sat down on the floor between Kat and Kegan in a crude circle, which unfortunately placed me across from Denise.

"Okay, so what do we do?" Denise asked, turning away from me and looking at Kegan.

"We should wait for Quinn, I guess," Kegan said.

"Why wait? Shouldn't we get started on something?" Denise gave him the kind of smile that turned other guys into idiots, but Kegan was immune. I loved it.

"I want to know why I should believe any of this is real." I looked at each of them. No one said anything so I leaned forward to look directly at Emily. "What makes you think she was right about you being a shapeshifter?"

Emily shrugged. "I wouldn't have called myself a shapeshifter, but I can totally see it now. If there's a certain thing I want to be a part of, or see, I somehow fit in."

Kat perked up. "How would you change your appearance? Did you just do the clothes and make up, or did you really shapeshift?"

"Mostly it was just the way I dressed and acted, but . . ." Emily stopped for a second. "I've never admitted this before, but there were times I could've sworn I was a little taller or shorter depending on the circumstances." Leaning closer to me, she said, "There was one time at a party that all the guys were ogling the chest of one girl. I went outside, adjusted my bra and pushed them up a little. When I went back in to see if I could get them to ignore her and pay attention to me — just to make her jealous — I was bigger. I would have said it was just 'cause I had adjusted my shirt and bra, but now I'm pretty sure they grew."

Kegan made a strange choking noise. I looked at him in time to see his face go pink, then red.

"That would be a handy trick." Kat glanced down at her own chest and its obvious lack of cleavage. I had a hard time not giggling at the longing in her voice. When Kat saw Kegan's mouth drop open, she crossed her arms over her chest and asked, "What else have you done?" Her blush wasn't nearly as deep as Kegan's. I wondered how much more he could take.

Emily must have noticed his discomfort since she described changing her height to ride certain amusement park rides. She claimed she'd never thought about how she had done it — she had just willed it so, and it was.

That would be so cool. I had always been one of the shortest in my age group. There were so many times I wanted to change my height.

"I don't think I've ever done anything that cool," Kat said. "I thought about those things Quinn said yesterday. One perfume I made was really good at getting the attention of a certain guy I wanted to impress. A friend borrowed it to see if her boyfriend liked it. He didn't, but the one I had in mind when I made it started to flirt with her. Maybe it was a potion made specifically for him."

Emily smiled. I leaned back and put my arms behind me on the floor. A love potion would rock. I'd never use it, of course, but still.

"A few of my friends used a face cleanser I made that cleared up their zits faster than the prescription stuff they'd been given by their dermatologists, too," Kat added.

"I'd say that was pretty cool." Emily smiled. "Love potions and beauty potions. Much better than changing the size of your boobs." Kegan was trying to look anywhere but at Emily's chest. I elbowed him. He elbowed me back.

"Where do you think your knowledge comes from?" Denise asked. "Does it really come from the earth like Quinn said?"

Kat shrugged. "Maybe. I like nature and being outside more than inside. I'm a vegetarian and can't stand the idea of eating animals. I've always been good with living things. I have my own garden and I can even get things to grow that wouldn't normally in this climate."

"If you get your power from the Earth," I asked, "have you ever felt something when you do your garden things?"

Kat thought for a moment. "Nothing that I know of. Kinda proud of myself for being nice to the world, but not really power."

"How are you able to know the things to add into your potions?" Emily asked.

"It just happens," Kat said. "I guess I'll have to pay better attention to what I do."

We sat quietly for a moment, lost in our own thoughts.

"So what about you guys?" Emily asked.

I figured I should share something. "The full moon is the hardest on me. It's when I'm angriest. I've never turned into a werewolf, or attacked anyone, but even my parents step lightly around me."

"So do you ever have any good days?" Kat asked.

"Depends on what you consider good." I shrugged. "There are days I don't feel so angry. Until something sets me off."

Denise snorted. I clenched my teeth and automatically started my counting.

"What kind of elements do you see, Kegan?" Denise asked.

"I don't see elements, really. I just have a sense to how things work. I like to pull things apart and then put them back together." He pushed his glasses further up his nose. "I can also put things together without looking at them. Just by feel, like I know where the pieces are supposed to fit. As if they were magnets pulling together."

"Nice," Denise said, fluttering her eyelashes at him.

"Don't bother, Denise. Kegan's not gonna let you suck his energy," I said.

Denise stiffened a little. "I don't suck energy from the guys I date. It's just an emotional high. I broke up with Blake and I feel fine, not weak or anything. There has to be another explanation for what Quinn said."

"Sure there is." I tried hard not to roll my eyes. She probably didn't want to believe herself to be a vampire any more than I wanted to accept the werewolf idea, but still she had to realize she sucked something from them. "You could have killed all those guys you've dated, you know."

"I've never harmed them," Denise snapped. "They're always fine after we break up."

"I saw what happened to Blake yesterday while you sucked him dry. His energy flowed to you, making you glow with it, and then something oozed back to him."

"Liar!" Denise shouted. "You can't see energy."

"I did. You're dangerous. You shouldn't be allowed anywhere near people," I snapped.

"What is your problem?" Denise glared at me.

"You are. Everyone worships you, but you're awful. Maybe there could be something good about being a werewolf. If I'm the only thing that can stop you, then I will."

"Go ahead and try!" Denise said.

I stood up and beckoned her over. The hairs on the back of my neck and arms rose. The excitement of what was coming thrilled me. I couldn't wait to see what I could do. If I were her mortal enemy, this would be the chance to see who was more powerful. I was sure I was. Denise was only good at sucking the life out of her boyfriends.

She looked at me and shivered. *It must be out of fear.* Then the shiver was gone, and she looked confident. *Maybe not.* That sent a shiver of fear through me as she grinned. I thought back to all those times in this very room, when I wished I could tear into her. Those memories, combined with the sight of her, overcame the fear and brought excitement and energy.

As I glared at Denise, my vision sharpened. Her complexion was flawless. *No fair!* I saw the emotions rippling off me, like what I'd seen on a hot day over asphalt. *Is this like what Kegan sees?* Some smaller waves came off Kat and Emily, joining mine and flowing to Denise, wrapping around her. She could take our energy just by being in the same room with us!

A flash of anger burned deep inside me. I clenched my teeth to keep from growling at her. The sharp poke of my canines hitting my lower lip sent my heart into overdrive. Had they grown? I ran my tongue across my teeth and my heart stopped a moment. They had lengthened. Impossible! I was *not* a werewolf. I shook my head in denial and breathed in deeply.

I could smell things I hadn't noticed before. Denise's perfume, the gel in Kat's hair, the lotion Emily wore, Kegan's deodorant, the fabric softener on my clothes even. The acrid scent of smoke like that from a freshly lit match registered in the back of my mind. The fruity scent of Denise's gum kick-started a memory of every time our parents had forced us to play together and she never shared her gum once.

The sudden influx of emotions into the room must have given Denise confidence. I saw the strength in her arms and legs increase as the energy ripples surrounded her.

Kat raised herself onto her knees and said, "Whoa, guys. I think you'd better calm down."

Denise leaned toward me and grumbled something vicious under her breath.

I lunged toward her, a small part of my brain screaming at me to stop. I couldn't help myself. The instinct to hurt her was too strong.

CHAPTER FIVE

Denise moved to the side, avoiding me. My frustration at missing her was only slightly stronger than my relief that I hadn't actually made contact. I debated trying again, noting the look in Denise's eyes. She was ready for me. Next time, she would meet me in the attack. The element of surprise was gone. Denise took a step forward and I clenched my fists.

"Stop!" The echo in the room startled me. I hid my hands behind my back and clamped my mouth hard, feeling my teeth against my lips. Denise dropped her hands she had raised in response to my attack.

Principal Quinn stood between us, quivering with rage. How did she get there so fast? I didn't even know she had been in the room. Her hair seemed thinner and her eyes looked ready to glow. Something was definitely wrong with her.

"I will not have this! Understand? You're no good to me dead." Her body shook as she stared us down. "If you die by violence, your souls will languish in eternal misery. Do not thwart my plans." Quinn rolled her neck. The cracking of her spine punctuated her words. She gasped and struggled for breath as if she faced some inner turmoil.

"What's wrong with you?" I asked. She glared at me before continuing.

"I will use your animosity to my benefit, but you must learn self-restraint. If you give in to your basic desires and cross over, you will fall. Fallen supernaturals are under the control of the demon lord."

"What?" I looked at the others. They seemed surprised as well. "There is a demon lord now?" My voice rose. "What other lies are you going to tell us?"

"You know these aren't lies, Claire. You've seen enough to know. If you hope to survive what's coming, you'd better learn how to embrace what you are."

I shook my head. I refused to believe it. *Completely.*

"You must learn or you'll become servants of a demon." Quinn looked into my eyes as if trying to read my thoughts. She pursed her lips together for a second. "Now, we can use what you two just learned about each other for our first lesson. What did you see?"

Denise said, "It was weird, but I was very aware of the emotions in this room. I knew I could use that energy for myself and take her on."

I snorted, jerking my chin up. "Good luck with that."

"Someday," Denise promised.

Quinn looked at me. "Claire, what about you?"

"It was the anticipation of something coming," I said after a moment. "The angrier I got, the more I couldn't wait to tear into her." I looked at Denise with a wicked grin. No way I'd admit she might have more power than me.

"If she had been a helpless mortal, you could have easily hurt her," Quinn agreed. "With her abilities, it wouldn't be so easy. It's too bad I couldn't let you two battle it out. The outcome would be fascinating." Her eyes met mine, and a sudden eagerness to learn everything about what she claimed I was overcame me.

"It is very unusual to have a vampire and werewolf right here. Your kinds don't normally stay in any proximity to each other," Quinn said. "You'll have to figure out a way to control your desire to kill each other while still learning to surrender to your abilities enough to access them."

She turned to me. "Although you have lots of potential power now in your human form, you will need to learn how to shift into a wolf to survive when things get really tough."

She couldn't be serious. I wouldn't turn into a real wolf. It was impossible. I knew I was short tempered and all, but this was ridiculous.

Quinn turned from me. "Kat, what did you just learn from this?"

"It bothered me," Kat admitted. "Why can't they find a peaceful way to resolve it? Who cares if they're mortal enemies? If they're able to deny their inner desires as vampire and werewolf in life, why can't they control that animosity toward each other?"

I crossed my arms over my chest and snorted. I'd done an excellent job at not killing Denise over the years. I'd been controlling that animosity every day since we first met. Some days I did better than others.

"I thought it was fascinating," Emily said eagerly. "I could see Claire . . . bristle almost." She tried not to look at me, but her eyes kept coming back. "It seemed like she was just dying to rip Denise apart. I could see her hair standing on end. Watching her as she got really into her anger, I had an idea on how to try to transform."

Quinn moved closer to her and whispered something. Emily shook her head, listened again to what Quinn said, and then nodded vigorously.

Quinn turned quickly toward me. The look in her eyes reminded me of hunger. She wanted something badly, but what? I looked to Kegan for support, but he looked just as excited as Quinn. A feeling of betrayal washed over me.

Emily looked at me. "I'd really like to try to turn into a wolf. Don't know if I could do it, but maybe with practice. Wouldn't it be amazing if I could become something else entirely?"

"Are you saying you think you can turn into me, and then into a wolf?" I asked. "No way." She was crazier than I thought.

"As you got angry, it seemed like it was just on the surface. If I tried this while it's still kind of fresh in my mind . . ." she suggested excitedly.

"Let's get to work," Quinn said.

If she knew how to do it, then maybe she could help me learn how to transform.

Emily stood up to look me over. Even though I wanted to protest, I was dying to see what she could do. A small part of me hoped she did change so I would have someone to transform with. Something deep within me was dying to get out, but I'd been clamping it down so hard for so long I didn't know if I could. If she failed, then I'd have an excuse when I failed too.

Emily's gaze roamed over my hair, body, makeup, and clothes. I shifted uncomfortably, running my fingers across the back of my neck. My scalp tingled under my short hair. Goose bumps covered my arms. Emily watched my movements, making me nervous. A familiar irritation began to rise. I automatically turned to my breathing techniques.

Emily's face scrunched up and she dropped her shoulders. "Gah, you killed it. I can't find what I'm looking for. Get angry again."

"Whatever," I said, bristling, my heart rate rising. "If you can't change, don't blame me."

Emily stood over me and smiled. "There it is," she said. "Stand up." She offered me her hand.

I frowned.

"Do it," Principal Quinn said.

I rolled my eyes but stood slowly. My hand automatically went to my hip in irritation. Emily stared at me. My eyes widened when I realized she was shrinking. She'd been at least four inches taller than me. She opened her mouth slightly as if uncomfortable, but not in pain. Once she had settled into her new height, *my height*, her muscles changed as her body copied mine. Her shirt hung on her instead of hugging her curves as before.

She focused on my hair and began to make the change. It started at the roots and slowly bled out to the tips. She closed her eyes, scrunching up her nose as the color changed from her black, with some dark burgundy highlights, to my deep caramel tones.

Reaching up to pick up a strand of her hair, she appraised the color. Shifting it again, she grinned at her results. It wasn't exactly the same color, but it was close.

Emily stopped for a moment and looked like she was thinking things through. She tugged at the hair she held and closed her eyes again. Her new hair began to shrink. When it was my length, Emily slowly brought her hand up to the top of her head.

"I did it," she giggled. "I actually got it to shrink."

It was even styled like mine. I touched my hair, surprised that she'd copied it so well, but then I dropped my hands quickly.

"How did you do that?" Kat asked.

"How do I look?" Emily asked, bouncing on her toes and looking at all of us in turn.

"Kind of freaky. Your face still looks mostly like you, but you have Claire's body," Kat said.

"Crap, I forgot about the face. What do I need to do to change it?" Emily asked as she touched her cheeks and eyed me again.

"You need to change your eye color," Kegan said. "Yours are gray, but Claire's are brown." He glanced at me before looking back at Emily.

Emily closed her eyes. She opened them slowly and looked at Kegan. "How's that?"

"Awesome." Kegan grinned. "That is the coolest thing ever." He looked at me, comparing us. Then he said to Emily, "Now your face. She's kind of angular, while yours is soft."

Emily's features shifted until she looked like what I'd only seen in a mirror.

She raised her arms and twirled slowly as she tried to get a look at herself from every angle. "Did I get it?" Emily turned to look at everyone.

They all cheered and congratulated her. *Holy crap, this is real.* I just stared, with my teeth clenched tightly so my mouth didn't drop open. At least my canines were back to their normal size.

"Awesome!" she said.

Denise stepped closer to Emily. She looked her over closely as if trying to find something wrong. "She looks exactly like Claire. She doesn't smell like Claire, though."

Kat stepped closer to Emily and sniffed her, and then she moved over to smell me. I pulled back slightly. "Yeah, you're right. They do smell different." Kat looked thoughtful for a moment.

Kegan said, "There's something different about the air around them." I looked at him and then at the other me, feeling very weirded out about it. I couldn't see anything wrong in the air above her, but then I wasn't an elementalist.

Quinn nodded at Emily. "Can you change into the wolf?"

Emily closed her eyes and stood still. We all watched closely. My face on her body wrinkled as she concentrated. Nothing changed. I hoped she wouldn't be able to do it right away. If she did, I'd probably be expected to do it now, too. *I am so not ready for that.*

Emily sighed and dropped her shoulders in defeat. "I can't find it."

Quinn looked disappointed. "We'll try again later. Kegan, tell me more about this difference you see in Claire and Emily."

"I can't really explain it," he said as we settled down into the same places we'd been sitting before. "They just look different by the air around them. It's almost like the air around Emily wants to stay where it had been before she changed shape."

"Interesting," Quinn nodded. "What did you learn as you watched Denise and Claire in their altercation?"

"Nothing that might relate to the elements. I could tell Claire was really pissed at Denise, but I couldn't understand why," he looked at me apologetically, "besides the fact that she's always hated her."

"You didn't see anything different about Denise?" I asked. "No energy ripples being absorbed by her?"

"No," he said. The others shook their heads when I turned to them. I frowned and didn't say anything else, unsure if I'd really seen it now.

"Kegan, I want you to try something," Quinn said, stepping closer to him. "From what I know of Elementals, you should be able to distinguish between temperatures. Tell me what you see when I do this." Quinn held her hand up with the palm facing forward.

Kegan leaned forward. "Whoa! How did you do that?"

"What did you see?" she insisted.

"Your hand looked normal, and then all of a sudden it looked like it was covered in flame."

"Did any of you see flame?" Quinn asked us. We all shook our heads and looked at Kegan with interest.

"That will come in handy."

"Handy for what?" I asked. "What are we training for?"

Quinn snarled at my question. Her face changed suddenly to a brief glimpse of glowing eyes and sharp fangs. I reared back in surprise but her face went back to normal, like nothing had happened. I blinked hard and looked at the others. They didn't seem to have noticed at all.

"I'm trying to teach you about your abilities. I don't want you to fall and become enslaved by a demon," she said through clenched teeth.

"But if we've never done anything like that before, why would we now?" The only one I had ever wanted to kill was Denise, but that was only after what she'd done to Paul. With most people, I could keep it at intense dislike.

"Now that there are five of you, there is too much of a change in the balance of things. Others with power will manipulate you if they discover you. I'm trying to train you in order to keep you out of trouble."

The other four nodded in agreement at what she said and looked at me like it was obvious what we were doing. I growled in frustration. She wasn't telling us everything and they didn't even care.

"Why does it matter that there are five of us?" I glared at the principal. "I want answers."

Chapter Six

Quinn narrowed her eyes as she studied my face. I wasn't going to back down. She would give me answers.

She pursed her lips, inhaling slowly as she stared at me. Finally, she nodded as if she'd come to a decision. "The reason the five of you are important is because you each represent a point on the pentagram."

Kat sat up straighter. "You mean the thing used in pagan ceremonies where they killed people?"

"No, the history behind the pentagram has been skewed. It is a potent protection against evil and demons. It is a symbol of safety." She rubbed her arms briskly. "Centuries ago, confused men associated the symbol with demons. So now, instead of being seen as good, it is thought of as evil. This is exactly what the demons wanted. It stopped being used against them."

"And we are supposed to be points on a pentagram?" Kegan asked. "How exactly?"

Quinn smiled. "Look at how you're sitting. Now imagine a straight line drawn between you. Kegan to

Emily to Claire to Denise to Kat and back to Kegan, completing the five-pointed star of the pentagram."

"That's just a coincidence," Kegan said, scooting back slightly.

"Is it also a coincidence that the home you moved into is in line with Emily's, and Emily's home is in a straight line to Claire's, and Claire's to Denise's, and Denise's to Kat's, and then back to yours? You all live in the same neighborhood, in the same pattern you are sitting in here. You are each a point of the pentagram."

"No way." Kat grabbed her phone and pulled up Google maps. When Denise crawled over to her and peeked at the phone, I scooted back. They pointed out their houses on the satellite picture.

"Holy stink," Denise whispered. "They are in an exact star."

"A pentagram," Quinn corrected.

"But how did we become supernaturals?" I insisted.

"You have always been. It's just been in its latent form. Until you began interacting with others with powers, it remained hidden. Now that you are all here together, it is becoming stronger and stronger."

"So it's Kegan's fault for moving here?" Emily said with a twinkle in her eye. Kegan gave her a side glance.

"It would have happened eventually. Either another supernatural would move nearby, duplicating one of your talents, or you would have moved near another. Every supernatural eventually has to face their ability."

"So since each of us are different, what does that mean?" Kat asked.

"You each have unique talents and abilities. They relate to the five senses in a way. The elementalist deals with sight, the vampire with taste, the werewolf with hearing, the shapeshifter with touch, and the witch with smell."

So that's why I can hear things so much better now.

"How did this happen? Were our parents like this?" Emily asked.

Quinn shrugged. "Your parents must have each carried a recessive gene. Once combined, it formed the basis of your abilities. You are all only children, aren't you? Nature has developed a way to keep the number of supernaturals to a minimum. Once a supernatural is conceived, some chemical your body releases while in the womb shuts down a mother's fertility. She will never bear another child."

"You're saying it's my fault my parents can't have more kids?" I asked. I thought about all the arguments my parents had about trying to have another baby. *Great, one more reason for them to hate me.*

"Basically, yes. If any of you had another sibling with the same abilities, you probably would have killed it in its infancy."

My jaw dropped. *I would have killed a baby?*

"So we are bad?" Kat asked, looking around at us. Her eyes met mine and glanced away quickly as if she was worried.

"You have the potential. Stronger desires than mortals. How you respond to your situation will determine the outcome."

"And why are you here exactly?" Denise asked.

"I want to help you learn to control your abilities and desires. It would be in everyone's best interest to avoid having you fall and become servants of the demon lord." She clenched her fists and shivered.

"How do you know all of this?" I asked.

"I've been around," Quinn said quietly before she looked at her watch. "It's nearly time for school. Come prepared tomorrow to tell me more of what you have learned. If you are to succeed, then you must do some preparation on your own time."

She turned to walk away, but then she paused. "I had doubts at first, but I now think you can do this. If Emily is able to transform this quickly and her ability is the weakest of you all, then just imagine what you can accomplish."

Emily's eyes narrowed as she looked at Quinn's receding back. "I'm the weakest?" she asked Kat.

Kat patted her on the shoulder. "Don't take her seriously. She's trying to give us all a pep talk. It just happened to be in a very rude and demeaning way."

"You'd better change out of my body," I said. "There is no way I want to have people wondering why I'm wearing those clothes."

"Right," Emily said with a smirk. "These look much too nice for you." She closed her eyes as if concentrating. Soon her body transformed. Bones stretched, muscles shifted, her features became softer, and her hair color darkened again.

"That is so cool," Denise said as she watched.

"Yeah," I grudgingly agreed. I turned to Emily. "But your hair is still short like mine. You planning to keep it like that?"

"No. It's really not that good a cut for me." Emily shook her head like her hair was wet, and it returned to its original length.

"What did that feel like?" Kegan asked.

"Kind of a tingle on my scalp, with a slight sensation of pulling," Emily said.

"Do you think you could transform into other people, too?" Denise asked. "Like Kat, or me?"

"Maybe. It might take me some time to figure it out, though. For Claire, it just seemed to make sense. I knew what I needed to do to look like her, but for you guys, I don't get the same feeling."

A tingle of fear shot through me. *How could she read me so well?*

"I wonder why that is?" Kat mused. Kegan started walking away and motioned for me to follow him.

"Who cares?" I snapped. "Just don't do anything while you look like me, or you'll regret it."

Emily blinked at my tone.

I ducked my head, wanting to apologize but refusing to back down at the same time. "See you later," I grumbled as I grabbed my backpack off the bleachers to join Kegan.

Kegan glanced at me and then looked at the door Quinn had left through. "Don't let it get to you. Just because she says you're a werewolf, it doesn't mean you'll eat others."

I clenched my teeth. That was exactly what I was afraid of. Trying to change the subject, I asked, "What did you see around Quinn?"

He stopped walking for a minute as if trying to remember. "You know, now that you mention it, she was completely missing the same kind of aura I see around you guys."

"There is definitely something wrong with her. I don't trust her."

"Really?" he asked. "Why not?"

"Have you ever noticed she doesn't seem completely human?"

"She looks normal to me."

I raised my eyebrows.

"Well, besides the lack of aura." Kegan pushed his hair off his forehead and nodded. "Maybe you're right. I'll have to pay close attention tomorrow."

***

After school as I gathered stuff from my locker, the ugliest kid I'd ever seen slid past me through the crowded hallway. Not wanting to stare, I watched out of the corner of my eye and saw his profile. Through the zits on his huge nose, I saw what looked like a second nose underneath, as if he wore some sort of sheer mask that attempted to hide his real face. Darker, and more pointed than the one I could see clearly. *What's up with my vision? First, Quinn seems to almost change forms, and now this kid? I thought my hearing was supposed to be enhanced, not my sight.*

I turned carefully to track him as he walked away. Leaving my locker open, I took a few steps with a book held forgotten in my hands and followed the ugly boy at a distance. The back of his head, covered in mats and tangles, looked like he'd just climbed out of bed. His back appeared lumpy, like he had something under his shirt. He walked purposefully down the hallway in the direction of the office.

Stopping at the water fountain, I pretended to get a drink while watching him. As he turned the corner, I hurried around the other students, making it to the window of the main office in time to see him admitted into Quinn's office.

"Claire?" a voice said.

I jumped in surprise, dropping my book. I turned to see Kat looking at me with raised eyebrows.

"What are you doing?" she asked.

"I just saw some strange-looking student walk into Quinn's office," I whispered before stooping to pick up my book.

"So?" Kat asked.

I glanced back at the office door. "Have you ever noticed something odd about the way Quinn looks?"

"Besides her being shaped like a supermodel but having a plain face?" Kat asked.

"No. She kinda flickers, changing the way she looks. Like this isn't her true form," I said.

"No, I haven't noticed anything like that. Maybe it's something with your powers manifesting." Excitement filled her eyes.

"Maybe," I said. That would make sense on why she couldn't see it.

"This is so cool, isn't it?"

I frowned and shook my head. "I don't want anything to do with this."

Energy waves rolled off Kat. I guessed them to be a little fear, mingled with lots of excitement. I wondered if Kat's being a witch instead of a werewolf made her more excited about it. Everything I'd ever heard about witches sounded much better than werewolves.

"Do you want to come over to my house this evening?" Kat asked. "I'd like to see what else I can do and think having someone to work with would help."

"I don't think I have time for that tonight," I hedged.

"You could figure out your powers and when you and Denise are paired tomorrow, you'll be more powerful than her," Kat said with a wink.

I thought about it for a moment. "I could probably squeeze in some extra study time."

"Great," Kat said. "When do you want to meet?"

"How about eight?"

"See you then," Kat agreed and walked off after giving me her address.

I looked back at the principal's door, wondering what was going on in there. I decided to leave it alone for now. The school counselor's office door opened and my heart skipped a beat when I saw Paul laughing at something the counselor said.

"Yeah, if it were that easy, I'd have half my college credits by now." His voice was smoother and deeper than I remembered it.

When had that happened? He'd also gotten taller. He was still distracted enough with the counselor that I didn't worry about him seeing me watch him. I'd never given myself permission to look at him or be anywhere near him for fear I'd start yelling again. Keeping myself at a distance helped with the hurt, but it was always there under the surface. The chance to really look at him again made me realize what I'd been missing.

The moment he turned to leave the office, I bolted down the hallway. I didn't want to test my resolve if he actually tried to talk to me now.

CHAPTER SEVEN

I slipped out of my house a few minutes before eight. It wouldn't take me long to get to Kat's house, but I still hurried down the steps and sidewalk into the dark night. The cool autumn air hadn't turned cold yet. My light jacket kept me sufficiently warm. My parents were too busy arguing about another work trip Dad had coming up to notice me leave.

I'd gotten better at letting my parents know what I did, but my habits of disappearing and ignoring my parents came back easily. I had put my pillows under the comforter to make it look like a sleeping body just in case they decided to check on me.

Even if my parents did discover me missing, they would think I'd gone off on my own to work things through. I'd done that often enough before my dad forced me into therapy. They'd probably just figure I was having a relapse and make me talk to the therapist about it. At least they no longer screamed at me.

Checking the address I'd scribbled onto my palm at school, I walked a few more blocks to Kat's large two-story home. The soft glow of the porch lights illuminated the sidewalk and steps. Autumn decorations, including corn stalks and pumpkins, littered their porch though we were weeks away from October. Knocking loudly on the door, I waited impatiently for someone to answer it, automatically beginning to count in order to keep my temper. My moods changed too quickly. Each day leading up to the full moon got more difficult to handle. Then as the full moon began to wane, I felt better. That stupid journal proved it.

Looking up at the moon again, I frowned. I'd always stayed inside, feeling sick, curled up into a ball on my bed during the full moon, never going outside during that time. What if I went outside? Would the full moon actually cause me to transform into a hideous beast?

Now I had a supernatural telling me I must transform into the thing I had been unconsciously suppressing my entire life. Just to save myself from something I still didn't fully understand.

Repressing the urge to bang on the door again, I listened closely to the movements going on inside the house. Footsteps approached so I took a small step back.

Kat opened the door. "Hey, thanks for coming," she said, smiling at me.

"No problem," I mumbled, not wanting to admit I wanted to be here, or that I appreciated the help Kat offered.

Finding myself in the kitchen of the house and being offered food put me at ease. Just a little. I was still nervous about what we would be attempting to do. I wondered if any of it would help, but a snack was just what I needed.

Kat pulled out cheese, nuts, crackers, sliced meats, and a cold soda from the fridge for me and fruit for herself. Was she bothered by me eating the meat? *Why the heck did you offer it to me?* I picked at it at first, but then started to enjoy it despite Kat's glances at me.

"Did you like the snack?"

"It was fine."

"Just fine?" Kat asked, looking disappointed.

"Yeah, why?" I raised an eyebrow.

"No reason."

"What?" I asked, leaning forward, ready to demand more information if Kat didn't deliver.

Kat sighed, "It's just that you seemed so tense, so I tried a small spell on the food hoping to calm you down." She shrugged. "I thought it worked because you seemed so much more at ease . . . until I asked you about it."

"Oh," I said, leaning back and trying to smile. "I think it did help. Sorry, I'm just really antsy about all of this."

"Me, too," Kat said. "I was trying to show off and see what I could do. I wanted you to tell me how great I am."

"Actually," I said, "you are pretty cool, but don't do any more spells on me, okay? We should get started."

"If I help you transform, are you gonna eat me?" She said it with a giggle, but something in her tone made me think she was worried.

"Who knows?" I sighed. "I've been trying so hard to keep my temper lately. But I always thought the worst thing I'd do was hit someone when I lost my cool. Now I'm told I've got a monster inside me that wants to get out. I have to let it, and then train it."

"Come on downstairs," Kat said. "We'll go in my room and see what we can figure out. But no more spells unless I ask first, I promise." Kat took me by the hand and led me to a closed door.

"You live in the basement?" I asked with a smile. "A witch with a room in the basement sounds kind of creepy."

"Yeah, you should see the skeletons in my closet." Kat winked.

The descent into the basement was far from sinister. The textured walls were painted a creamy brown, with small rectangular lights spaced every four steps. A worn handrail, smooth from use, lined the left wall.

Kat opened the door to her room. The cleanliness of her room surprised me — no bottles of body parts, animal by-products, or nasty-looking liquids there. I breathed in slowly, enjoying the light scent of the lavender candle burning on her dresser.

I'd never known a candle could be so helpful, but it probably wouldn't work in my room. I'd have to use a shovel to get all the clothes and shoes off my floor. My closet was the cleanest part of my room, because everything was on my floor instead. Her closet was probably as tidy as the rest of the room. Very few things looked out of place.

"Should we get started?" Kat sat on her bed and patted it for me to join her.

I gritted my teeth but focused on relaxing. I didn't want to dig into my inner workings, afraid of what I'd find. I glanced down at my hands, so small and fragile-looking. How could I possibly be some terrible monster?

"According to Quinn, you were born under a new moon so that's why the full moon bothers you," Kat said.

I shrugged.

Kat gave me a look of pity.

"You don't really believe all this, do you?" I asked.

"I kinda do," Kat said, "after seeing what Emily did this morning. Even you can't deny you saw her change into you."

She had a point. "Yeah, but I'm not gonna turn into a wolf," I insisted. "It's never happened before."

"Maybe that's because we didn't have all of us together like we do now."

"Could be." I wasn't going to believe it till I saw it. And if I just stayed home during the full moon, I'd be fine.

"So what do you think we should try?" Kat asked after watching me closely for a moment.

"I have no idea."

"What if we try some meditation? Something where we can get deep inside you and find out what makes you tick."

"I guess," I said with a shrug. That didn't sound dangerous.

She rushed over to her closet and opened it quickly. An avalanche of junk poured onto the floor.

"Aaah!"

I grinned at her. "And here I thought your room was so nice."

"I shoved it all in the closet trying to hide it from you, and didn't think about it in my rush to get this." She dug through the junk and then held up a gray box.

"It's a white noise machine. My mom got it for me a while ago when I had trouble sleeping. It helped me clear my mind."

It almost sounded like the ocean. Not exactly, but

close enough to remind me of it. Kat returned to her pile and pulled out a dark purple yoga mat. She yanked off the Velcro strap, unrolling it onto the floor in front of me. Kat stepped lightly onto the mat, crossed her legs while standing, sat down into a folded pose, and patted the mat beside her.

I dropped to the floor, much harder and a whole lot less gracefully.

"Sit with your legs crossed like mine and breathe."

I closed my eyes and listened to the fake waves, focusing on my breathing. At first, having Kat next to me interrupted my attempts at calm. Eventually, I matched my counting to my heart rate. I tried to ignore the different rate of Kat's breathing, focusing instead on my own pace.

In ten counts ... out ten counts...

Time became measured by my breathing. It didn't seem as obnoxious to be doing this with Kat as it had with Dr. Lowe. My tension slipped away. The muscles in my shoulders relaxed. I slid my hands off my knees, resting them on the floor between the folds of my legs with my fingers touching. The warmth of my fingertips against each other conjured up memories of walking hand in hand with my mother as a little girl.

Things had been so simple then. Mom and I always had so much fun together. We would go to the park, or on play-dates, or just hang out at home. When

Dad came home we'd eat dinner together and play games until my bedtime.

I smiled at the memories.

Too bad things couldn't have stayed the same. Soon my parents started arguing. I didn't realize until years later that it was because they were trying to have another baby. *And here it turns out it was all my fault.*

Dad kept telling Mom she was too obsessed with kids. He started spending more time at the office. Not long after that, we moved here. Dad's job relocated him, and Mom decided to go back to work when I started school. They no longer had time for me so they tried to force me to make friends. It hadn't worked, but they kept pushing. With Denise in particular.

Just the thought of those first few years here brought painful memories to the surface. I immediately clamped those images down and attempted to force them into hiding. I didn't want them.

My anger battled my pain. My breathing sped up. The white noise irritated me, bringing to mind all the empty noise of my house. The TV blaring in Dad's den. The radio in the kitchen as Mom tried to make up for not being home with pots and pans banging in her attempts at dinner. There was always noise of some kind in the house. Never any quiet moments. My outbursts and shouting just added to their fights. I guess they thought the outside noises they brought into the house would keep them from screaming at each other.

Each fight crowded into my already overloaded mind. Money, *my therapy sessions took a lot of that.* Housework, *I didn't do it right.* Who'd taught me bad behavior, *Mom's a shouter and Dad is emotionally unavailable.* And on and on. Kat's breathing beside me was slow and steady. Mine progressed erratically and I was incapable of slowing it down as I gasped for breath.

My heart beat faster. My palms began to sweat. All my senses were raw. The lavender candle that had soothed me before now turned my stomach. The white noise hurt my ears. I wanted to yank it out of the wall. The spongy mat beneath me wasn't thick enough. I clenched my eyes shut tighter, trying to keep myself in some state of meditation. Soon tiny pinpricks of red light invaded my darkness.

I bowed over my legs, tucking my head into the hollow between my thighs. Every muscle tensed. I wanted to fight something, but I didn't know what. I tightened my jaw and forced my breaths through bared teeth.

The hate, anger, bitterness, disappointments, betrayals, and hopelessness threatened to break me. Tears stung my eyes. A hot glow burned deep inside. It built with every emotion as they washed over me like waves on the beach, in sync with the white noise machine. The glow wanted to take over me, to destroy me.

The hot ball of emotions inside my soul beckoned me to seize it and end my misery. A flash of inspiration hit. If it wanted to take me, I'd let it. I'd let myself be overpowered by it all and slip into quiet oblivion. Then I wouldn't have to worry about it anymore. I wouldn't have to feel the disappointment and regret about Paul. I could get the hatred for Denise out of my system. I could finally be done. No more struggling for control. I'd be free.

I sat up straight and gathered all my consciousness around me. I reached out with my soul, opening myself up to the fire within. I didn't care if it burned me to a crisp.

The pulsing emotion ball began to retract, making me livid. I finally decided to do something about it, and it retreated? No way. It was mine! I wrapped my soul around it and my mind exploded.

I howled in pain.

In ecstasy.

The wall I'd built up around my core had burst. Sharp stinging — as if the debris from the imaginary wall rained down on me — covered my skin. My muscles quivered with energy, yet my heart beat slowly. There was no adrenaline rush, not like other times my muscles felt this ready. Only power.

On the edge of my awareness, Kat startled and move away from me. I couldn't stop howling. It was animal and uncontrollable. It was me. I knew I sounded creepy, but I didn't care. I felt free. Strong. Powerful. I had finally done it.

The howl lasted longer than I could have ever done on my own with my lung capacity. The sound came from my very soul, not just my mouth. My eyes were still clenched tight when a thought silenced me. Had I transformed?

Kat was still in the room. I could hear her breathing and heartbeat, but didn't smell fear. Her smell was pleasant, but a little tight. She seemed cautious, but not afraid. Perhaps I hadn't shifted into the shape of a wolf. I slowly touched my fingertips together. Still the same. I reached for my arm, feeling my skin, slightly damp from exertion, but it was still just my skin. I opened my eyes and gazed at my hands in front of me. Bringing them up to my face, I touched my cheek, my chin and lips, and up to my eyes and hair. I was still me. I hadn't lost myself.

The thunder of footsteps running down the stairs shocked me out of my self-absorption. I jerked my head to Kat in surprise. Her eyes were wide.

Her mother burst through the door holding a TV remote like a weapon. I knew she posed no threat, but my body tightened, ready to spring.

"Geez, Mom, don't you knock?" Kat asked, putting her hand over her heart.

"I heard screaming. Sounded like someone was dying." She looked around the room frantically, not seeming to believe she saw us sitting on the floor apparently unharmed.

"Oh, that..." Kat shrugged. "I just asked Claire to help me with an audition piece. My theatre class decided to do something fun for Halloween, and we're doing some dramatic readings. She was showing me how to do a proper scream."

Her mother creased her eyebrows as if she didn't believe it, but she eventually turned around and closed the door behind her. Apparently, she didn't really want to know what we were doing. As long as no one was dead, she could go back to her life and ignore us. That's what I'd do.

Kat looked at me and let out a nervous giggle then rolled her eyes as if to say, "parents."

I smiled sheepishly, embarrassed I'd caused that. I thought it was strange her mom called it a scream. It sounded like a howl to me. Maybe that was just the way I heard it.

"So, what just happened?" Kat asked, leaning closer with excitement plastered all over her face.

"I'm not really sure, but I think it's good." I sighed, and then I laughed until my sides hurt.

This felt incredible.

CHAPTER EIGHT

The cool air blowing past my face was invigorating. I'd never been able to run like this before but I was sure I could shatter Olympic records. I'd already gone more than two miles in the five minutes since I left Kat's house, including a couple of laps around Paul's block just to see his house. Once I got going, my legs begged to continue, to test them. I wasn't even winded.

My sides had hurt more from laughing at Kat's house than they did while running. I'd tried to explain to Kat what had happened, but I couldn't put it into words. Eventually I just told her I'd see her in the morning and left without another word. Her mom eyed me a little oddly as I left, but I just bit my lip trying to fight the grin that threatened.

I longed to keep running, to test my new energy, but my parents would have a fit if they found me gone. I decided to take the long way and ran past the high school. It was only three miles away. It didn't take me long to get there. I slowed down to a jog as I approached the building.

For some reason, the sight of the school didn't bring the usual thoughts. I didn't dread it and actually wished it was morning so I could walk into the school feeling this good. The streetlights bathing the red brick made them almost glow orange. A huge maple tree swaying in the corner of the lot cast moving shadows on the side of the building. My eyes were drawn to that area.

I walked toward it until a movement out of sync with the tree's swaying caught my attention. I hid in the shadows of a bush lining the sidewalk on the other side of the street. Some inner sense told me to be still. I didn't know exactly what I was looking for or why I should watch, but something was happening. A shiver washed over me as a whiff of smoke passed my sensitive nose. I tightened my fist unconsciously.

Quinn stepped out of the shadows. Not out from behind the corner of the building into the light, but out of the shadow itself. She just appeared out of nothing. Fear gripped my heart for a moment, then my core pulsed and I squashed the fear down. *She's on my side.*

Behind her from the shadow, another form appeared. It was shorter and less intimidating in shape, but seemed more menacing. When it stepped away from the wall, the movement of the tree allowed the streetlight to illuminate his features. It was the boy with the terrible acne and the lumpy back I'd seen going into her office earlier.

So he's with her. What are they doing together?

I couldn't understand their words, but they looked about ready to rip each other apart.

Quinn shimmered in the flickering light. Her hair in the tight bun disappeared and a huge irregular bump took its place. Her bare scalp still looked shiny and slick, and as black as her hair had been. The red hair sticks poking out of the bun were actually sharp, thin red horns protruding out of the top of her head. My jaw dropped. I pressed myself closer to the center of the bush. What was she?

Her long chin shrunk. Her white teeth elongated, the tips sharp and glistening with spit. Her once plump red lips thinned out and made her look like she was grimacing. The skin on her face reddened. Her irises glowed burgundy. The black makeup around her eyes became dark skin surrounding her fierce orbs. Her thin neck lengthened considerably, and her shoulders developed short spikes.

She leaned back deeply as if stretching. Her arms thinned and her hands expanded. The red fingernails turned into sharp claws. Her legs lengthened again by half. Her muscles rippled as they stretched. Black stilettos morphed into hooves with spiked claws on each heel.

She breathed in deeply and exhaled as if she'd been freed from some tight binding. She tilted her neck to the side. The crunch of the tendons and vertebrae in her spine popping sent shivers down my arms.

My mind reeled. *My principal is a demon?* When my mind attempted to wrap itself around the concept, my eyes fought what they saw. I closed them tightly, feeling the tingle of my scalp as my hair stood on end. My nostrils flared as I caught another whiff of smoke. *Is that from her?* My eyes flew open. I stared at her again. I couldn't deny what I was seeing, but didn't want to believe it.

The ugly boy with her transformed as well, but he almost seemed to pop out of his already gross appearance. His skin was the color of dried blood and huge areas looked scabby, like they would flake off with the slightest touch. Ugly Demon Boy's face was just like what I'd seen under the top layer at the school. He growled something at her and gestured violently. Though I could hear them, I couldn't understand the words they used.

Principal Quinn, or what had been her, lunged for him and scraped her claws down his arm. He howled in pain, grabbed his injured arm, and then muttered at her as he backed away slowly. She raised her hand as if to strike again. The short demon threw up his hands, and turning around abruptly, he disappeared through the shadow. Quinn shook her head and unclenched her fingers. She popped her neck again and shifted back into her previous form.

I knew Quinn was different from what she claimed, but a demon from hell? She told us a demon lord was waiting for us if we fell, yet she was a demon. Maybe she wasn't actually helping us. Maybe she was helping him. If so, then why teach us about our abilities? It didn't make any sense. When I looked back to the shadows in the corner, Quinn was gone.

I stood up slowly on weak legs. I couldn't see her anywhere. I started running again, though awkwardly as I stumbled out of the bushes. I had to tell the others about this. Quinn was a demon hiding under the disguise of a woman. Halfway down the block, a figure jumped out of the shadow in front of me.

My heart stuttered and I darted to the side trying to avoid it. A hand shot out and grabbed me around the arm. I screamed and swung at it with my free hand, but I was caught.

"What are you doing here?" Quinn hissed, now in her human form.

"Nothing!" I squeaked. "Let me go." I yanked my arms, but only ended up hurting myself in the process. Her grip was too strong. There was no way to break free from her. The fear I'd pushed aside earlier came back in full force. Maybe she wasn't really on my side.

"Why did you come here?" she demanded again. "Are you foolish enough to try to spy on me?"

"No," I whimpered.

"There is no reason for you to be here now. What are you doing?" She shook me hard, making my neck hurt with the whiplash.

"I..."

"Tell me!" she boomed.

"I was just running," I gasped. "I figured something out tonight, and wanted to test it."

She let go of me and I dropped to the ground, humiliated. I'd thought I was so powerful yet I was nothing. She could break me any time she wanted. The hopelessness of it all hit me. She was a demon and I had no strength against her. Tears stung my eyes. I blinked them back. *I'm not gonna cry.* If I was going to die right now, I wanted to at least go out with some dignity.

"You learned something? Show me!"

Her excitement gave me a sliver of hope, but what if I was mistaken? I had nothing to offer. She'd just kill me then. I stared at her.

"Show me," she demanded.

"I can't. It's gone." I closed my eyes, waiting for her to grab me again.

"What do you mean it's gone?"

When nothing happened, I opened my eyes slowly to find her glaring down at me.

"I found something deep inside that made me feel strong and powerful, but now it's gone. You scared it out of me," I admitted, ashamed.

"But you found something there?" she asked. "You actually were able to tap something within you?" She sounded more hopeful than I thought she'd be with my admission.

"Yes. I could run so fast without getting tired. I thought I could do anything. I even felt happy. . ."

I stopped when she smiled. This smile transformed her severe face. She looked almost pretty.

"This is very good news. At first when you refused to accept what I told you and kept clamping down on your desires, I feared my cause was lost before it began. But now that you have actually made an effort, we may succeed yet."

"Succeed in what?"

"In stopping the demon lord from claiming you all."

"But you said we had to fall before he could have us."

"In normal circumstances yes, but things are different now that there are five of you. He will come soon — either to make you his, or destroy you."

"Why are you helping us?" I asked.

"Because I don't want him to gain more power. I want to break free of his control. If I have the help of the five of you, I'll be able to obtain my freedom. You must learn how to fight what's coming for you." She stared at me.

"How? I can't even keep a hold of what I have for an hour. How can I hope to learn to control it?"

"You either learn, or you die." She looked me over, pausing briefly when she met my eyes. "You will say nothing to the others about what you have seen here tonight." She touched me lightly on the head. She stepped back into the shadow and was gone.

If she thought touching my head and telling me I couldn't do something would stop me from telling the others, she was sadly mistaken.

Chapter Nine

As I jogged home, exhaustion set in. I didn't have the stamina to run the whole way now that I was back to my own strength. Eventually, I made it to my block and trudged up to my house. I stood outside, watching my home, listening closely to see if any noises came from inside. The lights were off. Parents were probably asleep. Lifting the latch on the fence, I hefted the bulk of the gate in my hands to avoid the squeak of the hinges and slipped into the house by the back door.

I moved quietly to my room and collapsed onto my bed without undressing. I kicked my shoes off and then wiggled out of my jacket. Pulling the blanket over my head, I was asleep before I had the chance to reflect on what had happened at the school.

The sound of my mother in the kitchen woke me from my stupor. I looked at the clock and swore. Only fifteen minutes to get to school or I'd be late for my lessons. I ripped off my shirt and threw on another, not bothering to change my pants. I yanked on my shoes and grabbed my jacket.

I nearly plowed over my mother in my haste to get out of the house.

"Sorry, Mom!" I said. "I'm late, gotta run."

"Wait," Mom said.

"No time!" I shouted back over my shoulder as I ran down the hall. "Tell me after school." I slammed the door closed, glad I'd escaped a rant.

I yanked the garage door open, ducking under the rolling door as it went up the track. *When will they buy a garage door opener?* I fumed. I jumped into my car, praying it would start. Dad paid for half of it after I'd saved up for four years. We bought it six months after I got my license. It had sat in the garage for months. Dad complained about the lack of use, but it was a piece of junk, and a gas-guzzler so I rarely drove it. Relief flooded through me when it sputtered to life.

I had to hurry and knew I wouldn't be able to run to school fast enough to be there in time. I didn't dare show up late now that I knew my principal was a demon. I wanted to get there early enough to tell the others.

My mind raced. I drove without really seeing where I went or what I passed. I stopped at the four-way stop a block from the school and shifted my foot off the clutch into first gear, jerking into motion just short of whiplash speed. Annoyed at my inability to drive a stick smoothly, I grumbled and gunned it, nearly hitting a car backing out of a driveway in front of me. I swerved to miss it, blaring my horn in irritation.

My veins flowed with adrenaline after the danger had passed, making my stomach sick. I turned into the school parking lot, heading to the student section. After I cranked my steering wheel and parked, I jumped out of the car at a run. A huge garbage truck rumbled past, nearly running me over. I reared back and banged my leg on my bumper, coughing on the exhaust.

"Today sucks!" I shouted at no one. Whatever awaited me in the gym wasn't going to be any better either. Looking both ways to avoid being run over again, I ran to the school, banging through the doors just as the others sat on the floor in the center of the gym facing Quinn. *Crap, no way to tell them about last night.*

They all watched me cautiously as I approached at top speed and slid into place, panting. Quinn watched me closely as if to see what I'd say. It wasn't her touch or command that stopped me. It was the look in her eyes.

"How are you?" Kat leaned over and whispered.

"Fine," I panted, not looking at her.

Quinn stared at each of us, as if measuring our abilities. "What have you learned?"

Emily said, "I figured out how to shift into Denise." She looked at Denise. Receiving a nod in response, she shifted before our eyes.

"Nice," Kat said.

Quinn nodded and waited.

"That's all for me," Emily said after a moment, sounding slightly embarrassed.

Quinn turned to Denise.

"I nearly killed Emily when she convinced me she was Claire."

"What?" I jumped up onto my knees. I looked to Emily for confirmation. She waved her hand as if it were nothing. "Why were you pretending to be me?" I growled.

"I wanted to help Denise access her abilities." She shrugged. "It worked better than I thought." She pulled up her shirtsleeves to reveal dark bruises on her upper arms.

"You attacked her?" I gasped. "What were you thinking?" Denise scowled. "No," I corrected myself. "You attacked me." I gripped my thighs and dug my nails into my jeans, trying to calm myself through my breathing.

"I figured out how to return the energy," Denise said.

Quinn nodded and turned to Kat.

"I learned how to charm food to calm someone, and how to set a ward around my room so I would know when someone was near. I also made things move without touching them."

I looked over at Kat, surprised at all she'd accomplished. Was that before or after our little get together?

Quinn smiled briefly and nodded. "Good." She turned to Kegan.

Kegan didn't say anything, but slowly stood up. He took his glasses off and hooked them in the neck of his shirt. Staring at the bleachers, he took a deep breath. He swept out with his hand as if shooing a fly. The books near his bag fell off the bench. The papers ruffled in a strong wind and then died down just as suddenly.

"Wicked," Kat gushed.

Quinn nodded with pleasure. Then she looked at me expectantly.

"I ... uh ... I tapped my core for a bit and had amazing speed."

"Can you do it again?" Quinn asked.

"I don't know how to find it. I tried again after I lost it last night, but it never came back."

"How did you get it in the first place?" Emily asked.

I looked over at Kat and shrugged. "Meditation."

"Really?" Emily asked. "So why don't you do it again?"

"It wasn't a pleasant experience," I said.

"Your speed wasn't pleasant?" Kegan asked.

"No. That was great," I said. "I just wasn't a fan of the process of getting that speed."

"You'd better find it soon. You'll need it today for what I have planned," Quinn said. Her eyes sparkled with excitement. The others shifted on the floor, wondering what was coming next. My gut told me it wouldn't be good.

"I'll be sending balls of fire at you today, and if you don't manage to avoid them, you'll be in agony." She grinned.

Holding her hand close to her stomach, she balled her fist and pulled like she was yanking something from inside her shirt. A red ball of flame hovered over her palm. She stroked it with her thumb. She tossed it into the air and caught it easily, then lobbed it to Denise. Denise squealed in alarm as she threw herself to the side, banging her elbow hard onto the floor. The ball still hit her thigh, and she howled in pain. Denise swatted at it and knocked it onto the floor. It rolled away without burning the varnish and disappeared.

"Holy cow. How'd you do that?" Kegan asked. He looked at his hands as if hoping he could do it too. The rest of them looked at Quinn with a mixture of fear and excitement on their faces. I started my breathing, trying to keep calm.

"This is one of the weapons you may face. It will burn a person, but only skin."

We all looked at Denise to see her sweating after the effects of the burn. Her pants looked fine, but she complained of the pain underneath.

"Kat, this is the charm to heal burns. Learn it and heal her." Quinn recited something in a strange tongue. Kat nodded and then bent her head to Denise's leg. Placing her hand on it, she mumbled the words and Denise sighed in relief.

"Do you all wish to experience it yourselves, or will you believe me when I say it is excruciating?"

"I believe you," Kat said. She looked shaken.

Quinn said, "Since Denise has already had a taste, I'll let her decide who will be first against me."

I didn't have to wonder who it would be. Since my breathing wasn't helping me calm down at all, I stood up and stepped forward before she had a chance to say my name. Denise looked surprised, but Quinn seemed pleased.

"Do I have a second to find my core, or do you start now?" I asked.

Quinn looked over at Denise and raised her eyebrows in question. Denise looked at me and nodded. "I'd say give her a minute. She'll never figure it out anyway, and then she can spend the whole minute building up her fear for what's coming."

I rolled my eyes but knew she was probably right.

Quinn chuckled and nodded. "One minute."

I closed my eyes and swallowed hard. I thought about what happened at Kat's, hoping to speed up the process. I'd started out by trying to calm myself but bad memories had flooded in, building up my hatred, anger, and irritations. Anger worked for me, so I might as well use it. I focused on my irritations and ticked them off in a mental list.

The garage door. The near miss with my car. The garbage truck. The look on Denise's face every time she had a new guy. The lost puppy look in Paul's eyes a few days after she'd dumped him. The whispers from the crowd after I'd slammed Jax into the locker. The parting of the halls every time I walked them. My parents fighting. The demon standing in front of me with a ball of fire.

My heart rate increased. I embraced the anger. I wanted it, knowing anger would be the only thing to keep me from harm. Anger always helped me deal with the way my parents treated me. Anger helped me ignore the hurt when Paul left me for Denise. Anger deadened the pain. Anger was my companion. My ally.

My center swelled and my core pulsed. The seconds ticked by. I didn't know how long it took, but time was running out. How could I hope to do this?

"Ten seconds," Quinn shouted.

"I'm not ready!" I shouted back. My eyes still clenched tight.

"Get ready!"

I opened my eyes, aware that my core still pulsed, but I couldn't embrace it fully. Quinn stood ten feet from me with a fire ball in her hand. She brought her arm up and hurled it like a fastball. I ducked in time to see her create another one and throw it at me. I'd never avoid it in time so I brought my arm up to block my face. The burn was incredible, scorching my skin along my arm just below my elbow. I ran to the side as anger built with each throb of the burn.

Another ball hit me in the back. I screamed in pain. They continued to come and Quinn shouted, "I'm not going to stop until you try."

I am trying! The hopelessness of failure fell over me. I ducked down, trying to fold myself into my core when it flickered. I reached for it with my soul. It infused me with energy and power in time to see a volley of fireballs descending on me.

I rolled to the side and grabbed one out of the air, knowing it would hurt but wanting it anyway. Pain was better than failure. I ignored the pain and threw it back with all my strength toward Quinn. She ducked in surprise and shot another at me. I zipped past it, avoiding them as they came faster and faster.

Eventually making it to her side, I rammed my fist into her gut. The ricochet of power blasted me back onto my butt. I slid across the floor until my head slammed into the bleachers.

Pinpricks of light floated past my blurry vision. A strange echo sounded until I realized it was someone shouting my name. Sitting up slowly I shook my head, trying to clear it. In the background, I heard clapping as if someone were impressed, if a little shocked as well.

Kat raced to my side and grabbed my hand in hers. She turned it over and looked confused at what she saw. I examined my hand, surprised the skin was undamaged. She shook her head. "I saw you grab that ball. Why aren't you burned here? You've got burns everywhere else you were hit, but not here."

I shrugged. "It hurt when I grabbed it. I don't know why it's not burned."

Kat ran her hands across my exposed skin where she saw the burns. Looking me over to see if she'd missed anything she asked, "I've got everything I can see. Anything under your clothes?"

I leaned forward and pointed to my back. I peered over my shoulder while watching her slide her hand slowly across my shirt. When she reached the area, she stopped as if she could see it through the shirt. She said her charm and the burn disappeared.

"How did you know where it was?" I asked.

"I can feel the heat through your clothes," she said.

Quinn cleared her throat. "Done yet?"

I stood up slowly and walked gingerly back to the center of the gym. My core had dissipated again, leaving me with just my normal strength. *When did it leave?*

"Nicely done, Claire," Quinn nodded. "I didn't think you had it in you."

"What exactly happened at the end there?" I asked, rubbing the back of my head.

"Nothing. Just a lucky shot."

"That wasn't nothing. Power burst from you!" I said, indicating how far it had thrown me.

"You attacked my center. That is where my strength is and you went right for it. Gave you quite the jolt, as we all saw."

"So will that happen every time I hit you there?"

Quinn didn't answer, but turned to the others. "Who's next?"

"I want to know more now."

"Kegan, how about you?" Quinn said, ignoring me.

"No." I said. "You need to tell them."

"Now is not the time." She glared and tried to turn back to the others.

"It is. Who knows when some demon lord is supposed to come after us, and you aren't going to tell them?" My voice rose in volume and pitch with each word.

"What are you talking about, Claire?" Kegan asked.

"She's a demon."

"Yeah, right," Denise snorted. Kat and Emily just looked at Quinn.

"I saw her! She transformed into a demon right outside the school last night."

Quinn stared at me with her lips tight.

"Tell them." I glared at her. She shook her head. Anger flooded my senses again and I grabbed her arm. "Tell them!"

"Do not touch me!" Quinn snapped and yanked her arm out of my grasp. Heat radiated from her.

"If you want my help, you'd better come clean or I'm gone," I threatened.

Quinn seemed to think it over before she snapped, "Very well."

The lights in the room flickered. Quinn's image shifted again, this time faster than it had last night. Her hair disappeared, replaced by shiny black skin. Her horns emerged from the tight bun. Her legs lengthened and her stilettos morphed to claws again. She looked evil and terrifying, but now that it was in the center of the gymnasium, she didn't seem nearly as intimidating as she had before. I even managed to find and keep a tenuous hold on my core.

Denise screamed and scurried back in an awkward crabwalk as Quinn turned toward her. I struggled not to laugh as Denise freaked out. I'd handled it much better last night. At least that was the story I'd stick to. Kat and Kegan stood open mouthed. Emily look curious.

"Wow, Quinn. You are one ugly woman," Emily said, giggling. I whipped my head to the side to look at her, stunned by her comment. She handled it much better than me.

"You have a lot of nerve to say that to me." Demon Quinn narrowed her eyes but waved her hand as if to dismiss it. "But I will let it pass. I need you alive and would hate to have to destroy you before getting what I want."

"You're a demon?" Denise asked just above a whisper. "But you said you were a supernatural like us."

"I fell and the demon lord claimed me. He's had me under his power for a long time. I want my freedom. I was supposed to try to make you fall as well, but when I saw you were able to deny your inner desires, I decided to have you help me break his hold on me. You'll save yourselves in the process."

Quinn watched us all as we adjusted to her revelation.

"Who's to say you won't just destroy us after you get what you want?" Kat asked. I couldn't believe I hadn't thought of that.

"I must do something selfless in order to break my chains of servitude. If I killed you, that wouldn't be selfless, now would it?" Quinn tried to smile, but the fragile skin around her mouth didn't let it stretch upward. It looked painful.

She looked at each of us. When her eyes rested on me, I didn't look away, though I really wanted to. She stared into my eyes for a moment. "I desire to escape my own prison enough that I will teach you how to defeat a demon. That puts me at risk of you trying to overpower me. The five of you can do it together, if you know how. By taking this chance, I hope you will allow me to live. If you free me, we will all vow not to harm each other. It's as simple as that."

Simple? Far from it.

"So you want us to free you, a demon from hell, and let you loose on the world?" Emily asked.

"Yes," Quinn said.

"What will happen to the world when you are free?" Denise asked.

"I honestly don't know," she said with a quick shrug. "I believe once I'm free of my master, I will no longer be a demon."

We all exchanged glances.

"I do know what will happen if you don't free me," Quinn said. Her expression made me want to hide, but I held my ground. "I will destroy you now and drag you down personally so my master can feed on your misery." The gleam in her eyes as she talked about destroying us made my stomach clench. The others leaned back a little.

"Enough of this. We must continue." Quinn stretched and shifted her demon body. Her legs shortened to their previous length. The spikes on her heal transformed into her stilettos. Everything returned to normal, but I could still see a difference in her. I knew what she was. The hidden features beneath the face she wore to fool the world were still slightly visible.

"I do not expect another demon to come here; however, the master is not trusting so he may send spies. You should be prepared just in case."

I was sure that ugly kid I'd seen with her last night was a demon. She still wasn't being completely honest. Before I could call her on it, she continued.

"Without my instruction, you will not survive. I must teach you how to destroy a demon before the Master's attack. If you do not destroy him, he will continue with his plan and take you down for his enjoyment. Believe me — you don't want that."

Quinn placed her hand in front of her belly again as if she were testing it for more fire. She grinned when she produced another fireball. "Now, let's continue with your lesson. As demons, we are connected to the center of the earth. The hot magma that burns there is nothing compared to what burns within us. Eventually, if a demon fights long enough without replenishing by returning to the core, our center is weakened and we are defeated. If our core is extinguished, we dissolve and are vanquished."

"How long does it take to tire you?" Kat asked.

"I could out last all of you individually. If you expect to beat a demon, you have to work together and overwhelm it." Quinn looked at all of us and grinned.

"Who's next?"

Kat volunteered. She managed to conjure invisible shields, but Quinn still hit her multiple times. Soon Kat had wrapped herself in a shield that Quinn couldn't penetrate. Poor Kat couldn't heal herself even though she tried, so Quinn did it for her.

Denise got hit more times than Kat and me together, but she started pulling energy from all of us — except Kegan — making the fireballs bounce off her and roll away without doing any damage. It felt strange to have my strength sapped and not be able to do anything about it. I tried to fight it, but couldn't shake it off. As she got closer to Quinn, Denise sucked Quinn's energy, and it stopped flowing from us. Quinn's fireballs became less intense.

Eventually Denise got close enough to grab Quinn by the neck and throw her across the room. She didn't quite bounce, but looked disgruntled at the change in circumstances.

"Well, I wasn't expecting that." Quinn took a deep breath and said, "Kegan, you're up."

Kegan strode to the center of the gym and took his glasses off again. Emily whispered to Kat, "He looks so cute without his glasses."

"He looks cute with his glasses," Denise said, staring at him absently. A perfect blush spread across her face when he turned and met her eye.

"Lucky for him he's immune to your kind of charm," I said.

"Shut up," she said. She ignored me as she watched Kegan and Quinn.

The first fireball thrown at him almost hit, but he somehow managed to use a blast of air to throw it off course. The next fireball dissipated more than three feet away. The third fireball was extinguished before it left her hand. Quinn gasped in surprise and set her shoulders to the task. She held her hand in front of her center for longer than any previous time until the fireball glowed white instead of the reddish orange of before.

Kegan placed his feet shoulder width apart, getting ready for the attack. Quinn flicked her hand as if whipping a Frisbee at him. Kegan threw his hands up, palms forward to blast the fireball back. It burst into millions of sparks, leaving blind spots in my vision. When I could see again, I was surprised to find Kegan on the ground looking stunned and Quinn in the process of standing up.

"We are finished for this morning," she said slowly, her labored breathing interrupting each word.

We all looked at Emily. She looked relieved but annoyed at the same time. *Does she want to fight her?* What could a shapeshifter do against a ball of fire?

Quinn adjusted her black suit. "Continue your independent study and we will resume tomorrow morning. Kat, figure out a way to help Emily. She's going to need some assistance when she confronts my fireballs tomorrow."

She'd gotten off easy.

Emily frowned. "I don't need her assistance," Emily said after Quinn walked away. "I'm ready now."

Quinn stopped and turned around slowly. "You think so?" She had a gleam in her eye as she produced a fireball.

"Yes," Emily stated simply.

Shrugging as if she didn't care how it turned out, Quinn threw the ball at Emily. I whipped my head to see, stunned when Emily just stood there without making any attempt to dodge it.

I flinched as the ball hit her directly in the face. It bounced off and rolled away, disappearing after a moment. Quinn threw another and another at her, hitting her head, arms, shoulders, stomach, and legs. But Emily just stood there, looking bored.

"How did you do that?" I asked when Quinn stopped and approached her.

Emily smiled a gorgeous smile. "I changed my skin. She said these fireballs burned skin, so I changed it. It took me a bit of practice to get it right. Luckily I wasn't the first one to have a go with her, but I have skills too." She looked directly at Quinn as she said the last part.

"I will no longer discount you," Quinn said. "It will be interesting to see what you can do with an actual blade coming at you tomorrow."

CHAPTER TEN

I glanced in the little mirror hanging in my locker before class and sighed at my wild hair. It stuck up in odd angles. I picked at it, trying to make it look a little better. In my rush this morning, I hadn't even looked at my makeup. My mascara was smudged, so I wiped my fingers under the bottom lashes to clean it up a little. My shirt looked rumpled from the demon lessons I'd just finished, and my cheeks were flushed from the exercise.

I shook my head, giving it up as a lost cause and closed my locker. I took a step and nearly ran into Paul.

"Gosh, give me a heart attack, why don't ya?" I mumbled, surprised to see him. He'd done this for months last year, but I always ignored him, still too mad at him for going to the dark side.

"Hey, Claire Bear, are you actually talking to me?" He smiled.

"Don't call me that. You know I hate it." I frowned, trying to ignore the small flutters in my stomach that his deep blue eyes always produced.

Having them nearly covered by his shaggy blonde hair helped until he brushed it back off his forehead.

"Sorry," he said, biting the corner of his bottom lip. I looked at those lips and wished things had turned out differently. Now that he'd been one of Denise's boys, even for a short time, his lips wouldn't be coming anywhere near mine.

"I've missed you," he said, leaning up against the locker.

"Hmm," I mumbled. I didn't dare get into a conversation with him. I'd shouted at him for twenty minutes after learning he was Denise's new love interest. He'd been so occupied with her, I wasn't sure he'd heard a word I'd said.

"We used to have so much fun together. Don't you miss that?" he asked.

I sighed, not sure what to say. Yeah, I missed it, more than anything. I missed the walks we used to take with his dog, the park where we'd play on the swings like we were little kids, the talks we had. The way he listened so patiently when I ranted about the newest irritation my parents had produced in my life. The once-a-week ice creams at the concession counter in the local grocery store. The study sessions for the classes we had together.

"Yeah, I do," I whispered. I knew it wasn't completely Paul's fault — Denise was a vampire, after all — yet I still wasn't ready to wipe the slate clean.

"Can I drive you home today?" he asked. I heard the hope he couldn't disguise in those simple words.

"No," I said slowly.

Paul frowned and looked down at his feet. He used the toe of his shoes to wipe at something only he could see.

I would have loved to see him suffer longer, but I decided to make an effort. "I actually drove today." I tried not to smile when his head popped up in response.

"You really drove that guzzler?" he asked in disbelief.

"Shut up. I was running late." I shrugged.

"Do you want to go get ice-cream? They have a new twisty flavored frozen yogurt," he added with a big grin.

"Um, sure," I said, feeling my traitorous heart beginning to forgive him.

"I'll pick you up right after you get home," he said.

"Actually, I can't do it right after school. I've got something I have to do first." *Don't want him to think my life is completely open.* "How about we meet there at five."

"Great," he said, sounding relieved I'd responded so positively. He lifted his hand as if he wanted to tug on my ear like he used to, but he let it drop without touching me.

"I'll see you later." I turned and headed to my class, reaching up to my ear and tugged on it myself.

After school as I approached my car, I dug in my bag to find the keys. I wove through the parking lot, ignoring the students gathered around their cars flirting or chatting with each other. When I finally found my keys, I looked up and saw Denise standing next to my car.

"Nice ride," she said, looking over the chipped paint, the dents in the fenders, the cracks in the windshield, and the torn upholstery.

"Bite me," I said.

"No thanks."

"What do you want?" I unlocked my door and threw my bag to the passenger seat.

"We should meet and work out some things." The way she said it made me think it was the last thing she wanted to do. I totally agreed with her there.

"I'd rather not."

"If we've got a demon after us, don't you think it would be a good idea to get a handle on our abilities?"

"Right. When?" I asked.

"I'm free now for a bit, or we could meet in an hour or so."

"Now's fine," I said, "Where?"

"Have you seen that trail that shoots off from the duck pond in the park? The one that twists through the trees?"

"No. I don't usually spend time at the park." At least not lately.

"There is a clearing about a quarter mile off the trail that would be secluded enough for us to try a few things without anyone spotting us." She smiled like she was remembering something.

"If that's the place you go to suck the life out of your boyfriends, I'm not going there."

"Fine. Where do you suggest we meet?"

"Well," I said, glancing around. "I'm not sure I'm ready to actually hash everything out with you, so we don't need to be completely secluded, but there is that undeveloped field behind the new shopping center. No one would bother us there."

"Great, let's go." She walked over to the side of my car and tried to open the door. It was still locked.

"What? You're going to ride with me?"

"Yeah, why not?" She shrugged like it was no big deal.

"You would actually get into my 'ride' and be seen in public with me?" I looked around at the others in the parking lot who had been watching us as we talked. Everyone knew I hated Denise. Seeing us together was going to cause a lot of gossip.

"Who cares if people see me with you? It might actually improve your standing."

I tightened my jaw to keep back the growl that threatened, but the rumbling in the back of my throat couldn't be stopped. "Fine," I said through clenched teeth. At least they hadn't lengthened. Yet.

I ducked into the car, threw my bag into the back seat to open a spot for her, and unlocked her door. She slid in gracefully and connected her seat belt in one smooth movement.

I started the car, praying silently that I wouldn't embarrass myself with the stupid stick shift. I backed out with no problem, but the car stuttered when I pulled out of the parking lot into traffic.

"Not a word," I said as the car lurched forward, finally agreeing to maintain a normal speed.

"Wouldn't dream of it," she said.

I drove us to the empty field in silence. She just watched the road. I parked next to a section of chain link fence that had been peeled back to allow access for some large trucks a few weeks ago and never closed. Getting out, I walked around the front of the car and headed into the field. The tall grass and weeds came to my elbows. Denise lifted her arms away from her body slightly and ran her hands across the tops of the weeds as we made our way in. In the center of the field, I stopped and turned around to face her.

"So what did you have in mind?"

"Not really sure," she admitted.

"You don't have a plan?"

"I'm still surprised you actually agreed to come." She shrugged. "I just think we ought to figure some things out so we're ready for tomorrow. Who knows how soon we'll need to fight off a real demon?"

"Quinn is a real demon."

"Yeah, but she's not trying to kill us. Someday one will."

I nodded and waited for her to say something else.

"Quinn said we'd be facing blades tomorrow, didn't she?" Denise asked.

"Yeah, but how do you fight with swords or knives?"

Denise shrugged. "I talked to Kat about her shield she used to cover herself from the fireballs and she's going to see what she can do to cover us as well. Emily might be able to make her skin hard enough it wouldn't be cut either. Kegan will probably just blow the sword to the side. I don't know what to do for me. You might be able to outrun it, or even dodge the blows, but what happens if you can't reach your core in time?"

"I'll be cut," I said. "It takes a bit to get my core built up. But this morning was much quicker than last night."

"Maybe if you and I practiced setting each other off, we could learn how to gather our strength sooner and we could have a better chance at stopping Quinn."

"Right, so what do you want me to do?" I asked.

"Get mad," she said simply.

"Ha. Usually that would be pretty easy, but since you aren't acting anything like you normally do, I don't feel the need to tear into you."

"Well, what do I usually do to tick you off?" she asked.

"You suck the life out of everyone you come in contact with."

"I do not," she said. "Just the hot guys." She winked at me. I scowled back.

"You've sucked energy from all of us. I can see it when you pull it to you."

"What does it look like?"

"It sort of shimmers, like heat waves on a hot day. Your body just sucks it up like a sponge." I shivered at the image, jealous of the power she got so easily.

"Well, it feels incredible," she sighed. "The best is when it's brand new with a fresh guy. I've actually gone back to one or two that I really liked the sensations with, but it isn't the same as a new one." She had a dreamy look in her eyes.

"You're disgusting."

"Why? Because I like the feel of the power and energy? Do you get disgusted when someone eats a meal and feels good afterward? What's the difference?"

"You are taking it from a living person!" I nearly shouted.

"I've never drained anyone dry. And I don't bite people. They're in no danger."

"But still, they come away from their time with you like they've been drugged, and it takes them days to recuperate." Thoughts of Paul trying to come out of it invaded my memory.

"They never complain. They feel deprived when I let them go." She crossed her arms over her chest and looked down at me.

"That's because you leak some euphoric feelings back to them. You make them feel good as you slowly kill them."

"I don't kill them!"

"You will when you crave so much you take it all." My core flickered. "You like the feeling of that power way too much. When you pulled it from Quinn and us this morning, you glowed. You'll take too much!"

Denise slapped me hard enough to make my face go numb. The slow, creeping rage came full force and burst into flame inside my core. I wrapped my soul around it and claimed it.

I clawed at her, missing her face, but catching her hair in the process. Denise howled in pain and lunged at me. I jumped out of the way, avoiding her completely.

She turned around fast and grabbed me by the arms before I could move. Denise lifted me in the air, but I forced my arms open, breaking her grip. She set me back down on the ground, but managed to regain a hold on my biceps. I clawed at her hands with my nails. She screamed in pain, but didn't let go. I forced my fingers underneath her palms, scratching my own arms in the process. Once I got my fingers under her hands, I yanked up making her joints pop.

She released my arms and swung her legs behind mine, knocking me to the ground. She fell on top of me in the process, knocking the breath out of me. I wheezed in painfully. She pulled small amounts of energy from me. I bucked under her, not wanting to be drained. It wasn't anything like what I'd seen her pull before. I snarled in triumph and hit her in the face. She covered her nose with her hands, rolling off me. I scrambled up quickly into a crouched position, ready to launch at her with a moment's notice.

She held her face in her hands, rocking back and forth. "I wasn't trying to kill you," she mumbled thickly through her hands, now dripping with blood. "I just wanted to help you find your power and access mine."

I relaxed my position slightly and sat on the ground, panting from the exertion. "But you always have access to your strength. You've never had a problem getting it."

"I can't just call it up at will. I have to feel threatened to defend myself. The guys I'm with give it freely. I can't just take it from others without feeling like I need it," she said. She removed her hand from her face and gingerly touched her nose.

"Is it broken?" she asked, moving closer.

I leaned forward, not wanting to get too close because I still wanted to hurt her. I fought the urge to knock her out while she was down.

"I've never seen a broken nose before, but it doesn't look crooked or even really swollen."

"You cut my lip," she said as she used her tongue to lightly feel the edges of her mouth.

"I'd say I'm sorry, but I'm really not," I said with a shrug.

Denise surprised me by laughing. "I'm not either. That was awesome. I had more fun with you just now than I did when I threw Quinn across the gym." Why was she saying things that made me hate her less and less? If I wasn't careful, I'd have to rethink my vendetta.

"Now that was cool." I grinned at the image of Quinn sailing through the air.

"Not like when you grabbed that fireball out of the air and threw it back at her. She was stunned. Then you managed to knock out her fire for a moment when it sent you flying across the room. She wasn't able to grab any more fireballs, though she tried repeatedly. Not till after she'd rested for a bit."

Denise wiped her hands on the weeds we sat in and looked around for something to stop the bleeding with. Somehow in our scuffle, I'd lost my shoe. I yanked off my sock and tossed it to her. She looked at it cautiously, but she folded it up and held it to her nose.

"I've worn it for two days," I said, hoping it didn't stink. "But you probably can't smell anything anyways."

"Nope. But that's gross."

"I didn't have time to change last night before passing out on my bed." I pulled my shoe back on over my bare toes.

"Whatever," she shrugged. "Maybe we should head home. I'm not up to sparring with you anymore today. We'll have to see what we can do tomorrow."

"Hopefully we can come up with some way to avoid her blades." We worked our way back to the car and watched the road until it was empty before we climbed inside.

"I'm sorry about your face," I said softly in front of her house.

"I don't think it will be too bad. Maybe I'll call Kat and see if she knows how to take down swelling and heal cuts as well as burns." Denise pulled the bloody sock away from her face. The bleeding had stopped. She held the sock out to me.

"Keep it," I said, leaning away from her. "I've got another one just like it."

Denise chuckled and climbed out of the car after checking to make sure no one was around.

I couldn't believe my emotions. I still really disliked her, but the hate was gone, replaced by a healthy dose of caution and a little bit of respect. Maybe finding out we were mortal enemies would improve our relationship.

Chapter Eleven

I drove the short distance to my house, and managed to do it smoothly enough to keep the car from jerking while shifting gears. I smiled to myself as I climbed out of my car and headed into the house. I threw my bag onto the counter and stuck my head in the fridge, looking for something to eat. The steaks Mom had thawing looked really good. I contemplated eating one raw until my mom coming down the hallway brought me back to my senses. *I almost ate raw meat?*

"Claire!" she gasped. "What happened to you?"

I turned around quickly to see her staring at me and leaning around trying to see my back again.

"What? Oh, this." I brushed the dirt and weeds off my pants. "It's just . . ."

"Have you been in a fight?" She eyed me closely to see if I looked damaged in any way.

"No. It wasn't a fight … it was … my shrink . . ." I stopped and took a deep breath before rushing through. "My shrink told me it would be very helpful for my anger issues to do some physical exercises to help release some of the tension. I went running through a field then lay down to rest for a second." I reached up and pulled a piece of grass out of my hair.

She watched me closely as I gave her my excuse. It wasn't completely made up. He had told me to exercise. I kept my eyes on her, noting the opening and closing of her mouth as she tried to respond. "Okay then."

Dr. Lowe sure is helpful at getting me out of discussions with Mom.

I grabbed my bag and a slice of ham from the fridge, clamping down the longing for that steak, and went to my room. My attempts at homework were pathetic. I soon gave it up as a lost cause and took a shower to get ready to meet Paul.

***

I slid into the bench seat in the dining area near the deli at Lisa's Marketplace moments before Paul arrived.

"Thanks for meeting me," he said.

"Can't pass up the idea of ice cream." I tried to smile, but was still not sure how I felt about him or how much I wanted to make him suffer.

He led us back to the table after we'd ordered and let me slide into the bench. I stayed close to the edge, to keep him from sliding in next to me like he used to do. I was impressed when his frown disappeared quickly as he sat down across from me.

When I looked up into his big blue eyes, I realized my plan would backfire. If he were sitting next to me, I wouldn't have to look at him. Now all I could do was remember all the longing I'd felt over the years. I hadn't been brave enough to let him know how I really felt about him, but I had no problem letting him know livid I was that he dated Denise.

He seemed clueless about it after she dumped him and he started trying to hang out with me again. When I'd shouted at him about his betrayal, he hadn't said anything. I didn't leave him enough time. The haunted look on his face when he realized he'd hurt me continued to bother me every time I thought of it. *Was I too hard on him?* If I wasn't careful, I'd forgive him completely and even let him know how much I had longed for him.

I took a spoonful of my ice cream and watched Paul take a huge scoop. He had changed subtly over the last few months. His muscles had solidified, and his hands were bigger. He had more freckles. I almost smiled at the newness of him, frowning when I realized where my mind was going. He bit his bottom lip and acted like he was going to say something. He took another scoop instead.

I searched for something safe to discuss. "So how are your classes?"

"Good," he answered around a mouth full of ice cream. "How about you?"

"They're okay. Nothing too hard."

"I wish we had some classes together this term."

"Hmm," I nodded noncommittally. I didn't think it would have been a good idea. "Maybe next term."

"What classes are you taking next term?" he asked.

"Most of the same since they are those dang all-year ones, but I do have a couple electives. Not sure what they are right now. Trying to get through this term before I start worrying about next one." Maybe I wouldn't even be around next term to worry about the stupid classes.

"True. I'll keep my fingers crossed." He smiled, and I returned it easily.

"There it is. I've been hoping to see you smile again." He gazed at me as I blushed.

I took another scoop. "How's Max doing?"

"He's still jumping up on everyone who comes to the door." He shook his head and leaned back against the seat. "You know, come to think of it, you were the only one he wouldn't jump up on. He knew you wouldn't take any crap from him, I guess. He treated you better than he did me."

I nearly choked on my ice cream. Max had probably known all along I was part dog and thought of me as a buddy.

"He's a good dog," I said. "Maybe we could take him for a walk. I kind of miss him."

"That would be awesome. He's missed you lots. Maybe even as much as I have." The look of longing in his eyes made my stomach flip.

"Sorry," I mumbled. "I just needed time to sort things out."

"Yeah, I know." He lowered his eyes and dug patterns into his yogurt. "I wanted to apologize for what I did to you. I didn't know me going out with . . . her would upset you so much. I mean, I never thought you and I were…"

"We weren't," I said quickly. I sighed and swallowed the bitterness that threatened to come. How could I explain to him my irrational hatred for Denise without telling him what we were? "I just have some issues with Denise and probably reacted a little harshly. I just thought you, of all people, would understand how much I hated what she did. I mean, I ranted about her every time she switched boyfriends." I stopped talking as my anger rose.

"I know, it's just when it became a possibility for me, I couldn't help myself. I was in it too far to pay attention to what was going on in the world the whole time we went out. I even forgot to do homework and had to do some major catching up after we were through."

"I don't really want to talk about it anymore." I frowned and sucked on my spoon.

He nodded and dug a deeper trench into his yogurt. After a moment, he looked up at me through his long eyelashes. "Are we good?" he asked hopefully.

I sighed. "I don't know for sure yet, but I think we aren't in a bad place."

He nodded thoughtfully again. I hurried to add, "I'm not mad at you. But I'm not sure if I'm ready to just go back to how we used to be. Things have changed. I've changed." I swallowed hard. He had no idea how much I'd changed. I still didn't quite understand it myself.

"Can we start over?" he asked.

"Do you really think we can?" I was willing to, but wondered if it would actually work. Would I be able to forget it all?

"I want to try. Will you give us a chance?"

If he wanted to start again, I wasn't going to go back to being best buds and be treated just like one of the guys. He'd have to work for my friendship.

I sat quietly, looking into his hopeful eyes. After nearly losing myself in them again, I reached my hand out to him. "Hi, I'm Claire."

Chapter Twelve

Quinn stepped in front of the five of us and smiled wickedly. "Are you ready for your next lesson?"

I swallowed hard and looked at the others. They all nodded slowly, but none of them seemed any more excited than me.

"Good," Quinn said. "Emily, you will be first since you went last yesterday. I'm sure you are eager to prove yourself."

Emily nodded. The rest of us moved to the bleachers. Quinn pulled a long gleaming blade from out of nowhere. She raised it high and slashed downward. It made an ominous sound as it cut through the air in front of Emily. She stepped back slightly, but then she firmly planted her feet shoulder width apart and faced Quinn with determination.

I couldn't tell if she transformed into anything or changed her skin. Quinn brought the blade forward slowly to press it against Emily's stomach. The muscles in Quinn's arms flexed as she pressed harder, but Emily slid backward with no damage. She had to take a quick step to keep from falling over. Quinn pulled the blade back and swung it at Emily's arm. Emily took the blow with no sign of injury. The sound it made as it struck her almost sounded like metal on metal.

Quinn smiled and began hacking at her from every angle. Emily withstood every strike. Eventually, Quinn stopped and took a look at her blade. "You have damaged my sword," she said as if surprised.

Emily shrugged. "Sorry." She smiled, looking very pleased with herself, and walked over to the bench. "Kat, will you see what you can do with these?" Emily stuck her finger in a couple of the larger holes in her clothes. Her skin may have been untouchable, but not her clothes.

"Who's next?" Quinn asked.

Kegan handed me his glasses. "Hold these, will ya?" He jumped up and jogged to the center of the floor.

I reached over and touched Emily's arm. Though cool to the touch and very firm, it still looked like her flesh. "How did you do that?" I whispered.

"Just a bit of tweaking my body's chemistry. I practiced last night and didn't do so hot at first." She held up her hand to show a fresh scar across the length of her palm just under her fingers.

I gave a low whistle. Kat shook her head.

"I tried it myself since I didn't think I could

convince my mom to come at me with a knife." She grinned. "It took a while, but eventually I got it. It was a different change than the one to keep from burning. That was more on the surface. This was deeper inside."

"Cool."

"I know, isn't it? This is really kind of fun, don't you think?" Emily said.

"Sure. Loads of fun," I said, rolling my eyes.

"Shhh," Denise whispered. "She's ready to start on Kegan."

I let go of Emily and looked up at Kegan. Quinn lifted the blade and raised her eyebrow at him.

"I'm ready," he said.

She tightened her hold on the handle of the sword and brought it forward. Not fast, but definitely not slow. As Kegan motioned with his arms, the blade stopped its progression. Quinn tried again. He stopped her before making contact. She gripped the sword with both hands, attacking with much more energy. He continued to stop her and soon advanced on her. She stumbled a couple of times until I saw a shield of light form around her. Kegan gave up the offense and returned to defense but eventually began to slow down in his responses. He wasn't panting, but he looked tired. *How much concentration did it take to move the air?*

Quinn sped up, forcing him back. When he stumbled, Denise gasped even louder than I did and nearly jumped up. He regained his footing to keep Quinn at bay. She pressed her advantage, upping the intensity of each stroke as she pummeled him with the blade. Kegan looked around the room wildly as if searching for something to help him. I don't know what he saw, but he smiled and spun around. His fast circle reminded me of a discus thrower as he hurled what I could only assume was air at Quinn.

It must have hit her right in the center because she fell back hard onto her butt, the sword falling out of her hands and clanking on the wood floor before coming to a stop a few feet away.

Denise stood up and whooped loudly, cheering for Kegan. I was surprised she didn't do a double-Dutch and punch the air for him. Kegan leaned forward, his hands on his knees, breathing deep. When he returned to the bleachers, the satisfied grin made me chuckle.

"Next," Quinn grunted as she stood up.

Kat stood up and walked forward. "I'll try it, though I don't think I'll be anywhere as cool as you two."

She joined Quinn on the floor and mumbled something under her breath too low for even my improved hearing to catch. Quinn stepped forward, going for the stomach first. About three inches in front of Kat, the blade stopped. Quinn pulled it back and tried a different place. Kat stopped her again. She swung the blade around and attacked from all angles. It always stopped three inches away from making contact with Kat's skin.

Kat had a look of intense concentration, as if it were difficult keeping the shield around her. Quinn seemed to notice it as well and attacked with renewed vigor. The blade got closer. Still Kat prevented it from touching her skin. Sweat beaded on her forehead and she panted with the exertion it took to keep her shield up.

When Quinn chanted something, Kat's shield wavered. Shimmers in the air surrounded her. Why could I see it now and hadn't seen anything like it before when Kat formed her shield in the first place?

Shouting something unintelligible, Quinn used one hand to swipe at the air, and then brought her blade slowly to touch against Kat's neck. Kat stood as still as she could through her panting.

"You would be dead if I were truly trying to kill you," Quinn said sharply. "You must maintain your shield at all times or it will be no use to you. Not many demons are able to use a counter spell to negate the one you cast, but some can. Don't let them. You have to hold it longer against everything that comes at you, and maintain it while casting offensive spells."

Quinn looked at us.

I didn't know how I'd manage to survive this practice, but I knew I would have to do this on my own. *No one else needed help. I'm not going to ask for any either.*

I looked over at Denise. Instead of looking smug, she looked worried. *Great, I can't even count on her to make me mad enough to access my core.*

Quinn sent Kat to the bleachers and cocked her head to the side as she looked at Denise and I. Raising my hand in a fist as if to indicate we should decide by rock, paper, scissors, Denise shrugged and held hers in a fist as well. We rocked it off and came up the same for the first three times. I growled and clenched my teeth. Was she reading my mind somehow? On our fourth time, she got rock to my scissors.

"Best out of three?" she asked.

"No, I'll go." I said, hoping my irritation would help me find my core. I stood up and walked forward. As I approached Quinn, the realization of what I was about to do hit me. I swallowed hard and looked directly at her blade. Maybe it would throw me into some kind of angry fit and then I could access my core. It looked even worse up close. The sharp edge had some dings in it from her hacking away at Emily earlier, but it still looked wicked enough to cut me up with no problem.

Quinn smirked. "You don't have anything like they did to protect yourself. You are going to have to come up with something more primal to get out of this."

Primal? Before I had time to think it over, Quinn flicked the sword at me and ripped through the shoulder of my shirt. She didn't break the skin at all, but the blade made an inch-long gash in the material. She then flicked the sword toward my leg. I flinched to the side, but not quickly enough to avoid the tear she made in my pants.

"You're ruining my clothes, Quinn." Irritation was a good step toward the anger I needed.

She swung the sword to the side, and I ducked just in time to avoid a hit. I jumped up and ran to the left. Quinn followed, advancing on me with the sword.

"So you aren't even going to play fair and give me a sword?" I panted.

"No. Why would a demon want to play fair?" she said as she swung at me, almost catching me again. "You knew what to expect today and yet you came empty handed. You must learn to prepare better or fight with what you've got."

She lunged toward me. I jumped over her using her shoulders to propel me further than I would have ever managed on my own power. My core pulsed, but embracing it was still difficult. I dropped to the ground and rolled away as Quinn attacked. She anticipated my motion and brought her sword down near where I had been. If I'd been any slower, she would have hit my upper thigh.

I scrambled up. Dodging to the side, I ran away from her. She moved quicker than expected and intercepted me before I made it across the gym. I slid to a stop and kicked at her arm holding the blade, hitting her in the elbow. She nearly dropped the sword so I punched her in the face and then grabbed my hand in pain. Hitting Denise in the field yesterday was nothing compared to this. Quinn didn't seem effected at all.

I still hadn't been able to embrace my core. The pain in my fist took all my focus away from protecting myself. Quinn took the sword in her other hand, letting the other arm hang limply. *Yay, a point for me. Damaged elbow.* She swiped at me as I grinned. Warmth covered my arm. I looked down and saw blood dripping onto the floor at my feet. The opening of the wound was eerie to look at. A three-inch gash left a flap of skin open. Layers of fat and muscle were visible, but luckily no bone.

I stared at it in confusion. *Why don't I feel pain?* Maybe my core could help me avoid pain. What would happen when the core disappeared? I looked up at Quinn. She frowned and opened her mouth. Before she could speak, something hit me from the side and knocked me to the floor.

A flash of blonde hair was all I saw before a body crushed my chest. I thrashed underneath the weight and recognized Denise as she leaned toward my arm. In shock, I realized what she was doing just moments before her mouth covered my wound.

I screamed in rage at the idea this vampire was going to taste my blood. My core enveloped me as my pulse skyrocketed, sending fire through my veins. I grabbed her long hair and yanked with all my strength. Denise screamed in pain and fought against me, but not to get away. She pulled against my hand and kept leaning toward my arm. Her mouth was red and she wanted more. I didn't think she had bitten me but she was in a blood frenzy. Her eyes didn't look normal, but glazed over with addiction.

Using my good arm to pull on her hair again, I brought my knees up to try to push her away with my legs. I failed, howling when she brought her lips against my gash. I could feel her sucking the blood and was freaked that she would end up biting me. Or would she suck me dry first?

I wasn't nearly as strong as her efforts to stay latched to my arm. Was my weakness from her sucking my blood and energy, or was her strength from finally tasting blood? I let go of her hair and brought my hand to her face, reluctant to get anywhere near her teeth. I'd heard vampire venom was deadly to werewolves, but didn't know if that was true or not. I didn't want to test it now. I grabbed at her face, getting my fingers under her chin enough to grip her jaw. I pushed with as much force as I could, but was ineffective. My anger flared. I reached back and punched her in the jaw as hard as I could.

That did it. She screamed, an eerie call that sent shivers down my spine and brought a growl in response. She left my arm and lunged for my face with her hands outstretched. I brought my good arm up to block her and used my knees to throw her off course. When she came at me again, I kicked her with my legs, sending her sprawling. She lunged at me faster than I could have imagined and would have caught me if I hadn't been just as quick.

I rolled to the side and came up into a crouch. Denise lunged again. I brought my good arm up to swipe at her head as she neared me. One good hit knocked her flat on her back. With my good hand, I grabbed her around the neck, placing my knee across her ribcage. The span of my hand wasn't big enough to cut off her air by itself so I leaned forward, putting pressure on her throat.

She struggled, clawing at my hand. I wasn't going to let her up. She looked in my face, but her gaze shifted. She stared at my arm as it dripped blood. She hissed and bucked, trying to get out from under me.

Quinn cautiously stepped forward and pinched Denise's nose closed. Denise squirmed as her eyes darkened with hatred.

Quinn spoke slowly as if to a child. "You are overcome. Stop now or I will let Claire have her vengeance. Come back to yourself now."

Denise closed her eyes and tried to hold still. It seemed like her mind struggled against her instincts. I knew she wanted my blood, but she was trying to get herself under control. I hated to admit it, but I was impressed that she was able to do it.

Once she stopped bucking, I loosened my hold on her neck. I didn't remove my hand nor take my weight off her. I didn't want to give her too much freedom to go for me again. I glanced at Quinn. She nodded. I slowly took my hand off Denise's neck. When she didn't react violently, I again looked at Quinn and then moved my knee off Denise. Quinn kept her hand over Denise's nose.

Denise held still and breathed slowly through her red-rimmed mouth. I stepped back, breathing hard. I looked up to see Kat and Emily clinging to each other's hands as they watched us. I attempted a smile, but my heart wasn't in it. Kegan stared at Denise, irritating me that he seemed more concerned for her than for me. I closed my eyes and shook my head. *I'm not going to let her ruin another friendship with a guy.* Denise struggled occasionally with Quinn, but she didn't try to get up.

I looked down at my arm and then gripped it with my hand, trying to stop the flow of blood. Luckily there were no spurts, but it bled freely. It almost tingled, but the pain seemed to be blocked by my core. I hadn't lost it yet.

Kat approached carefully as if afraid to upset me. "Do you want me to try to help you?"

"Yeah," I said, wincing. "Do you think you can close skin up?" I opened my hand to show her the flap of skin.

She nodded hesitantly. "I think so." She reached forward slowly and touched the skin. She pushed it back up until it closed. She looked ready to pass out.

"Are you afraid of the sight of blood?"

"No, blood doesn't bother me."

"Then what's wrong with you?" I snapped. Kat blinked in surprise before glancing down at my arm, and then over at Denise. "Oh," I said, the anger lessening slightly.

Emily approached slowly and watched my face for a reaction of any kind. When she got closer, she gasped. I thought it would have been the sight of my arm, but her eyes never left my face.

"What now?" I huffed.

Emily just shook her head numbly as if afraid to tell me.

"What!" I shouted, causing Emily and Kat to both flinch. Kegan glanced at me before he looked away, staring at Denise.

"Your eyes, they've changed," Emily whispered.

I opened my mouth to ask what she meant, but Emily just shifted her eyes to show me the color of mine. They were no longer my dark brown. They had softened to a brownish gold with slight flecks of green near the pupil. They looked creepy.

"No. That's not possible." I shook my head in denial. "Do you think they'll stay that way? My parents will freak, thinking I'm doing drugs or something. Everyone will think I'm possessed."

Emily and Kat watched me without a word. Kat looked back at my arm and mumbled some chant. Her hand felt warm as she poured some sort of healing power into me. An intense itching started. Like all the itching of a cut healing was crammed into one tiny moment, and then it was gone. Kat removed her hand and I looked at my arm. Blood was everywhere. Kat tried to wipe most of it away with her hand as she had healed me. A long pink gash, the color of a week-old scar, replaced the fresh gash. Yet it wasn't healed completely.

I cautiously touched it, wondering if it would hurt. It was only a little numb. I pressed on it, feeling a slight twinge, but it was a vast improvement on what stitches would have been like.

"You're handy to have around," I said to Kat.

She sighed in relief and smiled. "Are you really okay?" she asked.

"Yeah, now that you've put me back together. Why?"

She looked back at Denise, still held down by Quinn. "I thought one of you would end up killing the other. At first I thought she'd be the one coming out on top."

"Thanks a lot." I frowned. Why would they think she'd be the winner?

"She didn't end up biting me so I think I'll be okay."

"But why would she drink the blood of a werewolf?" Emily asked. "I can't imagine it appeals to her. Aren't you guys supposed to be deadly to each other?"

"No clue. I can't imagine why—"

The sound of Denise retching interrupted me. She had rolled over onto her side as she heaved up the contents of her stomach. The splash as it hit the gym floor turned my stomach. I was glad her body blocked the view from us. Kegan stepped back. Quinn leaned away from her, but kept a hold of her shoulder as she vomited.

"Wonder if your blood didn't sit well with her," Emily said.

"Either that, or she realized what she did," Kat said. Emily nodded. I shook my head thinking it was just too nuts.

Quinn turned to look at us and said, "We are done for this morning. Go."

We went, more vomiting sounds following us.

Chapter Thirteen

Classes were torture. My head spun from the shock of this morning. When Kat had asked me how I felt, my core was still wrapped around me. It disappeared as soon as we left the gymnasium. Sickness replaced it. My arm alternated between throbbing and numbness. I kept getting sideways glances from people, but no one spoke to me, even more than normal. *Is it my eyes?* Kat had repaired the gashes in my clothes before classes started, and luckily there was no blood on them.

A strange echo accompanied the bell that rang to release us from fifth period. I stood up to leave, but light-headedness forced me down. I put my head between my knees, breathing slowly.

"Claire? Are you feeling okay?" Mr. Sandts asked. "You look a little pale."

"Yeah, just stood up too fast." I slowly tried standing again and felt better, but still odd.

"You eat lunch today?" he asked.

"No, I had to catch up in English," I mumbled.

"Well, you'd better get something in your stomach or you'll pass out if you don't watch it."

I just nodded as I left the room. I heard him mutter, "Girls."

In the hallway, the ebb and flow of the students moving made me dizzy. My stomach churned as I stumbled toward my locker. Less than six feet from it, I crumpled to the ground, surrounded by gasps from those around me.

Faces from every side showed concern, smirks, or judgment. As I stared at them, they spun around me. I tried to sit up but couldn't get my hands under me to push myself up.

"Claire, are you okay?" someone asked.

I stared blankly, trying to find who spoke. I couldn't pick out anyone until Paul's blue eyes peeked out from his blond hair as he leaned over me.

"Claire. What happened?" he asked.

"I don't know," I mumbled. I'd been slowly feeling worse as each hour passed.

Paul touched my head and pulled his hand back in shock. "You're hot."

A snicker from the crowd made Paul turn around and snap. "Shut up!" He placed his hand on my neck as if to feel for my pulse. "I think we need to get you to a doctor."

"No!" I tried to shout, but it came out more of a gasp. "I'm fine."

"You're sick. We need to get you to the office at least," Paul said.

Maybe that would be best. Quinn would probably be able to tell if it was from blood loss or something else. "Help me up."

He grabbed my hand and placed his other hand under my elbow. His fingers brushed the scar from this morning. I hissed in pain. He flinched, knowing he'd hurt me but not sure how. I glanced down at my arm and blinked. The pink scar looked white surrounded by the flaming tissue around it. An infection. Made sense.

Paul carefully helped me up and wrapped his arm around my waist as he held me upright. I couldn't have made it more than a few steps if he hadn't been right there. I ignored the spectators and focused on Paul. It was different than the last time he'd put his arm around me. He had obvious strength now, not just potential.

I breathed him in and nearly collapsed again, this time from emotion, not weakness. Something about his scent reminded me of home, before it got stressful. It was a smell from my memories that gave me quiet warmth instead of the overwhelming heat I was most familiar with. He'd always been there for me. Until a succubus lured him in.

I'd missed him. Why did I let him go? Why did I ignore him for so long? Being without him had been torture.

"Paul, I don't want to start over," I mumbled.

He paused in his step. I nearly stumbled with the sudden change. He grabbed me tighter to keep me from going down. I clung to his arms and found myself staring into his face. He frowned and I realized what it must have sounded like.

"I wish I could take back these months. I've been such a jerk." I couldn't bear to look in his eyes anymore, afraid to see his response. I mumbled against his chest. "I miss you too much. I need you. More than anything."

His hold on me tightened, wrapping me with comfort. I looked up into his eyes full of emotion. He still cared. I let everything go and just melted into him.

**

"Claire. Claire, can you hear me?" Paul shook me but I couldn't see him. I tried to open my eyes. They were too heavy. I flailed my arms when my legs were swept up in his grasp. "Hold still or I'll drop you," Paul grunted.

I gave up and enjoyed being cradled in his arms. Sounds from around us begged for attention. I ignored them as Paul carried me through the halls.

"What is this?" Principal Quinn's voice penetrated my mind. I managed to open my eyes. The room looked blurry and didn't want to hold still.

"She collapsed in the hallway and is burning up," Paul said.

I tried to join the conversation, but I only managed to moan. My mind was alert yet my body betrayed me. I couldn't do anything with it, but inside I felt wonderful. Paul lay me down on the cold cot in the nurse's station. I shivered at the loss of his warmth.

I managed to keep a hold of his arm, not willing to let him go.

"Paul, you may leave now," Quinn said.

"No." I gripped him tighter, surprised at the strength in that action. I felt a strange response from Paul that I couldn't quite describe.

Quinn approached me and leaned close to my ear. "We need to take care of you, and Paul should not be here for that." I caught her meaning but still didn't want to let him go. I needed him. He helped me remember who I was, not what I was becoming.

"Paul, why don't you go find the nurse? She's probably in the faculty room. I'll just get Claire comfortable and call her parents."

I reluctantly let go of Paul's arm. He softly tugged my earlobe like he used to. "You'll be okay. I'll come back, I promise."

I bit my lip and nodded, afraid I'd say something I shouldn't. I closed my eyes so I didn't have to watch him leave. When the door closed, Quinn stood over me again, gripping my arm.

139

"This is not good. I should have thought about this before. I didn't think she'd poison you. She never managed to bite you — just supped on your blood."

"I've been poisoned?"

"Some of Denise's venom has entered your system. If she'd bitten you, it would have manifested much sooner. The small amount that you received during your altercation has finally become too much for you to handle. If you'd been able to maintain your core, you could have burned it up without much harm. Since you reverted to your normal self, it is poisoning your system."

"Will I turn into a vampire, too?" I gasped, terrified at the idea.

"No, your werewolf portion would not allow that. You will die if you don't get this poison out of you."

"What?"

"You must access your core and burn this off or you will die," Quinn stated simply.

I focused deeply within myself and felt my center at peace, even with the threat of dying from vampire venom. I doubted I could seize my core in this state, but I tried anyway. I grabbed for it, noticing the difference as it slipped out of my grasp. I tried again passing it without even touching it.

"Denise did this to you," Quinn said. "Is she going to take Paul again?"

I howled in pain at the image that brought. She'd suck him dry. Kill him! I had to get her poison out of me. I clawed at my chest, trying to get to my core with my own hands. My hardened fingernails ripped through my shirt and scratched my skin underneath. I thrashed, screaming again in pain and anger.

I stopped trying to grab it with my hands. I had to seize it within myself. It was still different, but I could sense something strange about it. As if my inner core was coated in something warm and euphoric. Like when Blake passed me after making out with Denise.

Denise had tainted my core. I held onto my anger, fed it more, and felt the fuzzy core begin to crack.

"That's it. Fight it. Don't give in," Quinn said.

I fought for it. Imagining all the things I'd like to do to Denise. It cracked more.

I'd let my guard down.

No more. She would never do this to me again. I'd never let her get near Paul again. He was mine and I'd do whatever I could to keep him.

I sat up, panting with the internal exertion. I couldn't fully clean off her slime from my core. My arm burned from the poison still in my system. The strongest concentration was there, even though it had moved to other parts of me. I used my claw-like nails to rip open the scar. I clenched my teeth, not wanting to scream out but barely managing to keep my gasps of pain from becoming too loud. Once I'd torn through the scar, yellowish pus oozed out. I gagged, but I milked it until the blood flowed freely.

The difference was immediate as the venom seeped out and the heat faded.

"Is it working?" Quinn asked.

"No!" I said through clenched teeth.

Quinn slapped me across the face. I grabbed her arm before she could hit me again. She brought her other hand up and hit me upside the head. My heart pounded. My core pulsed, weak but breaking through the venom. I kicked her in the gut, knocking her back a few steps. I stood up, ready to defend myself from her should she attack again. She lunged at me, using her legs to trip me. On my way to the floor, she hit my back.

I jumped up and swung at her as she came forward. She blocked my attack easily and used her free arm to hit me again. I clenched my teeth and grabbed my core. It was hard to hold onto, but it was at least accessible. She was fast in the little room, but I managed to keep out of her reach. I didn't want her to hit me again.

"How about now?" she smirked.

I tried not to smile but knew she'd helped. "Much better." The core had enveloped me, and the sickly slime that had coated my center dissipated.

"Good. Now that you've burned off the venom, you should be fine. Paul will be back with the nurse soon. How are you going to explain what happened and why you are well now?"

I had no idea. My arm still bled. The cut wasn't as deep this time as before, but I didn't dare get Kat to close it up for me. I wanted to make sure all the venom left my system. I didn't care if it bled all over the floor except for the fact that it would raise questions.

Quinn must have thought the same thing because she grabbed paper towels from the dispenser on the wall, handed them to me, and laid some on the floor under me.

"Just bandage this." I held my arm up. "I'll say I scratched it too hard when it was hurting earlier."

"This doesn't look like a scratch. Come up with something better."

The gash I'd made looked almost like the knife wound Quinn gave me. It wasn't as deep, but it still looked nasty. I looked at my fingernails and gasped when they looked more like claws than nails. I clenched my hands into fists, trying to hide the claws.

"Just bandage it. I'll figure out something later."

Quinn grabbed the first aid kit and wrapped my arm with some gauze. "And the other?"

"I skipped lunch?"

"Paul knows you had a fever. He carried you in here."

"Oh, right." I sighed. I had no idea how to take care of this. "Sometime fevers come and go, right? I took some Tylenol and the fever went away. Is there an icepack?"

Quinn grabbed a cool pack and broke it on the counter. The chemicals inside mixed together as she shook it and handed it to me. I placed it on my head and lay down. My core was still there, and I didn't let it go. I might not have gotten rid of all the venom yet. Maybe the core would keep me hot enough to fool Paul. It was the best I could do.

I briefly thought it was too bad Paul had carried me in here, but there was no way I was going to regret it too much. The way he'd cradled me was too important to want to forget or wish away.

I heard voices outside and knew the nurse was close.

"Your shirt?" Quinn asked as she wiped up the blood on the floor.

"Crap." I'd forgotten I'd ripped it. I quickly flipped it around so the tears were in the back. It looked a little odd, but nothing unusual for the way I typically dressed. Quinn nodded. I lay back down to watch the door.

It opened and the nurse rushed in. The look on her face made me wonder what Paul had said to her.

"I'll go call your parents now that she's here." Quinn left the room.

Paul slipped in past her. He seemed panicked until his eyes met mine and saw I was lucid. I smiled, feeling embarrassed suddenly as I remembered what I'd said to him.

How much of my admission was from me, and how much was influenced by the venom?

The nurse checked me over. "Tell me about what happened."

I glanced at Paul and then looked at the nurse and lied. "I didn't eat lunch and started to feel a little funny during class. Kind of light headed. I passed out by my locker." I looked at Paul again and rushed on. "Paul helped me in here and Principal Quinn gave me some crackers and this icepack since I felt a little warm." Paul raised his eyebrows, but kept quiet.

"What happened to your arm?" the nurse asked as she placed a thermometer in my mouth.

"Oh," I said and blushed at the idea that came. I mumbled around the thermometer. "I didn't want Paul to leave to go get you, so when he left I fell off the cot and caught my arm on the edge. It scratched me so Principal Quinn bandaged it." I grabbed my arm and patted it gently. "It's nothing."

"I'd better take a look at it," she said.

"It's fine." I spoke more harshly than I should have so I cleared my throat and tried again. "Really, it's fine."

The nurse took the thermometer when it beeped.

"Just over 100 degrees. You should go home and take it easy. If the fever doesn't go away with some Tylenol, you'll definitely want to go see your doctor. Get something to eat and don't skip meals from now on."

"Right." I nodded.

"Just lie down and wait for your parents to come get you. I'll let Principal Quinn know you should go home. She'll contact your teachers and get any assignments you may need to take home." She left the room.

Paul stood near the door just watching me. "Are you sure you're okay?"

"Yeah, I feel really good now. Don't know what happened, but I only feel a little off."

He stepped closer to me cautiously and reached toward my head. Moving the icepack, he placed his hand on my forehead, I felt the slight warmth of his hand next to my cool head. He touched my cheeks. His hand felt cool against my flushed skin.

"How did you get the fever down so fast?" he asked. "You were burning up."

I shrugged. "Thanks for helping me. I'd have never made it in here on my own right then. Maybe it was some strange fluke, but it seemed to pass pretty quick."

He just nodded and watched me. I smiled at him and tentatively reached for his hand. He let me take it and squeezed it softly.

CHAPTER FOURTEEN

Quinn couldn't get a hold of my parents, so she excused Paul from classes and told him to take me home. She gave me her number with explicit instructions to call her if anything else happened.

Paul kept his arm around my shoulder as he led me out to his car. I let him because he couldn't think I was suddenly healed. The way his arm felt around me had nothing to do with it.

He opened the door and helped me into the car. For a moment, I thought he was going to reach down and lift my legs, but he straightened and cleared his throat nervously when he saw my raised eyebrows. He walked around and climbed into the driver's seat. He gazed at me expectantly as if waiting for me to say something. Or did he want to say something? I couldn't tell.

I decided to give it a go. "Thanks for taking me home. I didn't want to stay on that cot waiting for Quinn to track down my parents."

"No problem," he said. "I…" He looked down at

the keys in his hands, and then he started the car. "I'm glad I was there to help."

"Me, too." I looked in his eyes and wondered briefly why he seemed so out of sorts. He kept looking away from me, but at the same time looked like he was trying not to stare.

Oh, no, I thought. *He's noticed my eyes. They haven't gone back to normal, have they?* I leaned toward the window and tried to see if my eyes were visible in his side view mirrors. It was difficult to be sure, but they did look different than my normal dark browns. They had definitely lightened up. They didn't glow or anything, but they looked very odd. *Should I say something about them, maybe lie and ask what he thought of my new contacts, or just pretend nothing's wrong?*

How on earth could I hope to develop a relationship with him? Here I was, fighting a battle against my own inner beast — a real monster, according to everything I'd ever heard about them — and I wanted to start up a romance with the guy I cared most for in the world. What if I attacked him? How could I keep him safe if I didn't understand what would happen to me? I clenched my teeth, relieved the canines were their normal length. My fingernails had returned to normal too. No claws for the moment. I hadn't even noticed when they changed back. So why had my eyes stayed different?

I sighed softly and tried to ignore the looks Paul gave me as he drove me home silently. When he pulled up to the curb in front of my house, he got out of the car and opened my door. He took my bag and walked me up to my front door.

"Do you want me to come in and stay with you till your parents get home?"

"Umm, no," I said, trying for casual. "I'll just go lie down and rest. I'm sure I'll be fine."

"You shouldn't be alone in your condition," he said.

"What condition? I just skipped lunch and passed out. I'm fine." I smiled, hoping to convey wellness with my words.

"But—"

"There is nothing wrong with me," I insisted. Well, except for the fact I was a werewolf that might eat him if I ever transformed. I didn't want to break away from him, but he couldn't get too close. Not that I'd do anything to him now, other than something that would embarrass me later. If we got too comfortable, I could hurt him. Until I knew more about what was going on, or how dangerous I could be, I had to be extra careful.

"Sorry," I sighed when I saw his frown. "I really am fine. I'll just go lay down. My parents would freak if you were here when they get home. They're weird that way."

Paul just stared. I knew he didn't believe me. He'd been to my house with my parents gone before I'd severed all connection with him.

"Besides, if I'm contagious, you don't want to get this." I should tell him to get lost, but I couldn't do that. I was too selfish. "I'll see you tomorrow." I let myself in and closed the door. I watched him from the window as he returned to his car. I wanted to beg him to stay, to hold me, to talk to me, to tell me it would all be okay.

I waited for him to drive away, but he just sat in his car watching my house. I lay on the couch under the window and thought of him until I drifted off to sleep.

I woke with a start as images of Denise, fangs dripping in blood, swam in my still hazy mind. She'd found a new boyfriend but hadn't stayed with her normal kissing. She'd killed him and the look of hunger in her eyes burned in my mind. I looked out the window and saw Paul's car there. The sun had moved, indicating it was much later than when he first dropped me off. Why was he still there?

I pulled out my phone and dialed his cell, hoping it was still the same number. I could have texted, but I wanted to hear his voice. His head jerked up, and he moved to reach for his phone.

"Hello?" he asked, in a husky voice, sounding like he'd just woken up.

"Why are you sitting outside my house?" I asked.

"You shouldn't be home alone." His head turned toward my house.

"And you think sleeping outside in your car makes me not home alone?" I tried not to smile, but failed.

"Well, technically I wasn't sleeping. I just closed my eyes for a bit."

"Uh-huh. You never were a good liar."

"And you always were," he said, but then quickly added, "That's why I didn't believe you when you said you were fine. Something's wrong and I want to help."

I didn't know what to say, so I turned off my phone and watched out the window. I didn't want to talk to him, but I was dying for some real human contact. I was afraid of losing my humanity. Would it be wrong of me to keep him? Could I keep him to help me keep myself normal without running the risk of hurting him?

My phone rang. I glanced at it, already knowing he was calling me back. Probably to apologize for calling me a liar, even though he was right. I ignored the phone, letting it go to voice mail. I went to the door instead. I hesitated a moment before opening it and stepping out onto the front porch. I sat down on the top step and watched him in his car. He stared at his phone as mine began ringing again. When he looked up and saw me on the porch, he put the phone down and the ringing of mine cut off.

I marveled at his courage in getting out of the car and approaching me. Why did he try so hard? Why did he think I was worth any of his time? There were so many other more deserving girls out there. The whole time we'd been friends, he'd put up with my rants, moods, and anger with no complaints. How had he handled me then? He walked slowly, as if afraid to do something sudden that would make me bolt and hide in the house.

I gazed up into his blue eyes. He didn't seem bothered by mine anymore. Had they gone back to normal, or was he used to them? We stared at each other for who knows how long. I tried to read him, but I didn't know how. "Why are you so good to me?" I asked.

"Because you deserve it."

I shook my head in disbelief. That was so far from the truth. Paul sat down next to me, with a few inches separating us. It would be easy to reach out and touch him, but I didn't dare.

"No, really. You stand up for the little guy. When Jax picks on a kid at school, you put him in his place. When we were in elementary, you stopped those kids from hurting that three-legged cat. When Max got hit by a car and we were worried we'd have to put him down, you came over and slipped him bits of bacon to cheer him up."

I chuckled at the memory and couldn't help the tear that formed.

"What's going on with you?" he asked softly.

I laughed out loud, surprised at that simple question. He raised his eyebrows, surprised at my response. "Sorry, I wasn't expecting that," I said, trying to explain my outburst.

He stayed still, waiting for me to answer. I started playing with my fingernails, thankful again they were still normal.

"Don't get angry or anything," he said softly, "but I've been watching you forever, and I've noticed some things are different with you lately."

I stared at him in shock. "You watch me?"

"I always have."

"Wow." I shook my head and looked at his car.

"You aren't mad?" he asked.

"Not really, though I know why you'd think that. I'm always mad."

"Not always."

I looked at him again in surprise. I always felt mad. What did he see in me? "I'm actually more surprised."

"Why?"

"Well, because there has to be a lot more interesting things out there to watch," I said, not daring to look at him. "I wouldn't want to watch me."

"I can't help it. I've always been fascinated with you."

Unable to detect a lie in his words, I stayed quiet.

"So are things okay with you?"

"Yes and no. But I can't really talk about it."

"That's fine," he said after a moment. "But just so you know, I'm not going to let you push me away this time. I learned my lesson. You won't get away with ignoring me for too long. I'm going to prove to you I am worth trusting."

"I do trust you," I whispered. "But it might not be in your best interest to be involved with me. At least for a little while."

"Ooh, involved. That's something I'd like to consider." He smiled.

"Not like that. Well, yes. And no. Crap!" I threw my head back and expelled a forceful sigh. "I'm dealing with some things right now that I can't really talk about and I don't know how much time I can spend with you, or how safe it would be for you to be around me."

He raised his brows and took my hand in his. "I'm staying as close as you'll let me. You tell me when you want your space, and I'll give it to you. But I won't disappear completely. I'll always be around."

I pulled my hand out of his, feeling bad at the disappointment in his eyes. "That is really nice of you. And I'm going to hold you to that. If I tell you to 'get lost' for a bit, I expect you to do it." To soften the harsh words, I leaned over quickly and kissed his cheek. He looked at me in surprise. I smiled. "I'm going inside now. I promise I'm fine. Go home and I'll see you at school tomorrow."

"Can I give you a ride in the morning?"

"Thanks, but no. I have an early morning tutoring group so I'll do my morning run to the school. But I'd love a ride home after school."

"It's a date." He grinned.

I patted him on the knee before heading into the house. I didn't convince him to stay as far from me as possible, but at least I got him to agree to take off when I told him to. I wondered how well he'd listen.

Moments after Paul drove away, my phone started ringing. I smiled, sure it was him.

"Hello?"

"Claire?" Kat's voice sounded worried. "Are you okay? I heard about you collapsing in the hall."

"Yeah, just a funny reaction to this morning's lesson."

"But you're fine now?"

"Of course. I'm home, resting. I should probably get started on my—"

"Did you hear about Denise?" Kat said in a rush.

"No? What about her?"

"Quinn totally ripped into her. I listened in while she was chewing her out in the office. She was so mad at what happened. At first when Denise attacked you,

Quinn acted like it was no big deal, but then in her office, she was shouting at her and telling her that she should have been more careful. She insisted Denise get herself another boyfriend quick so she wouldn't be tempted as badly if there was any more spilt blood. I thought for sure Denise was dead."

"Wow—" I began, but Kat just plowed on with her story.

"So then Denise comes out and she looked like crap. You know how she usually looks so perfect and gorgeous and all? Well, her hair was a mess, and her eyes looked bloodshot. She didn't look like she'd been crying, but she looked so messed up. I think she's really freaked about what she did to you. So anyway, I watched her as she left the office and she looked around the hallway at all the guys passing by, but she didn't give any of them a smile like she normally does. She actually looked like she almost wanted to hit one of them. Kinda like you…"

She paused and cleared her throat before she rushed back into it. "Then she looked back at the office door and turned with this really pissed look on her face. She walked up to the first guy she saw and kissed him. He tried backing away, but she just gripped him so tight that he couldn't move. Everyone started whistling and making comments. She didn't even flinch. She just kept at it. After a couple minutes, she let go of him and he fell into the lockers behind him. Then Denise walked away, pushing her way through the crowd and left the school. I haven't seen her since. We were supposed to get together."

Kat finally stopped and I waited, expecting more.

"Did you hear that, Claire?" she asked.

"Yeah, I was just trying to take it all in."

"Why did she do that?" Kat asked. "I mean, why did she drink your blood in the first place, and why did Quinn tell her to get a boyfriend?"

I realized for the first time that Denise hadn't picked up a new boyfriend since dumping Blake. No wonder she'd lost control and come after me. Not that I was excusing her for what she did, but I could kind of understand it.

"Claire?"

"Denise hasn't had a boyfriend since the day Quinn told us what we were. She's probably kind of hungry."

"Oh, right. Of course she'd want to drink blood if she wasn't getting any energy. It's amazing that you can be so calm about this."

At that, my heart skipped a beat and sped up. Was I still too calm? Was Denise's venom in me still? I grabbed my core and felt it infuse me with strength. My sigh of relief was immediate. My calmness must be in response to Paul.

"Well, there isn't anything else I can do about it right now," I said. "I'm just not going to bleed in front of her again. You guys should be careful, too. And I'm not so sure she should be loose around guys after today."

"No kidding," Kat agreed. "Well, anyway, part of the reason I called was to see if you had any idea where Denise would be. I have to meet with her. Quinn wanted me to find out how she was doing and to *encourage* her to take care of her energy needs in a more *appropriate* way."

I snorted at the thought and said, "I don't really have any clue where she'd be. Have you tried calling her cell?"

"Yeah, but she's not answering."

"Well, I really don't know ... oh, wait." I suddenly flashed on the place she'd suggested we meet at the park. I explained to Kat how to get there and wished her luck.

It's going to really suck keeping tabs on this stupid vampire.

CHAPTER FIFTEEN

I ran into Emily in front of the school in the morning. After asking me about yesterday, she said, "Do you think she'll do more with blades or fire balls?"

"Denise never had to do the blades, but I don't know if Quinn will want to run the risk of any more bleeding. Of course, if she cuts Denise none of us would attack her." I definitely wouldn't.

"True. What else do you think a demon would use to fight with?"

"No clue. I never thought she'd use blades. Fire balls, I can understand, but a blade? You don't think she'd use other real weapons, do you?" I asked.

"Who knows? I always thought of them doing more of the possession thing, but maybe you don't get possessed by a demon unless you are going to be turned into one. That's the impression I got when Quinn said if we fell we'd end up like her."

"What do you think it takes to fall?" I asked, opening the door. "I mean, since Denise has tasted blood, if she goes for it instead of just sucking energy, will she fall?"

"Probably. What do you think will happen to us if we lose her?"

"We'd have less chance of success without all of us."

Emily looked me over as if appraising me. "You're going to have to keep an eye on her. We will too, but you'll be the only one strong enough to really keep her in check."

I moaned. "Great. I don't want to constantly watch her and make sure she doesn't end up eating someone."

"You know it's for the best," Emily said softly.

"I know, but still…" I shuddered at the idea of watching her make-out sessions. Could I ignore the grossness by thinking of it as food? No, that would make it even worse. I'd be freaking out for the guy she was with.

"Hopefully Kat found her. She'll be able to help, I'm sure."

"Yeah," I agreed, though I didn't know what Kat could do to help a vampire who'd finally tasted blood. At least she hadn't bit me. Or killed me. Maybe things would still be okay with Denise. I wasn't looking forward to seeing her though.

***

Quinn stood motionless before us, just watching. Denise had yet to make eye contact with me. She whispered with Kat. Emily got her to say a couple of things. Denise only glanced once at Kegan, and ignored me. That was fine with me. I didn't want to hear any insincere apology or pretend to accept it.

"Today we will do something different," Quinn said. "I'm going to access your minds and give you a taste of what you might experience from some who may come after you. A few demons are able to give horrid nightmares. They confuse you so they can attack without you fighting back."

Quinn cleared her throat and continued, "To accomplish this in a short amount of time, I will need to do it simultaneously. And to make sure none of you freak out and hurt each other, I'll give you a sedative that will wear off within twenty minutes. If you can fight the sedative and get out of the mind trap, you can be done early. Otherwise, those twenty minutes will be the worst of your life."

"You'll only be messing with our minds?" Emily asked.

"Yes. I will do nothing to you but give your mind something to fight."

"That doesn't sound too bad," Kegan said.

"You let me know if you feel the same way when I'm done." Quinn had a wicked smirk. I wasn't looking forward to what was coming after experiencing her fire and blades, but at least it would only be in my mind. I could deal with that.

I still reached for my core and let it envelop me. I felt so much better just having a hold of it. Quinn gave us each a small minty pill that left a nasty aftertaste. I cleared my throat, trying to get the bitterness to disappear, but it lingered. I swallowed hard and closed my eyes. When I opened them again, the room began to sway.

Kat's head had rolled forward. Emily tilted her head sideways and adjusted her shoulders like she was uncomfortable. She kept squirming. She never moved places or changed forms, just fidgeted. Denise sat stiffly with her eyes wide open as if she didn't dare close them. Kegan lay on the floor and propped his hands behind his head as if looking at the clouds on a nice afternoon. I grinned at him. He winked.

The sound of someone hitting the floor made me turn to see Emily flat on her back. She hadn't done it on purpose like Kegan did, I was sure. Kat collapsed forward and her head hit the floor in front of her folded legs. She managed to stay in a sitting position, sort of. Denise propped herself up with her hands to the side of her but looked very unstable. I focused on myself, but I didn't really feel too much different. I figured I'd be able to stay upright but decided a little caution couldn't hurt. I placed my hands in front of me on the floor between my crossed legs just in case.

Quinn slipped quietly between us all and placed her little finger behind Kat's earlobe. She then did the same to Emily, and then me. Her hot finger behind my ear sent a shiver down my left side. I kept my eyes on her as she moved over to Kegan and then Denise who flinched, shaking her head as soon as Quinn removed her finger.

Denise clenched her teeth and widened her eyes even more if it were possible. She didn't look like she was going to give into this very easily. I tried to ignore her and focused on keeping my core wrapped around me. I pulled my cell phone out to see what time it was so I'd have an idea on how long this lasted. I figured it had been about a minute and a half since the pill, and I was still upright. That had to be a good sign. Kat and Emily had collapsed within moments of taking the sedative.

I sat there bored as I watched the others lying motionless. My core was doing awesome at keeping me from succumbing to the drug. A few minutes, later my phone rang.

"Claire, it's Paul. I need to see you right now. Can you meet me?" He sounded urgent. I looked up and didn't see Quinn anywhere. Kat and Emily were still out cold on the floor. Denise stared straight ahead without seeming to notice me at all. Kegan looked like he was studying the ceiling.

"Yeah. Where are you?" I asked into the phone.

"I'm outside the school. I've got to talk to you."

I stood up quickly, amazed at how easy it was to avoid this sedative with my core wrapped around me. Quinn wouldn't be able to take advantage of me as long as I could access it. I glanced back one more time to see if she were anywhere around. No sign of her.

I rushed out the gym and jogged down the hall until I came to the outside doors. I pushed them open to find Paul leaning against the concrete wall of the planter box lining the sidewalks. He stood up quickly and rushed over to me. I was surprised when he took me into his arms and hugged me tightly.

"Paul?" I pushed back but he didn't let go.

"I'm so glad I found you! I've been thinking about you all night. I had to come."

"What's wrong?" I asked, slightly confused.

He took my face in his hands, brushing his fingers softly across my jaw line. "I need you." He smiled tenderly at me.

I didn't know what to say. I stared at him and watched in awe as his eyes told me everything. He wanted to kiss me. Did I want that? Yes. If I were truthful, I'd always wanted that, but *now*?

"Don't be nervous," he whispered. "Nothing will happen to us. We're meant for each other. You've always known that. It just took me a little longer to figure it out, too. And now that I have . . . I'm not going to let anything stand in the way."

My core began to slip. I grabbed hold of it tighter. I couldn't let it go. The sedative couldn't take effect now of all times. I had to stay awake for this.

Paul slowly leaned in. His eyes, never leaving mine, drew me in deeper. I held my breath, not daring to believe this could really be happening. His eyes closed as his lips inched closer to mine. I was about to ask if he was sure he wanted to kiss me when his mouth took mine.

I closed my eyes and melted in his kiss. His lips were soft and tender. As the kiss deepened, my body shivered with anticipation. My arms found their way around him, pulling him closer. My core pulsed and I felt more alive than ever. He snaked an arm around my waist, pulling my body against his. His mouth, leaving mine now, moved along my jaw line and across my neck.

My heart beat faster. I let go of any fear or reserve I felt about kissing him. I was safe in his arms. For the first time, I just let myself *feel* . . .

Every part of me was alive. I shivered and held back the moan that threatened to escape. My lips found his once more and I kissed him with everything I had. I didn't want this moment to ever end and let myself become lost in the joy.

The slamming of a car door jolted me out of my bliss. I looked up to see Jax getting out of his Camaro. He glanced at us but didn't say anything. Good thing. I looked back at Paul, fighting an embarrassed smile. Jax gossiped more than any girl I knew.

From the corner of my eye, I saw the gym doors open. Denise stepped out slowly. She walked stiffly, as if in a dream, staring straight ahead. Her eyes locked on Jax. He walked toward the building with his gym bag over his shoulder. Paul stood over me, slowly smelling my hair as I watched Denise. A shiver of fear gripped me. Denise didn't look in control of herself. Her face held no expression.

Denise approached Jax and took him by the hand. He let her lead him to the bushes with no argument. I watched in horror as she wrapped her arms around him and began kissing him. Jax seemed to enjoy it, but Denise seemed possessed. She barely let him come up for air. When he began to struggle, Denise held him tighter. His life force left as she intensified the kiss. He moaned, more in pain than ecstasy. Jax pulled back from her. Denise went for his throat, dragging him to the ground.

"No!" I shouted.

I tore out of Paul's embrace and sprinted to help Jax. Denise raised her head, blood dripping from her lips. It was even more terrifying than the dream I'd had of her killing some guy. I could smell the blood. I quickly looked at Jax, lying halfway under the bush. His foot twitched slightly once, and then he didn't move. Denise snarled at me and crouched over Jax.

"He's mine," she hissed.

"No, Denise, you don't want to do this. You can control it. You have to stop now."

"Why? This is fantastic. So much better than what I did before. I can have eternal life this way. I can have it all."

"That's not true. Not that way. The demon lord will claim you. You don't want that," I said.

Her eyes flicked briefly away from me. Her grin widened. "Fine. You can have him." She slowly moved to the side, away from Jax. Was he still alive? Denise kept her eyes on me as she circled around, trying to keep out of my reach.

I realized too late what she was doing. She shot out of the bushes, knocking me down as she jumped at Paul.

"No!" I shouted again. This time I was faster as I pursued her. I grabbed her arm before she reached him.

I dodged the blow she aimed at me and shouted

at Paul. "Run. Get out of here now!" Paul just looked at me as if I was crazy. He glanced into the bushes and saw Jax's feet poking out.

"What is going on?" he shouted.

"Just run!" I had to stop Denise. I infused myself with the energy pulsing from my core and felt myself begin to change.

"Run, Paul!" I shouted more in fear of him seeing what I was about to become than for the possibility of Denise attacking him. My skin rippled as my body changed. My hair rose, coating my arms in a coarse fur. My fingernails hardened into claws gripping Denise tight. She fought against me but couldn't break free. The transformation was unstoppable. I was becoming what I dreaded most. My teeth pressed against my lips, forcing me to open my mouth. My muscles quivered as they morphed. My back arched. My arms and legs changed until they matched each other in length. I couldn't keep a hold of Denise through the change and she darted forward. I tried to shout for Paul again, but instead I howled.

Paul stared at me in horror, completely ignoring the fact that a vampire was bearing down on him. She hit him from the side and knocked him down, going straight for his neck.

I lost all consciousness and gave myself completely up to the beast. I tackled Denise from behind, ripping her off Paul and began tearing into her flesh. She tasted awful, but I continued to rip her apart. She didn't stand a chance against me. Soon I had her by the throat and tasted blood. It wasn't hers. It was human. It was delicious. I wanted more.

I left her lifeless body and moved slowly away, sniffing the air, sensing something living in close proximity. It smelled of the blood I tasted. I wanted it. I raised my head and saw a man pressed against the wall of the building. He held a hand to the side of his neck, looking worried, but he didn't move. This would be so easy. I could take him in an instant. I crouched low, looking for any sign of danger but sensing none now that I'd disposed of the vampire. I could take my time with this and really enjoy it.

My paws moved forward slowly as I bared my teeth. The heart inside the man beat frantically. His blood smelled delicious. The vampire might have started on him, but I would finish him — kill him before he had a chance to be poisoned by her venom. Exactly what I was made for.

I prepared myself to pounce when he spoke. "Claire?"

He still looked worried but confused as well. No matter. I'd soon stop anything he had to worry about.

I jumped and slammed against him, knocking him to the ground. He lay pinned between my weight and the brick wall of the building. He pushed against me, but he wasn't strong enough to move me at all.

As I came forward to deliver the killing blow, he gasped in fear. "Claire, No! Stop!"

I ignored him and bit into the soft flesh of his neck. When the blood flowed into my mouth, it felt wrong. I came back to myself and screamed in shock at what I'd done. I jumped away from him and stood up in my human form. His big blue eyes stared lifelessly at the clear sky above me.

I threw my head back and howled.

Chapter Sixteen

The howl was deep and desperate. I wanted to die. If Denise could just … but no, I had killed her already. I dropped to my knees and slammed my hands against the floor. The sobs tore from me. I couldn't believe what I'd done. I closed my eyes tight in a futile attempt to block the images that kept crossing my mind.

Jax's feet poking out from under the bush.

Denise ripped apart.

Paul's dead eyes.

I'd transformed into the werewolf and lost myself completely. I had no control in that form. I was evil, and would be a servant of a demon, or worse, a demon myself. Another howl escaped me, heartbreak ripping through my throat as I screamed in agony. I had killed two people. One deserved it, but the other… He was innocent. He shouldn't have been there. I shouldn't have gone for him. I loved him, yet I let my inner beast take control. I had done the unthinkable.

I lay prostrate on the ground and sobbed, wishing I could cease to exist.

"Claire," a voice said in the distance.

I ignored it, not wanting to acknowledge anyone for fear I'd revert to the wolf and kill them, too.

"Claire." The voice was now firm and impatient. "Claire. Come back to yourself. Time is up."

Was the demon lord claiming me now?

"Claire, don't make me give you the antidote. You won't like it." Quinn's voice finally registered with me.

I rolled over slightly and looked up. Quinn stood above me in the gym. I scanned the room for the others. Kat sat upright, looking groggy. Emily bowed her head, rocking as if trying to comfort herself. Kegan paced back and forth. I focused my attention on Denise. She was extremely pale, and her face looked even more expressionless than when I'd seen her going toward Jax.

Wait? It had all been in my mind? I had actually succumbed to the effects of Quinn's mind control. I hadn't really watched Denise kill Jax or attacked her myself.

And Paul?

Paul was alive? I hadn't done anything to him. I hadn't seen him.

The sobs took over again and I cried, this time in relief.

***

I went through the images over and over all morning long, sickened at what I'd become. I couldn't get my mind off it as I walked with Kegan down the hall between classes.

"Practice sucked this morning, didn't it?" He shuddered. I nodded.

"How much of it could be real, and how much of it was to prepare us for the worst?" I finally asked.

"I don't know. What did you see?"

"I turned into a wolf and attacked a couple people." I didn't look up from the floor as I walked.

"Wow. Who?"

I shook my head, not willing to get into it. *But maybe Kegan would understand what I did. No. Telling him I killed Denise would bother him.*

I really didn't know what to think about myself. The emotions when I'd kissed Paul in my vision kept coming back to me. I couldn't get them out of my head. I wanted to be with him, hold him, kiss him, to be kissed by him. Every time I allowed myself to think of it, the memory of his arms around me turned to him pushing frantically against my wolf body as I closed in for the kill.

My stomach clenched. I swallowed the bile rising in my throat.

"Claire!" Paul's voice seemed to echo through the hallway. I saw him from the corner of my eye but was too freaked to talk to him.

"I've got to go," I whispered to Kegan and bolted to the bathroom. Fear of everything I might become rushed through my body making me sick. I puked into the toilet and stared at the contents in fear. When my eyes registered what I saw, I laughed hysterically at my relief that there was no blood. I hadn't actually eaten a vampire or anyone else. I flushed the toilet, then sat on it, pulling my feet up and wrapping my arms around my legs. I buried my head in my knees and cried at what I was.

I managed to avoid Paul all morning, but by lunchtime, he cornered me. I contemplated grabbing my lunch and leaving the table, but chickened out when no excuse came to mind. I didn't want to hurt him in the way I had to. Because of my weakness, would I end up killing him?

In my vision, I'd been able to still think clearly until I embraced the actual beast. Once I started to rip Denise apart and enjoyed it — loved the taste of the blood — that's when I lost myself. I remembered everything about my wolf attacking Paul. Almost like I could see it from outside my body but couldn't stop it. The wolf had completely taken over. *If I hadn't tasted the blood, could I have kept my mind?*

"Claire, are you okay?" Paul asked.

I startled then blurted, "Fine."

"You look terrible. Are you sure you're feeling well enough to be at school?"

"Rough morning. But I feel better now with you here in front of me." I smiled, swallowing the lump in my throat. *I will not cry.*

"Really?" he asked with raised eyebrows. "It seemed like you were avoiding me this morning. I called your name a couple of times between classes."

"Oh, sorry. Guess I didn't hear you. Maybe I am still feeling a little off." I shrugged, trying to avoid more questions.

We sat quietly through most of lunch. I don't know if it was the expression on my face, or that I wouldn't meet his eyes for more than a second at a time, but he didn't push me. He had to know something was up with me, but I loved him even more for leaving it be and not pestering me to explain.

"Do you want to meet me by my car after school, or should I find you by your locker?" he asked.

"By your car."

"Okay," he smiled. "Enjoy the rest of your day." As he got up to dump his tray, he reached slowly toward me and softly ran his finger along my earlobe. He tugged the ear gently and I smiled, thinking how funny it was that he still did that. I couldn't even remember when it started, but I always thought of it as his way of giving me a hug, or a high five, or even a kiss goodbye. It was sweet when I thought about it.

On my way to meet Paul outside, I saw Denise standing against a display case. She stared blankly at the people passing by. I debated with myself about stopping and talking to her, but didn't dare. I still didn't trust myself after my vision.

For the first time in my memory, she was practically alone. No one came to her. No swarms of people vied for her attention. The students in the hall passed by, almost oblivious.

I wove my way through the crowded hallway and stopped against the lockers about three feet away from her. I didn't want to get too close.

It took a few minutes, but eventually she acknowledged me. We didn't speak, just looked at each other. At first, she seemed upset by me being there. I stood my ground quietly, just watching her. I interpreted the change in her eyes from a blank stare to anger, then worry, then resignation when I didn't move from my spot.

I raised my eyebrows and tapped my forehead. She nodded and her expression softened. What horrors had she seen? Had she seen herself feasting on the people around her? Had she killed anyone?

I whispered, "Sucks, doesn't it?"

She frowned and narrowed her eyes. When I realized my choice of words could be taken wrong, I bit my lip trying to keep the smile from forming. "Sorry," I whispered.

Denise frowned again but nodded as if accepting my apology.

"We can do it, you know. We'll be able to fight this off. Look at what we've accomplished so far." I spoke it quietly, but I knew she could hear me even though students surrounded us.

"That's easy for you to say. You haven't attacked anyone," she whispered back.

I flashed on the vision of killing her and Paul. I had to take a deep breath before saying, "Not yet, but it is very possible. Just brush this off, and try to get back to normal."

Denise snapped, though still a whisper, "We aren't normal. What I did wasn't normal. What I want to do isn't normal."

"But your boyfriends worked so well before to keep you *normal*. Come on, there has to be someone around here that you could hook up with." I glanced at the people passing by, noticing for the first time that the guys were giving her wider berth than the girls. They never looked at her, not purposely ignoring her, but almost instinctively keeping their distance.

"What if I don't want to?" Denise asked.

"Then you'll end up eating one of them when you just can't take the hunger any longer. As much as I hate to admit this, what you did before is so much better than what you could do. I won't say I'm excited for you to use these guys the way you do, but I'd rather watch that than the alternative again."

She whispered, "Again? Did you have a vision of me doing that?"

I nodded quickly and said, "Then I turned to a werewolf and killed you. I lost myself when I did it, and did something truly horrible." I shuddered at the memories that flooded me. "So take care of things, will ya? I really don't want to watch you to make sure you don't go too far. You've controlled it before, so go back to what you were doing. Just be careful."

Denise shook her head. I didn't know if it was to argue with me or because she just didn't want to contemplate what might happen.

"We don't have much time," I said, more harshly than I meant to. I took a deep breath and tried again. "We don't have much time to learn what we need to, so avoiding any setbacks would be very beneficial. Don't you think?"

Denise nodded and let out a defeated sigh. "I'll try."

I stepped back into the crowd, but watched her

still. She closed her eyes and took a few moments to just breathe before she opened her eyes and smiled. Something about her changed, and she seemed to radiate goodness. I could almost feel the pull of her charm as she focused her attention on those around her. They stopped avoiding her and shifted in closer as she began to participate in her former sociality.

People started talking to her in passing. Some stopped and talked momentarily before moving on with a spring in their steps. A slight shimmer surrounded Denise as more people interacted with her. She seemed to size up the guys and when she'd picked her next object, she turned on the charm full force. He stood no chance. Denise placed her hand on his arm, not possessively, but more like she was encouraging him to find her intriguing. She began walking with him and nearly started to glow with the energy vibes she pulled from those around her and the poor soul she had chosen.

It was so easy for her to suck people in. She didn't even seem to try. She just did it naturally. So much different than the way I could turn people against me just by entering a room. And as long as I kept myself from turning, I was much less dangerous to them than she was. Life wasn't fair.

Chapter Seventeen

Paul leaned back against his car, looking around the parking lot as I came out of the building. His position was almost the same from this morning when he'd leaned against the concrete wall. My vision flashed before me again. I tried to focus on the more pleasant part, wishing it had been real. It had felt so real that my belly tingled as I remembered the kiss.

I walked slowly toward him but the horrible parts of my vision crowded out the good. What would happen if he were near when I transformed? Quinn thought for sure I'd have to do it sometime. I wouldn't be able to fight off demons in my human form. But would I remember anything about myself, or would it all shift into the mind of a beast?

I stopped suddenly when I realized I had completely accepted the idea of me being a werewolf.

Paul looked concerned and ready to walk toward me, so I tried to shake off my inner turmoil and headed to meet him.

When I got to the car, Paul took my bag and

tossed it onto the back seat. He opened my door and walked around to his side.

"Sorry it took me so long."

"No problem. You're worth the wait."

I nodded my thanks and took in his smile. It did funny things to my stomach so I looked out the windshield to try to calm myself.

"You look like you feel a little better than you did at lunch," Paul said.

"I do? Thanks."

He paused with his hand on the gearshift and asked, "Do you want me to take you straight home, or would you like to come with me to the park to take Max for his walk?"

"I'd love to. It'll be fun to see him again." I grinned at the thought.

"Great. He'll be so excited to see you."

My grin faded when I realized Max might notice a difference in me. Would he accept me still, or find me a threat? It was too late now to back out, so I practiced my deep breathing to calm myself. I didn't want to have any wolfish tendencies when I met up with Max. When Paul pulled up in front of his house, I stayed by the car while he went inside for the dog.

"You sure you don't want to come in for a minute while I get his leash and stuff?"

"I'm sure. It will be funner to watch him come out

and see me." I wanted to have an escape just in case. And hopefully Paul would have the leash on him already. My hand stayed on the car door's handle so I could jump inside at the first sign Max wouldn't accept me. I didn't want to run the risk of changing in front of Paul if Max attacked. Better to hide in the car than turn into a wolf and kill Max in self-defense.

I waited nervously and took stock of myself. My fingernails looked normal. My teeth felt fine. I leaned down and looked into the side view mirror on Paul's car to see my eyes. Still a light brown, but nothing too creepy. Had my scent changed from the last time I'd seen Max?

I stood up quickly when I heard the front door open. Paul stepped out with a huge German Shepherd. "There she is Max. Go get her," Paul said excitedly. Max did as he was told and bounded down the steps toward me, his leash trailing behind him. I tensed up, but then I decided it was best to show my superiority and stood up straight. Max came right up to me and stopped just short of my feet. He wagged his tail, then touched his nose to my hand as if checking to see what I'd do with him.

I reached out and placed one hand on his head and scratched him behind the ears while my other hand rested under his muzzle. He licked my hand and whimpered slightly. He seemed genuinely happy to see me. *Man, I've missed you.* I really should have forgiven Paul much sooner. And not just for Max's sake. I got down on my knees and hugged Max. He licked my face and laid his head against my shoulder as if trying to hug me back.

"I told you he's missed you," Paul said as he came up. A huge grin plastered across his face.

I didn't dare say anything at first, too afraid I might give away my emotions at having something love me so unconditionally. I hugged him tight, standing up with the leash in my hand. I offered it to Paul, but he said, "You keep it."

We headed down the sidewalk, Paul next to me and Max following a few steps behind. His nose never came in front of my body. Paul kept looking back at him and shaking his head. Eventually he said, "He never stays behind me while I take him out. He's always pulling on the leash, trying to get in front, or even dragging me behind."

"Guess he knows I won't take any crap from him." I patted Max on the head. He looked up at me with adoring eyes and Paul chuckled.

"If we always go for a walk with you, I'll have to change my work out routine. This is so easy and laid back that I'm not getting my normal exercise chasing him through the park."

"I don't have to come with you if you'd rather

keep your normal routine." I shrugged, trying not to sound disappointed.

"No way, I'm bringing you with every chance I get," Paul said, taking my free hand in his. "Just pointing out that Max is a completely different dog around you."

I smiled and let him keep my hand, even though I knew I shouldn't. I just needed to live through the next few weeks and then see what happened with Paul. Why couldn't I focus on that? Why couldn't I just tell him I was unavailable? He'd be safer that way.

Because I was weak, that's why. Because I now knew what it was like to be loved by someone, even if it was his dog. I also knew what it was like to love someone. At least we didn't have any lessons from Quinn this weekend. We wouldn't meet with her as a group until Monday morning. I'd be free to pretend my weekend was just a normal one for a normal teenager.

Denise was totally right when she said we weren't normal. But I was going to pretend for a little while. It was so easy to pretend with Paul. He accepted me for what I was, or what he thought I was. He'd never be able to accept me for what I really was, but I'd have to deal with that later. If I were lucky, he'd never have to find out.

***

On the way back home, we passed Kat's house. She sat on her front porch with a huge book on her lap. As I got closer, I saw it was a book on plants and their medicinal uses.

An idea struck me. I told Paul I needed to stop and talk to her. He frowned at first but replaced it quickly with a smile and said, "See ya later."

I passed the leash to him. Max whined. "Don't worry, boy, I'll see you again." I smiled at Paul. "You, too."

When I joined Kat on her porch, she nodded in Paul's direction. "Cute."

"Yeah, he is."

She looked at me with a huge grin on her face. "So why would you leave him to see me?"

I cautiously asked, "Do you think there is a potion you could come up with to…" I couldn't decide the best way to ask this. It would definitely not come out delicately. Kat waited patiently.

Trying again, I said, "Is there a way you could think of to help me avoid desiring the taste of blood?"

Kat's eyes widened. I blushed. She opened her mouth to speak, closed it, and then sat quietly for a minute as if contemplating my question.

"Could you give me more specifics?" she asked. "I'm not quite sure what to try since I don't fully understand the problem." She said it so innocently that I decided to share my experience in my vision with her.

Her eyes widened and her mouth flew open more than once during my retelling. Tears were in her eyes when I finished. "And I thought my vision was bad. No wonder you were so shook up."

I nodded and waited for her to think of something to help me.

"I'm not sure if I have an answer for that right now, but I'll do some research this weekend and see what I can find." Kat stood up and hugged me. "You really are very strong. I know you can survive this. You'll come through okay. You won't let it take you over."

I was touched by her concern for and belief in me. Not one to normally like hugs, I hugged her back tightly, almost disappointed when she let me go.

On my way home, I felt much better about my chances. I had a witch on my side, and she was going to help me figure out how to keep from losing myself to the beast. I had more faith in her than in myself.

Chapter Eighteen

The weekend flew by. My parents were in a pretty good mood. Dad was actually home from his latest trip and they figured since my shrink made such a difference in me, they'd try some counseling. Paul took me for ice cream on Saturday. We walked Max at the park and spent most of our free time together. But the lessons with Quinn were always on my mind.

Paul seemed to notice I was preoccupied most of the time. I would catch him watching me each time my mind wandered. I'd smile shyly at him and he'd wink at me as if to say, "Welcome back." I tried harder to stay more in the moment with him, but little things would remind me of my vision, or of the fireballs, or the blade and Denise's venom, and I'd be lost in thought for a while.

Paul never tried to do more than hold my hand. I made the mistake of daydreaming about the kiss we'd shared in my vision. It always led to the events that happened next and I'd end up almost as devastated as the first time I saw it.

When Monday morning came, I was relieved to get back into training. I wanted this thing over with, to be done with it one way or another. Of course I wanted to live through it, but I couldn't wait until it was over so I could move on with my life.

Kegan caught up with me before practice. "How's things?"

"Good." I felt a little guilty that I hadn't been spending much time with him since we found out what we were. Of course he didn't need me hanging around. He had other friends. "How about you?"

"Not too bad. Watch this." He held his hand away from his body, palm toward the ground. My skin began to tingle as he pulled on the ground beneath him. Pebbles started to bounce and skid across the sidewalk.

"Cool—" I started, but he shushed me.

"Wait."

I kept watching as the pebbles rose from the ground slowly as if being sucked up toward his palm. They spiraled like they were riding on a miniature dust devil.

"Now that is awesome. Was that earth or air?" I still didn't fully understand the way his elements worked.

"That was earth. I'm much stronger with air, but I've started to try things with earth, water, and fire." He let it drop and blew the remaining dust out of the way with a blast of air.

"I wish I could do something cool like that."

"I wish I had the strength you had. Then I wouldn't be such a geek."

"At least you aren't a freak of nature." I bared my teeth and pointed at my eyes.

He elbowed me softly. "We're all freaks. But in a cool way."

"Ha," I said as I pulled the door open. The gym had been transformed. Emily already stood there, looking confused. She shrugged when Kegan asked what was going on.

"I don't think today will be any easier than last week." Emily looked around the gym at the rock pillar jutting out of the floor. How had Quinn put it in here? Was it real, or just an illusion? She had placed other things in there as obstacles, too. Kegan stepped forward, touching them. Not an illusion.

Denise joined us. "She'll probably give us a huge workout today."

I nodded, trying to keep from making any rude comments to Denise. The habit was hard to break since I'd hated her for so long. Even our little talk Friday at the end of school hadn't changed my feelings for her by much. Maybe I should make a bigger effort.

Emily asked, "So how are things going with you and James? You keeping things under control?" I perked up to listen, wanting to know the answer.

Denise glanced at me briefly and sighed. "Yeah, it's not too bad. I have to really be careful and watch myself. I still get the same energy. I hate knowing there's a faster and easier way to get that energy."

Emily patted her arm. "Wouldn't it be much worse if you all of a sudden found out on your own that you craved blood and killed one of your boyfriends? Knowledge can be what saves you from yourself."

Denise didn't say anything, but I could tell she was thinking over Emily's words. I agreed with her, but knowing what was possible was also a big temptation.

Kat entered the gym carrying the huge book I'd seen her looking through on Friday afternoon. She dumped it onto the front bench and joined us. I looked at her hopefully, but she just shook her head. My heart sank.

She pulled me to the side. "I couldn't find anything in here or any book about how to make you not crave blood. The only thing I can think of would be bleach, but you'd have to have lots of it to mask the blood scent, and I don't know if you want to be carrying any bleach around."

I chuckled. "Maybe bleach would be a deterrent to the demons coming after us. I'll have to ask Quinn."

"Ask me what?" Quinn said as she stepped out from behind the pillar. Had she been there the whole time? Or did she just appear like I'd seen her do from the shadows that night in front of the school?

"Does bleach do anything to demons?" Kat asked.

Quinn snorted. "It might sanitize them, but it wouldn't harm one."

"What about holy water?" Emily asked.

"It does a little, but it won't stop them for long or melt them or anything you've seen in your movies," she said. "Plus you'd have to be a priest to really use it effectively. You don't have time to learn the holy things that work for them."

"What will stop them?" Denise asked.

"You will, if you work together. The five of you can combine forces and be more powerful than any demon." She shivered and took a deep breath. "You must fight in unison and maintain your integrity. You'll be tempted to choose the easy way out. If you do that, you'll doom yourself, and likely the others you abandon. If you don't help me break free from his power, I'll still be under his control, and more powerful than you. I'll make your existence miserable if you don't succeed. You won't just die, you'll be in eternal damnation with no relief."

"So by working together, we'll win?" Denise asked.

"It is your only chance," Quinn said. "And even then, it is not predetermined. There is still a chance you will be overpowered."

"Are you going to help us?" Emily asked.

"I cannot. I will be restrained from participating against my master. I can defy him through you, but when he actually comes forth, I can do nothing against him. The only thing I can do is to train you in what you might encounter and let you win on your own."

"Doesn't sound very hopeful," Kat said.

It didn't. It sounded like we were doomed before we even started.

Quinn shrugged. "Do you think you are unprepared now?"

"Yes," I said

"What if you had no idea what was coming for you and he just showed up? No knowledge of what you are or what he is?"

She had a point. At least now we had a slight chance of survival. If we worked together, we might survive.

"So," Quinn said, "let's get started. Today you will all fight against me. I spent the weekend building up my strength. I'll do things you could encounter when you fight the demon lord and his minions. Some things you've seen and some will be new to you. My only instruction to you in this matter will be for you to work together as a team."

I nodded and glanced at Denise. She stole a quick glance at me as well, but looked away quickly. It wouldn't be easy, yet I was willing to try. How much would she put into it?

Quinn chanted a spell and the lights went out. The only illumination in the room was from the skylights in the ceiling of the gym. Quinn stepped into a shadow and disappeared. I heard a gasp from the side of me, probably from Kat. I looked around the room more closely, trying to see what all was there.

Quinn had transformed it to look almost like a junkyard. Piles of broken wood scattered around the massive rock pillar in the center reaching up to the metal rafters. Some rubber tires lay strewn around, with a pile of dirt and a section of the floor coated in what looked like oil. As I took in the strange scenery around me, a flash of light in the darkness behind the pillar caught my attention.

"Watch out!" I shouted, embracing my core. Everyone turned to see. Denise ducked in time to avoid the fireball launched at her.

More fireballs shot out at us. With the five of us, it was much easier than it had been when we'd fought her one-on-one.

Emily must have changed her skin again because she didn't avoid the balls coming at her. She tried catching some of them but never managed to do it. Kat had a shield around her, making the fireballs bounced off. Kegan just blew them off course.

Quinn stepped out from behind the pillar, still producing fireballs with one hand while she held her wicked blade in the other. I shied back from it, not wanting to come near it. I looked over at Denise, who looked ill. She pulled a bandana out of her pocket and wrapped it around her nose and mouth, old western bandit style. I couldn't fault her thinking but wondered how effective it would be.

Quinn disappeared again and reappeared next to Emily. She struck her with the blade. It bounced off. Quinn didn't lose a moment as she touched the spot behind her car and Emily dropped to her knees screaming as if something were attacking her.

Kat rushed over to her and chanted something, and Emily looked up in relief. As soon as Kat stopped the chant, Emily screamed her inner terror again. Kat looked panicked as she realized she'd have to keep chanting to help Emily overcome the images assaulting her mind.

Quinn swung the blade at Kat. The force of the blow knocked her down, but didn't cut her. I rushed in to help, leery of the blade swinging freely. It couldn't be easy for Kat to hold onto her shield while still trying to perform another spell to help Emily with her visions.

Kegan sent a blast of air that forced Quinn to back away from Kat a step or two, but she resumed the attack and threw more fireballs.

Denise came toward us as well. Quinn threw fireballs in rapid succession. Sometimes at me, sometimes at Denise, but she didn't try to send them at Kegan. Instead she conjured a shield that his air couldn't penetrate. She continued to attack Kat with the blade, keeping her down on the ground. Kat panted from the exertion of holding onto both spells. As we came closer, Quinn shouted a spell. A chunk of wood from the pile of debris flew at us. I turned to see it just in time to duck, but the fireball hit me. I screamed in pain. She kept pulling random items from the room while throwing fireballs at us, forcing a retreat.

The only things that didn't fly at us were the rubber tires. I rushed over to them and grabbed one. Something about the rubber prevented Quinn from using them. I ripped one apart, stunned when I did it. Another fireball struck the back of my neck. The burn was excruciating, but I tightened my grip on my core and the pain faded away.

I picked up the half tire and turned around in time to deflect a fireball thrown at me. Denise was still being bombarded by the fire. She looked tired and began to pull energy from the room. To bolster herself, she drained the others.

I threw the other half of the tire at her, barely missing her head.

"Watch it!" she snarled at me through her bandana, the look in her eyes murderous.

"Use the tire!" I shouted. "It stops the fireballs." I held one up to block another ball as a demonstration.

She nodded quickly and dove for the tire, avoiding a fireball sent her way. She struggled to pick it up at first, but she managed to get it in front of her slightly as a shield. She reached her hand toward Quinn, pulling a snake of Quinn's energy and releasing mine.

Quinn looked winded for a moment. She stopped to gather her strength again as if pulling from an inner source. She cut off the flow to Denise, but Denise didn't seem to notice. She was completely energized again.

I grabbed another tire and ripped it into smaller pieces. I didn't know if it would help or not, but I started throwing them at Quinn. She used some force to block them, but couldn't make them fly back at me.

Denise and I approached her again, holding our tire shields in front of us. Kegan gathered a handful of dirt and sent it on a current of air. When it hit Quinn, it swirled around her face, making me choke in sympathy. Kat and Emily still struggled, but they looked relieved that aid was coming.

Quinn swatted at the dust storm and sent a fireball directly at Kegan. He looked stunned when it hit him in the head. She threw a chunk of wood at him, knocking him out cold. Denise snarled and ran to him. After looking him over, she turned to face Quinn, anger all over her face.

"Is he alive?" I shouted.

"Yes, but he's unconscious."

Quinn continued to produce fireballs for me while holding Kat and Emily back with the blade. Emily still couldn't seem to fight off her inner vision. Quinn's odd spells pulled different objects in the room toward us. The ripped tire helped me block most of the things coming at me, but when a broken piece of wood with a nail in it hit the tire, it deflected off and spun around, nicking my other arm.

I gritted my teeth against the pain and looked down quickly to see a small gash just beginning to bleed. I whipped around to find out where Denise was so I could protect myself from her. She glanced at me, meeting my eyes with a curious expression. Then I saw her eyes when she noticed the cut on my arm. She backed away, holding her breath. How long would that last?

"Stay away from me," I threatened.

Denise just nodded. We both moved to increase the distance between us, but Quinn gave no quarter. She kept throwing things at us while still attacking Kat with her blade. Kat finally had to stop her chant. Emily dropped to the ground, screaming.

Kat managed to say a spell to call a broken pipe to her. She grabbed it and swung it wildly until she knocked the blade to the side. Quinn kept swinging the blade and throwing stuff at us, but her fireballs were less frequent. Maybe she was getting tired.

Denise reached with her arm outstretched toward Quinn. Tendrils of energy flowed toward her. It wasn't nearly as strong as before, but she found a way to drain Quinn again.

Kat swung her metal pipe, hitting Quinn in the arm. She nearly dropped the pipe but kept hold of it in time to raise it again to block the blow Quinn directed at her. Kat fell to the ground and grunted, metal pipe flying out of her hands. Quinn brought her blade up above her head as if preparing to bring it down on Kat in front of her.

I dropped my tire and rushed into the fray, tackling her from the side. She screamed and lowered the blade toward me, missing me by less than an inch. If I could stay close enough to her, she wouldn't be able to hit me. I hoped.

"Claire!" Kat shouted and threw something to me. It was the metal pipe. I grabbed it midair by instinct and brought it down hard, hitting Quinn in the head with it. It bounced off without doing any obvious damage. She looked irritated, but not injured. So apparently hitting a demon in the head didn't do much to it. I didn't dare move too far away, but I leaned back to give myself room to try again. I brought the pipe up and swung it sharply into the center of Quinn's stomach.

A boom and a white explosion filled the room, knocking me back at least five feet. My head rang. My vision blurred.

I stood up slowly, to steadying myself by bending forward and holding onto my thighs just above the knees. Emily lay on the floor, gasping for breath but no longer screaming. Kat dusted herself off and stood slowly. Denise eyed me warily, breathing shallow while she kept herself across the room from me. Kegan moaned and rolled over, holding his head.

Quinn lay still on the floor with her blade lying next to an open hand. The pipe lay across her chest. The smell in the room reminded me of metal shop. The pipe melted where it had struck her.

The other girls looked at me in shock.

"Did you kill her?" Kat asked.

"I just hit her with the pipe."

Denise approached cautiously. Kat noticed her hesitation and then saw the blood on my arm. She looked at me and raised her hand slowly as if asking permission to touch me. I nodded. She put her hand on my arm and healed the wound. Denise sighed but kept her cloth wrapped around her face. Kegan stumbled upright and wobbled as he came to stand by her. Kat healed the burn on his face.

Kneeling down next to Quinn, Denise placed her hand on her neck to check for a pulse. "She's still alive, but it's pretty faint."

Emily joined us with an angry look on her face. She seemed upset still about her lack of participation in the fight since she'd basically been fighting herself in the vision. Kat put her hand on her shoulder, and Emily relaxed visibly.

"So what do we do?" Denise asked.

"No clue," I said, staring down at Quinn, still unsure what exactly had happened.

CHAPTER NINETEEN

Quinn eventually woke up. Her eyes widened to find the five of us crouched over her.

"You all right?" Kat asked.

"You accessed my center again?" She looked at me with raised eyebrows.

"Apparently."

"So why did it knock you out this time? Last time she hit you there, it just stopped you from producing fireballs," Denise said.

"I told you before," Quinn wheezed as she sat up slowly. "If you hit a demon just right and knock out their power source, you then have the advantage over them." She rubbed her stomach tenderly and looked up at me again. "That is one of the only ways to defeat a demon. You can decapitate one, but that isn't nearly as easy as you might think. But by stopping the flow of power to our center, you can then defeat us."

"So basically we have to get to your center?" Emily asked.

"Yes. Although it is our vulnerable spot, it isn't

easy to get to. You must have a very powerful hit to the area."

"So once we hit their core and knock them out, we have to decapitate them?" I asked.

"For some of the more powerful ones, you will have to do both. Unless of course you can take its head off without first stunning it through its core, but don't count on it. For some of the lesser demons, a direct hit to the core will end them immediately. I'm surprised Claire has been able to hit me there twice."

"Why didn't you tell us about this at first? Give us the directions we needed in the first lesson?" Denise asked.

"I didn't trust you yet."

"You don't trust us?" I said. She didn't tell us anything useful until we forced it out of her. "You had to do some spell to get us to agree to join you in the first place, then you didn't tell us you're a demon until I saw it for myself, and now we find out by accident how to defeat one instead of just protect ourselves. Why don't you tell us?"

"I am prevented from giving you information unless you figure it out on your own," Quinn said. "Once you get the concept, I am free to discuss it, but I am unable to even make mention of it until you've discovered it first."

"What?" Kegan asked. "Why not?"

"It's like having a key to the code and then being able to understand it all."

"How many more things haven't you told us?" I demanded.

"I can't say." Quinn looked sorry about that, but it didn't do anything to help me feel better.

"So why are you able to train us with the fireballs, and to teach Kat those healing spells, and the visions you gave us?" I asked.

Quinn narrowed her eyes at me. "The healing spells are things that don't relate to demons themselves, so there is no problem with something like that. And I've always used fireballs in my other duties for my master, so I am allowed free use of those." She stood slowly and winced. "About today's lesson. Emily, you were completely incapacitated by the vision. You must learn to put those things out of your mind so you can be a part of the real thing." Emily opened her mouth to say something but Quinn ignored her and turned to Kat.

"Kat, you gave up too much of your ability to fight by trying to help Emily. Either learn how to cast a more powerful spell to free another from their problem, or don't attempt it. You could have been a stronger opponent to me had you not been spending your efforts on Emily."

"But you said we had to work together," Kat argued.

"I said the five of you must work together. By pairing off, you risk your own survival or effectiveness," Quinn snapped. "You must choose the best way. If it will end up lessening your own effectiveness, you must abandon the other."

Kat looked at Emily. From the look on her face, I knew Kat would do whatever she could to help one of us, even if it killed her.

"Denise, a cloth? Really?"

Denise didn't say anything, but looked uncomfortable.

"Your sense of smell is too powerful. Don't waste time on things that are of no use. Maintain control through other ways. You still need to breathe so get desensitized to it or learn to ignore it. You had many opportunities to attack me, but wouldn't because of the chance Claire's blood would entice you. You know what it did to you before. You would never do that again, so don't be timid around blood. You also had enough strength by absorbing it from those around you making you less hungry for the blood." Denise looked relieved when Quinn explained it that way.

"Kegan, you did well at first, but got cocky and thought you had me beat. Once you let your guard down, I had you. Never think you've won until the battle is completed.

"Claire, why didn't you access your true power?

You could have made a much better attack on me had you not been in your vulnerable human form. The fireballs would not affect you as a wolf. They are meant to harm human flesh. You'd also have much better reflexes as a wolf than a girl."

We all listened to her continue to tell us what we did wrong. Some things could have gone better, but we had managed to all stay alive. I was only cut slightly, and I took her out of the game within eight minutes. She wouldn't praise us, but a small part of me knew she had to be impressed we'd stopped her so soon. The look on her face when she first gained consciousness after I hit her with the pipe was enough to confirm her surprise.

***

I was on a high all morning long. We managed to defeat her and all came out of it pretty well. We might survive if we managed to improve at the same rate we'd done during practice. Quinn never said when her master would be coming, but I didn't know if that meant she was keeping it from us or if she didn't know for sure.

I needed to get with Emily to figure out this transformation thing. I wanted to have control over it. Relying on getting upset to change meant I ran the risk of losing my mind to the beast. Emily felt pretty sure she'd be able to transform into a wolf as well. She hoped that it would be something that could help me with my own.

At lunch, I purposely sought Paul out. He smiled when he saw me.

"You're in a good mood," he said.

"Yeah. It's nice. Maybe I should have good days more often." I took his hand. He seemed surprised, but didn't say anything. He held onto my hand tightly for a moment before softening his grip and rubbing his thumb across my thumb.

"We still on for Max's walk after school?"

"Yup. I wouldn't miss it."

"Are you sure you aren't just using me to get closer to my dog?" Paul teased.

"Oh, man. You caught me. Now what will we do? It's going to be so awkward to have you there since I've been trying to steal your dog from you," I said, bumping him in the arm with my shoulder.

"He wouldn't mind. He adores you."

"I love him. He's the coolest dog ever." I smiled at the memories of the weekend when we'd taken him for a walk, stopped at the park, and threw a Frisbee for him. He caught it every time.

"He probably wouldn't even notice it if I didn't come."

"Why, Paul, I'd almost say you're jealous."

"Not completely, but I do get close every once in a while. Maybe I should take you out without bringing Max."

I grinned. "That would defeat the purpose of going to the park to walk him."

"No. I mean on a real date."

I looked up into his eyes and got slightly nervous at his expression.

"Will you go to the homecoming dance with me?" Paul asked.

"I don't know if I can." I really did want to go out with him, and homecoming would have been the perfect place, but it was the night of the full moon. I still didn't know what would happen to me on a full moon if I were exposed to it.

Paul's face fell. My heart clenched when I saw it.

"It's okay. I understand," he said as he tried to take his hand out of mine. I didn't let him.

"No, you don't understand," I nearly snapped. I took a deep breath and tried to speak softly. "I would love to go with you, it's just that I might have a problem with that particular night."

"Like what?"

"Will you give me a chance to work it out and let you know in a couple of days?"

Paul looked away from me into the mass of

students walking around us on the way to the cafeteria. My heart had a different kind of reaction.

"Or do you want to ask someone else?" Who would be his next choice?

"No, I wasn't going to ask anyone else." He shrugged. "I just thought it would be great to go with you."

"I'd love to, but I'll still have to double check something." I squeezed his hand, hoping to show him how much I meant it.

Paul nodded and we walked quietly the rest of the way to lunch. We tried to open up new conversations, but I could tell he was disappointed. What was I doing? Why couldn't I remember to keep my promise to myself and stay away from him? I had to protect him in case I couldn't control myself when I transformed.

My journal showed my moods. The days leading up to the full moon were always more difficult than the previous, but things never really got bad until the actual night of the full moon. Now that I knew what I was and knew a little more about how to handle it, I would probably be fine on Saturday night. Plus being with Paul was always a mood lifter.

I stood up quickly, surprising Paul. "I'll meet you in the parking lot after school."

I rushed out of the cafeteria, headed straight to Quinn's office. Her door was locked. The secretary said she'd slipped out for a bit and would be back soon. I paced the office, trying to figure out what to ask. Would she even know if I'd really transform on the full moon? She seemed to think I had a choice in it.

The secretary watched me as I paced back and forth. The expression on her face wasn't hard for me to guess. She probably thought it was funny that over the last couple of weeks, I'd purposely sought out the principal. I'd never done that before. I'd always tried to stay out of the office, and now I was here waiting for Quinn to return. I smiled at the irony of it.

***

"Ask me again," I said to Paul as I joined him at his car after school.

"What?"

"Ask me." I smiled. "What you asked me before lunch."

"Oh." He looked me over and taking in my smile, he must have felt more confident this time. "Will you go to homecoming with—"

"Yes!"

"Really?"

"Yeah, things should be fine."

"Cool. We'll go out to dinner before the dance," he said. I nodded in agreement. Paul opened the door for me and when he joined me in the car he had a new idea. "What if we do our pre-dance activity on Friday night before the homecoming game? Then we can go to dinner on Saturday night before the dance. That way I get to take you out twice."

I smiled at him, excited about his idea. "It sounds like the perfect weekend."

"Good, it's two dates. I'll pick you up on Friday at three and we'll go do something, then go to the game together."

Max greeted me at the door, excited to get out. He barely moved so Paul could open the front door wide enough for us to get in. He barked once in greeting and rushed past Paul to get to me. I scratched him behind his ears and leaned down to him.

"Who's a good boy?" I asked as he whimpered with joy at seeing me. "You want to go for a walk? Huh, I bet you do. You just can't wait to get out of this cramped house and go explore again. I don't blame you. I'd be miserable stuck in the house all day like this."

Paul watched me with Max. "What?" I asked when I noticed.

"Nothing really, I just still can't believe how Max is around you."

I shrugged it off, knowing why Max probably felt the way he did toward me. I was a perfect blend of dog and person to him, but he didn't find me a threat. That comforted me a lot. Hopefully it would never change.

Paul grabbed the leash off its hook by the coat rack and hooked it onto Max's collar, and then handed me the leash.

"You should keep it," I said, hoping to make Paul feel better.

He shrugged and kept the leash. Max looked up from Paul to me as Paul opened the door. He didn't start walking until I did, and even then he whimpered as I left. "Come, Max. We're still walking."

Max looked at Paul again, whimpered once more, hung his head, and followed us out the door. When we got to the sidewalk, we turned toward the park. Max lifted his head, wagging his tail. I chuckled at Max's hopefulness. When he realized I was coming, he stopped whining but I had to correct him to stay behind Paul like he'd done for me.

By the end of the walk, I'd given in and taken the leash. I wanted that connection, that control. I wanted to feel that someone totally worshiped and adored me. It was shallow, but it felt good.

Paul took my hand and led me over to a park bench. Taking Max's leash, he tied it to the leg of the bench so he couldn't wander off. We sat down quietly. At first I kept a couple of inches between us. Paul simply slid over and put his arm around me. I sat stiffly for a moment, confused at my conflicting emotions.

Would I ever be normal? I'd finally figured out how to behave normally only after learning I was a werewolf. How twisted was that? I couldn't even let myself enjoy my life. I had to worry about whether it would be over in a couple of weeks. Or if I'd kill someone.

It wasn't fair to Paul. I was being selfish, and I knew it. I wanted to know what it was like to feel human completely. I wanted to have something normal to remember.

I closed my eyes and leaned my head back, intending to rest it on the back of the bench. Instead, I found my head pillowed on Paul's arm. Forcing the images of the whole werewolf thing away, I let myself take in my surroundings.

Max breathed slowly as he lay on the ground next to the bench. He seemed so content. His heartbeat matched my own — calm and relaxed. I breathed in deeply, smelling the tanginess of the leaves changing color. The cool air felt refreshing and the warmth radiating from Paul sitting next to me was so tempting. I allowed myself to snuggle in closer to him.

He shifted slightly as he adjusted his body to cradle mine. The hint of soap and his own personal smell were intoxicating. His breathing slowed slightly, but his heart rate did a few odd things. It sped up, then slowed down. When I leaned my face closer to his shoulder, his heart rate changed again. I tried not to smile, but felt a little smug knowing that my closeness affected him. This was totally new. I loved it.

He turned his head toward me, but since he was so much taller than me, even sitting down, his chin rested on top of my head. He breathed in slowly, turning so his cheek was against my head.

Contentment filled my soul. I hated to admit it, but I loved him. I had allowed him into my heart. I allowed myself to feel emotions more deeply than I'd ever imagined possible.

This feeling for Paul was so different. I would do anything for him. He had been so constant and had forgiven me for not forgiving him. I needed him more than I dared to admit, yet was terrified that I was wrong for him.

I reached up to my shoulder to hold Paul's hand as it held me close and tucked my feet under my legs. When I moved, Paul shifted to accommodate me again. I could stay like this forever, next to him. For a moment, I could forget about the future.

Paul took his other arm and brought it around me in a sideways hug as we sat on the bench. A smile came at the thought he wanted to get closer to me. I'd never been the kind of person who liked being held close, or confined, but this was different than expected.

I glanced up toward Paul, causing him to lift his

head. He looked down at me with his deep blue eyes. I stared into his eyes, trying to interpret what they held, surprised when he leaned in closer. His eyes were inches from mine.

Our foreheads nearly touched. He glanced down briefly, looking into my eyes with a question in his own. I stared more deeply, feeling lost.

Paul moved slowly closer, hesitating slightly for a moment as he kept his eyes on mine. Was he testing me? *What's he asking with those eyes of his? Why can't I think?*

His breath felt warm on my face, reminding me how cold the evening had become. It smelled of mint. And of promise. It smelled of him. Delicious. I remembered the kiss we'd shared in my vision. This was so much more intimate than that. This was real. This was right. This was what I wanted. Wasn't it?

When his lips brushed mine, the flash of him lying dead on the ground invaded my mind. I panicked.

"No!" I blurted, leaning back. My face flushed with fear.

Paul let me go.

"I can't," I choked. I shook my head and stood up. "I'm sorry. I've gotta go." I looked around frantically, trying to figure out where to run. When I finally got my bearings, I took off running without giving Paul a chance to say anything.

Max jumped up and tried to follow but was stopped short by his leash. He barked as if begging me to come back for him, to wait so he could come, too.

"Sorry," I whispered and kept running, not daring to turn around. I couldn't see Paul. I grabbed my core and let its energy surround me. I needed this help. I didn't want to think about what I'd almost done. I had to make sure I could always stay in control.

Yet as I ran, I wished I were still there in his arms. We could be kissing right this moment. Instead, I freaked out.

Paul would probably change his mind and tell me to forget the date. He should. He should go find someone more worthy of him. A girl who wouldn't turn into a monster without notice. Someone who wouldn't hurt him. I kept running, though tears blurred my vision. I didn't need to see. I could have run home with my eyes closed.

Eventually, the cold air as it hit my wet face brought me out of my emotions.

I needed to be strong, to be something more than me. I was human but needed to find a way to blend it with the werewolf parts of me. I had to learn how to access my wolf form while keeping my mind about me. I would do it. I had to. Otherwise, any future with Paul was impossible. I would never let myself hurt him. I could never let myself get too close to him without being sure I could keep myself under control.

The change in my emotions with him would affect the way I could hold onto myself. If I got too careless and didn't keep myself under control at all times, then the possibility of me turning into the beast was too real. If I could change and keep my mind about me I'd be fine. Paul would be safe.

I needed to practice.

CHAPTER TWENTY

Instead of running home, I took off toward Emily's house, hoping she was home. I pounded on the door, barely winded from my run. It was amazing what my core could do for me. I felt strong and invincible.

Emily opened the door, surprised to see me. "Come in," she said.

"Actually, can you help me work on transforming? I have to see if I can do this and keep my mind. Quinn says I have to transform when the demons show up. It might even happen on a full moon now that she's done that weird spell on me, but I don't know. I want to learn how to do it so I can learn how to *not* do it." I took a deep breath and knew I had lost Emily somewhere. "Can you transform to the wolf?"

"Every time I've tried, I keep getting blocked," Emily said. "The times I thought I could do it were when you were really angry and fighting with Denise. I can shift into almost any human, but can't quite get an animal down."

"Can we try?" I didn't want to beg, but I needed this. I had to keep my mind about me when the change happened.

"Give me a minute," Emily said as she ran into her room. She came back with her jacket and the keys to her car. We climbed in and I gave her directions to the secluded area of the park where Denise had suggested we go before. It was on the opposite side of the park from where I'd left Paul and Max, so I hoped I wouldn't see them. Being in the secluded spot with Emily didn't bother me as much as it would have with Denise.

I got out of the car and ran around the area to make sure we were alone. Emily suggested we go even higher up into the trees to avoid being seen by any joggers using the trail. I agreed. We walked for ten minutes before finally stopping. I embraced my core again and listened for things that might indicate we weren't alone. After a few minutes, I knew we were safe and asked Emily how her shifting worked.

"I just tell my body what to do. I think of all the things that need to be different and make my body do it. To change the color of my hair I just think about it, and it happens." Her hair shifted quickly from brown to blonde and then to red. "How about you? Didn't you say you transformed in your vision? You haven't done it for real though, right?"

"Just in my vision." I frowned at the images that followed.

"How did that happen in your vision?"

"Denise turned into a vampire and was killing someone. I went to save him, and partially turned. When she attacked someone else, I got really mad and gave in to the desire. I was a wolf before even making contact with her. Then when I stopped her, I tasted blood and lost my mind to the wolf. I was no longer myself."

Emily eyed me cautiously. "Well," she hesitated. "I don't think I'll transform into Denise then."

"No," I agreed. "That wouldn't be a good idea. I can muster up enough anger without seeing you act like her. It would probably be a good idea for you to do something to your skin like you do for Quinn's lessons."

"Right." Emily nodded and changed her skin. I could see a subtle difference, but it wouldn't be obvious to someone without my heightened senses.

I closed my eyes and started to breathe, taking in everything about myself. My jacket felt tight. I took it off and enjoyed the tingle in my arm as the goose bumps rose. The change in temperature helped me to notice my body better. I thought back to my vision with Denise and let myself relive it, paying close attention my feelings in the vision. I tried to make my body do the same thing. Having an immediate threat helped me before, but I could pull up those images and feelings with no problem. They were always there in the back of my mind.

I remembered my anger when Denise went after Jax. The goose bumps on my arms weren't from the cold anymore.

As Denise got closer to Jax in my memory, I focused on how she made me feel. She took Jax into her embrace and kissed him. A shiver climbed my back. As he enjoyed it, I felt myself beginning to change, knowing what was coming. I ran my tongue across my longer teeth. My fists clenched, pushing the hardened fingernails into my palms. I kept my eyes closed and felt what happened. The cold chills were gone.

Denise dragged Jax to the ground. I ran to try to stop her. Air brushed past me as I ran to save Jax in my memory, yet I felt the soft ground under my feet as I stood on a pile of fallen leaves.

Again, my mind saw Denise look up from her kill with blood dripping from her lips. I focused on Denise looking crazed with the blood lust.

I took a deep breath, slightly relieved when the smell of the real world around me in the forest was stronger than the blood in my vision. The whiff of blood in my memory was enough. I tried to shift, imagining my body as a wolf. I had been a wolf in my vision, so I could clearly picture how I should look. I willed myself to change. The hairs on my arms and the back of my neck stiffened, but I was still human. My body wouldn't obey.

The vision continued. I knew what was coming next. Maybe the terror of watching Denise attack Paul would be enough to tip the scales. It played out in my mind. I circled her again, glancing at Jax as he lay dead under the bush. Denise would turn on Paul any second. Why hadn't I noticed her intention the first time? It was obvious now as I watched it again.

When she lunged for Paul, I chased her. My real body followed my memory. I darted forward, eyes still closed. I knew I was really moving, not just watching things happen in my vision. In my vision, my body transformed. Why couldn't I do it now? Denise made contact, and I flinched back in terror. I knew what was coming for Paul. I willed myself to really change. My memory was clear. I knew how to do it, but it wasn't happening for real. I felt it almost there. Like when I knew the answer to something, but just couldn't spit it out in the right words. I growled in frustration.

Shivers ran over my entire body. I tingled everywhere. No change. I watched myself attack Denise, living through killing her again. I hated it in my real mind, but felt the joy and satisfaction of ripping at her through my memory. The conflicting emotions made me question my resolve. Did I want to let myself transform if it meant I would enjoy destruction?

The taste of blood was so real. I ran my tongue over my teeth to double check. I couldn't quite let myself go completely, too afraid of what would happen. If I shifted into a wolf right now, could I come back to myself? I let myself experience the remainder of the vision and attacked Paul. The look of betrayal in his eyes sent physical pain through me. I hadn't noticed it before. Though he looked confused at what had happened, he still seemed to think of me as me, and not as a wolf. It wasn't until the end, when I bit him, that he finally looked truly scared.

Paul still could see me, past the werewolf. Had my mind come up with that on its own or was it really possible? Would he still think well of me even if I turned into a monster?

The vision ended and I felt much better than any other times I'd gone over it. Instead of focusing on the killing of Paul, I focused on the hope that maybe Paul might still care for me even if he knew.

A twig snapped nearby. I jumped up quickly, expecting something dangerous. Emily paused and stood still, watching me cautiously with her finger to her lips. She looked me over from head to toe.

She tilted her head to the side, and then she changed. It was subtle at first. Her legs shortened. Her arms lengthened. She bent forward as she began to morph. The hairs on her body thickened and covered her entirely. Even her clothes changed — they didn't rip. They turned into fur. How had she done that? Before, she said she didn't think she could do anything with her clothes, but now she was able to take what was on her and change it to look like what she wanted. What would happen with my clothes? Her transformation was complete before I finished contemplating my clothing issues.

"You did it," I whispered in awe as I took her in. She looked amazing. The transformation was so complete. I wasn't afraid of her, but seeing a large wolf in front of me did make me pause and move cautiously.

"Can you still understand me?" I asked looking Emily the wolf in the eyes.

She nodded.

"Can you speak like that?"

The wolf made some funny whining sounds, a little higher and rougher sounding than what Max sounded like, but no words came out. The wolf shook its head, making a sound like she was clearing her throat. She tried to speak again. Eventually, she gave up and shook her head.

"I guess not," I said, coming a little closer to her. "But still, that's awesome. You look like a wolf but still have your own mind. You are completely you inside, aren't you?"

Wolf Emily nodded and sat down on her haunches. She looked into my eyes intently, as if asking me something.

"I tried," I said, answering the question I thought she must be asking. "I felt so close, but just couldn't do it."

Wolf Emily tilted her head as if to ask, "Why?"

"I don't know. Maybe it's because there wasn't a real threat to actually push me over."

Wolf Emily kept looking at me as if expecting me to give her more.

"In my vision, with the change, I lost my own mind completely. I'm too afraid of that happening again."

Wolf Emily shook her head, making me think she felt sort of bad for me. I stared in awe at the way she had fully transformed. If only it were as easy for me. Then again, maybe having me turn easily would be a bad thing. What I really wished was to transform with little difficulty and still keep my human consciousness.

Wolf Emily adjusted her position slightly, tipping me off moments before she lunged for me. I dropped to the ground instinctively and avoided her attack just in time. She hit the ground behind me and turned on me quickly.

"What are you doing?" I shouted. Maybe she really didn't have her full mental abilities. Maybe she was a wolf.

I grabbed my core. I'd let slip away from me as Emily transformed. It came easily and infused me with energy preparing me for her attack. When she jumped, I slipped to the side and brought my arm up. The force of my strike in her side made her grunt and whimper slightly in pain.

"Serves you right," I snapped.

Wolf Emily walked slowly and began to circle me as if looking for a good place to strike. I watched her, waiting for her movements to give away her intentions. I could easily beat her. I wasn't worried about her hurting me, just annoyed that she thought this would help. Now I had to defend myself against her simple attacks without hurting her as she tried to make me angry.

Wolf Emily snarled and jumped forward, surprising me when she went for my legs. She managed to bite one, drawing blood. I screamed in rage and pain. I swiped at her, hitting her across the back of the neck. She whimpered in pain again and I looked at my hand. My fingernails were claws and had blood and fur on them. She wasn't invincible as a wolf.

"Stop!" I shouted. "Kat's not here to fix you up." I tried to not breathe too deeply, hesitant to smell the blood just in case it did weird things to me. I definitely didn't want to lose control right here. I could easily kill Emily if I lost it now.

Wolf Emily just shook herself and began circling me again. She was determined, I'd give her that much, but she was stupid. Who in their right mind would purposely antagonize a werewolf?

After moving around me for a few minutes she seemed to finally agree that this was stupid. Emily changed back. She absorbed the fur into herself, and her clothes started to show through. I relaxed, crossing my arms over my middle.

"It's about time," I said, frowning. I looked up through the trees, trying to guess how much more daylight we had. With my attention off her, Emily quickly shifted back into the full wolf form and knocked me to the ground.

Her claws dug into my shoulder. Her muzzle and teeth were inches from my face. She looked angry, yet triumphant. She growled deep in her throat as if to say, "I've got you."

Her expression and her attitude pushed something deep within me. I growled back. My teeth lengthened. My fingernails changed. Wolf Emily suddenly looked less sure of herself and she hesitated for just a second. She must have seen something threatening in me because she went for my throat, not biting, but opening her jaw wide enough to catch my neck between her teeth.

I howled in anger and brought my legs up between our bodies. She still had her front paws on my shoulders, holding me down. I found enough room to get good leverage and kick at her. I used all my strength, pulling from the core within me to force her off. Her body flew through the air. I heard her hit a tree, followed by a second thump as she fell to the ground

I reached up to my throat, feeling the sting of the cuts I'd received as her teeth scratched me. She was going to pay for that.

I got up quickly, ready for her next attack, but nothing came. Emily was back in her human form unconscious under the tree. I rushed over, worried I'd really hurt her. Her strong pulse made me sigh in relief. It took her a while to come to, but when she did, she looked up at me with an embarrassed and irritated expression. I couldn't tell which emotion she felt more strongly.

"What exactly were you doing?" I demanded.

"I thought that if I could turn to the wolf, I could get you to try it, too. Better than helping you in my human form." She shrugged, wincing in pain. She brought her hand to the back of her neck.

"Let me see." I hissed in sympathy as she leaned forward. My claws had caused a lot of damage. Her shirt was ripped just below the neckline. Blood oozed slowly out of four long scratches. It wasn't as deep as it could have been. Maybe being in a wolf's body actually protected her from more harm. No, if she'd had her iron skin, she'd have been better protected. The smell of her blood didn't bother me. *That's good to know.* Maybe I really could keep myself together if there were blood. Of course, I hadn't tasted it, and that was what worried me.

Emily reached into her pocket and pulled out a tissue. "Here, will you help me with this?" She leaned forward again for me to wipe the blood.

"Maybe we should stop at Kat's on the way home?"

"Probably a good idea," Emily agreed. "Don't want to have my mom asking me how I got this."

I cleaned her up as best as I could. "Do you feel like you could get up?"

"Yeah, soon. Give me a second longer to rest. That sort of took it out of me."

I sat next to her and wiped my fingernails free of her flesh.

"Why didn't you change, Claire?" Emily asked, looking at me through her hair as she leaned forward.

"I didn't really need to. You weren't much of a threat."

"You were close. I could feel it coming from you."

"You can feel it from me?" I asked, dumbfounded. "How?"

"It's just there. You are so close. You almost did it before my shift. That's why I could do it myself. It was right there with you."

"I know I'm close, but I just can't let myself go all the way."

"You're going to have to, you know."

"I know," I said a little more sharply than necessary. She was only trying to help.

"Don't worry," Emily shrugged. She grimaced again at the pain. "We'll get you there soon. I'll give you something to fight against."

"No offense, but you aren't strong enough. I'll be holding back for fear of killing you."

"Yeah, maybe that's true in my wolf form. Next time we spar, I'll make my skin tougher."

Chapter Twenty-One

Quinn had moved on to a new lesson style. She no longer fought us personally. Instead, she built some fake demon bodies out of clay and performed a spell that animated them to fight against us. They were strong enough that they didn't just crumble when we hit them, as I'd expected at first. They were slow and not really threatening since they couldn't think on their own, but they didn't give up easily. The only way to stop one was to hit it in its core, but the location of each core was different.

She had us start by fighting them one-on-one, then she had more join in the practice and we fought multiples at a time until we eventually fought in a group.

Quinn threw fireballs and objects at us, but every time we approached her she'd disappear and reappear somewhere else. She never engaged us personally again. She would sneak up and try to touch us to start those awful visions. She managed to get Emily again, but Emily seemed to fight through it much better this time. When Quinn got Kat, she dropped out of the fight for a while until she could work her way out of the visions. She never got close enough to Denise, Kegan, or me to give us any visions to fight, but she focused her other battle skills on us while Emily and Kat were nearly incapacitated with the visions.

This was a much different style of fighting than we were used to, but we managed to hold our own pretty good. While Denise and Kegan kept Quinn occupied, I went for the clay demons. I took out five of them before they learned to avoid me.

When I got tired of the clay demons, I switched places with Denise and joined Kegan in the fight against Quinn. It wasn't nearly as fun. Quinn kept popping to different places. I missed the thrill that came when I actually felt threatened by her. These clay things started out as a bit of a challenge, but eventually they lost their intrigue. I wanted to really get into this, to let all this pent-up frustration out. I wanted to have a reason to change. I had to make sure I could hold onto myself when I did.

"Stop running from me!" I shouted at Quinn when she once again disappeared into a shadow and popped up somewhere else.

"You really want to confront me?"

"Yes! How will we ever learn if we only fight fake demons? I need the real thing."

"Very well." She said a spell, making the clay demons disintegrate. The others stopped mid-action as their opponents disappeared. "You four," Quinn said to them, "Sit and watch. Claire has challenged me one-on-one."

Emily gave a little cheer and high-fived Kegan. Kat shook her head as if she couldn't believe I was gutsy enough to do this. Denise just scowled at me. Was she mad?

"Prepare yourself," Quinn said.

"You, too."

Quinn disappeared and came up behind me, striking me in the back with her fist. Then she hit me with a fireball as my back arched at the pain. She moved too quickly for me to follow. She could pop from place to place so much faster than I imagined. Maybe telling her to fight me one-on-one wasn't such a good idea, but then again, I really needed to know what it would be like to fight something who was out to kill me.

Another fireball hit me. I wrapped my core tighter around myself. It helped to ease the pain of the burn but didn't take it away completely. That was okay. I needed that reminder and the anger it brought. I would shift this time. I'd make myself. The others could all access what they needed. It was time I did it, too.

I fought Quinn with as much energy as I could. I felt powerful, but not quite where the ability to transform developed. What was stopping me? Emily said it was just there on the surface. It had to be accessible. It came to me in my vision so easily but it was elusive now. Quinn kept throwing fireballs at me, but most of them missed.

The objects she threw with her strange telekinesis were a little trickier to avoid. I dove into the pile of junk around the room and grabbed a rubber tire in one hand to use as my shield again, and found a piece of metal pipe like I'd used before. It wasn't long, so I'd need to get closer to hit her with it. That left me no room to avoid the fireballs. She also ran the risk of getting hit by the debris she sent flying at me from all directions, so that slowed down slightly.

We managed to give and take for quite some time. Nothing made me change. She hit me with her fists. No change. She hit me with fireballs. No change. She hit me with objects. No change. She cut me and made me bleed. No change. Denise didn't even move from her spot so there was no threat from her to tip the balance for me. I hit Quinn with the pipe in the face. I swung at her stomach next. She deflected it easily. I hit her with my fists, but it only made my hands hurt.

Quinn moved back and conjured a fireball and threw it at my head. I dived to the ground to avoid it then rolled and jumped back up. I turned to face her. My core was getting stronger so when some of her other fireballs made contact they didn't burn as much.

I wasn't winning, but neither was she. I was a match for her. If only I could get myself to transform, then I'd have the upper hand. But if I did, how could I manage to hit her in her core?

A head butt?

Would that even work? Maybe being in wolf form would allow me to rip her head off. She did say once that decapitating a demon would kill them, but I didn't really want to try that with her right now.

We fought back and forth and my core kept me from getting tired. Quinn seemed to have unlimited energy now, maybe because Denise wasn't draining her powers. She had said, one-on-one, she could outlast each of us. Eventually she'd probably come out triumphant. I couldn't get the upper hand in this conflict.

I debated on calling a time out, but couldn't bring myself to do that. I wanted to test myself, to come up with something fantastic and new. I wanted to transform and see what I could do against her then. But I had no clue what was stopping me.

I attacked Quinn with renewed vigor. She stepped back in surprise at my accelerated attacks. I moved almost as fast as she did, without popping in and out of shadows. Releasing my mind slightly, I tried to go by instinct. I used emotions and feelings instead of trying to analyze things.

I was so close. I could feel the tension building as I attacked Quinn and fought off her attacks. My skin began to tingle again, a good sign. My teeth felt more like fangs. My claws ripped at Quinn. Finally I got a reaction from her. My arm and neck hairs rose. I glanced at my arms briefly as I brought them up to block another attack. My arms still looked mostly hairless. I wasn't as close as I'd thought.

When Quinn raised her arm to strike me, I grabbed it and without stopping to think, I bit her. I tore a chunk of skin from her arm before she could pull away. As she screamed with rage, I transformed. This was it. My arms tingled again. The hairs thickened. I reveled in triumph. I was changing, but I was still myself. My mind was still whole. I would keep it together.

My body began the transformation. My arms lengthened. I looked up at Quinn in time to see her place both hands in front of her stomach. She pulled something different than a fireball and hurled it at me. I had time enough to register that whatever it was, it couldn't be good before it hit me in the face. Everything went black.

***

I woke up in pain. My head screamed at me with each heartbeat. Muffled sounds added to my trauma. The skin of my face felt tight, almost burned. I longed to go back to the blackness and never come out of it. I didn't want to be alive if this is what it felt like.

My eyes were open, but I couldn't see much. *Am I blind?* No, it wasn't dark, it was all light. Some dark objects moved around me, but nothing looked solid — sort of like dark clouds roaming around in a bright sky.

Something touched my face. Words that should mean something sounded in my tender ears. *Kat must be trying to heal me. Good old Kat.* I closed my eyes and just let her at it. I focused instead on finding my core. It had disappeared, but I wanted it back. It always helped with the pain. Once I embraced it, the pounding in my head lessened considerably. While Kat worked on my head, I focused on the rest of me. I didn't really feel too bad, besides my head. A cut on my arm stung a little. Some minor burns didn't bother me much, and soon Kat would take care of them.

I opened my eyes again, happy to find my vision clearing. I raised my hands to my face to see if something close up would look better. It took me a while to focus on it, but eventually I saw my pink hands and short fingers. I wiggled them. My fingernails looked normal. I automatically ran my tongue across my teeth. They were normal as well. *I'm not a wolf.*

I had been so close. I was sure I could have transformed completely if Quinn hadn't done whatever it was.

I looked around for her, but still couldn't focus on things too far away from me. "Where is she?" I demanded of Kat.

"Right here," Quinn said, her blurry outline coming closer to me.

"Why did you stop me?" I growled. "You've been telling me all along to transform. I was almost there and you knocked me out!"

"I was protecting myself," Quinn said with venom in her voice.

"You what?" I couldn't quite comprehend that.

"You were hurting me. If you fully transformed, you would have been able to take me down right then. I can't allow you to do that."

"You really think I would have been able to destroy you?" I asked, surprised at the revelation.

"Yes," Quinn said, shifting her shoulders. She straightened up. "I've told you before. The key to our success is your transformation. If you do it now and destroy me, then the demon lord would come for you immediately. You can't survive yet. You still need more practice."

"But how can I practice and learn everything if I'm not allowed to transform? This is the closest I've ever been besides in my vision and you knock me out before I can even finish."

My eyesight cleared up enough for me to see the frustration on Quinn's face. The others watched me as well. Emily had a look of satisfaction and pride on her face. Kegan looked surprised. Kat looked sympathetic, and Denise looked … jealous? Was I reading that right? Could she actually be jealous?

"We are done for this morning. Tomorrow we will practice more with the clay demons. Maybe you'll even start *working together*. I'll try to make them more challenging to you, Claire, but I will no longer participate with you. It is too dangerous for us to do that. You know you can change, so if you can't manage to do it with the clay demons, you'll know how once the real battle begins." She turned to the shadows and disappeared, taking all her strange objects with her. The gym was bare.

I sat dumbfounded at the contradictions of Quinn's words now and before. Why would she stop me? I couldn't be strong enough by myself to defeat her. She said we needed to work together. I could have hurt her, I'm sure. My pride wouldn't let me deny that. But I wouldn't have killed her. I'd need the help of the others, wouldn't I?

Or would there be so many that we'd have to all work together to stop them? I couldn't believe how angry being stopped before I transformed made me. This was so different than the way I'd felt when she first told me what I was.

I thought back to the moment where I almost made the full transformation. I still had my own mind with me. I might actually be able to keep it when it really mattered.

Chapter Twenty-Two

I played over this morning's practice, testing my memory. Quinn tasted horrid when I bit her, like her blood was tainted. It hadn't turned me into a frenzy where I wanted to kill her. I was more focused on the act of transforming. By being cautious and staying focused, I had a good chance of keeping my wits. I thought again of the way my skin felt as the werewolf fur started to emerge. I ran my hands over my arms. The remembered sensations gave me cold chills.

I was so deep in thought that I missed Paul's approach until he was right next to me. He didn't say a word, just fell into step with me. I looked up at him, afraid to see his expression, but hoping it would be positive. After yesterday's botched kiss, who knew what to expect?

He looked curious but waited for me to speak first. I ventured something simple. "Hi."

"Hi." He smiled.

Maybe he isn't angry about yesterday.

I kept my eyes forward as we continued to the

cafeteria. He didn't try to take my hand, disappointing me slightly, but I totally understood why.

"How was your morning?" I couldn't stand the silence.

"Decent. Got my score from the quiz yesterday. Did pretty good."

"Nice."

"How about you?" he asked.

I flashed over the things in my demon fighting lessons and shuddered. "It started out pretty good, got worse, then better, then worse again, and now it's better."

"Well, I hope it stays good for you."

"Me too." I looked up at him. He looked around at the scenery, or others passing us, but never at me. I slowed down, suddenly self-conscious.

He stopped and turned to me. I looked directly at him, trying to figure out what to say. I opened my mouth multiple times, but just couldn't find the right words.

He took pity on me and shrugged as he said, "Don't worry about it."

"But—" I started.

"Seriously. I don't blame you. I shouldn't have tried that yesterday. It was probably too soon."

"I…" I couldn't think of what to say. It was too soon, but not in the way he thought.

"Someday," he said with a soft smile.

"Thanks," I whispered.

He took my hand in his and leaned closer to me until his forehead touched mine. "But please don't make it too long."

I grinned at him. "It won't be long. I just can't let myself give in now. I might end up going too far."

He nearly choked on his next words. "Too far?"

I blushed, completely stunned at the way it came out. I stammered for a moment before finally saying, "I mean I just can't kiss you yet. I have to keep my wits about me for something, and can't allow myself to be distracted by you."

He grinned with a blush that made him even more adorable. "I can totally see how you could find me distracting."

"You have no idea," I muttered.

I couldn't believe my relief that Paul had given me more time.

***

Joining Paul at his car after school Friday, I asked. "So are you going to tell me what we're doing?"

He smiled mischievously as he opened my door then paused like something just occurred to him. "You aren't afraid of heights, are you?"

"Not really. Why?"

"Good, 'cause I'm taking you indoor sky diving." He grinned.

"Really?" I squealed. "I've always wanted to do that."

He leaned into the car and tugged on my ear. "Perfect."

Butterflies in my stomach fluttered as we pulled up to the Fun Complex. When Paul opened the door for me, he offered me his hand. I took it, and we walked in together. Twenty minutes later I tugged on my jumpsuit and played with the straps of my helmet as we waited for the instructor to finish our training. I was dying to get in the wind tunnel.

Finally, we went in together and after the instructor gave us a few last pointers, we were on our own. Inside the wind tunnel, the monstrous fan beneath the grate sent a humming vibration throughout my body. Paul had done this before so he showed me some tricks and then joined me on the side again.

He took my hand, and we jumped into the center together. The wind lifted me into the air. I was clumsy and wobbled so much I nearly pulled Paul back to the ground. He placed his hands on my shoulders as he lay in the air, helping me learn my balance. Before long we were airborne, holding hands and doing all kinds of silly things. I smiled so much my cheeks hurt. Shouting over the sound of the air rushing past me was useless. Paul couldn't hear me.

He grabbed my hand and moved closer to me. I shouted in his ear, "This is awesome!" He smiled at me and raised his thumbs up. "Thanks for bringing me!"

He cupped his hand to his ear. I shouted it again. He still couldn't hear me, so he moved in closer. On an impulse, I kissed his cheek and shouted, "Thanks!"

He grinned and shouted back. "Glad you like it."

We spent the rest of our time doing flips and back flips. We even tried to stand on our heads in the air. It didn't work — more like a dive bomb — but it sure was fun, especially when he held me as he showed me what to do. I was reluctant to leave when it was over, but we had a game to go to. I'd still have lots more time to spend with him.

I'd never been to a football game before, so seeing Paul get excited as we entered the stadium got me kind of curious to know what I'd been missing. He waved at his friends as we passed them. Most nodded good-naturedly, some gave me curious looks.

The weather cooperated perfectly. I sat down next to Paul on the metal bleacher facing the field. I looked around at the crowd, trying to find Emily or Kat. They said they'd come together. Kegan said he wasn't going to come at all, something about a Star Wars marathon.

Denise was a cheerleader, so she would be here down on the sidelines. When I finally spotted Kat and Emily, they waved at me from the other end of the bleachers. I waved back and smiled. They seemed to be as excited as everyone else here.

No wonder Denise loved gatherings like this. She probably fed off the euphoria. With fifteen minutes until the game started, the marching band was on the field giving it their best. Our mascot, a red devil, marched around behind them, pretending to use his pitchfork as a trombone. Paul slipped away for a few minutes to get us some nachos and drinks.

Soon the drill team took the field and the devil joined the dance in a few places, bringing squeals of delight from the spectators.

As the dancers left the field, the announcer's voice boomed across the stadium. "Welcome to Daimon High! Home of the demons!" He introduced the teams, eliciting cheers from our school when our team ran onto the field. The opponents were announced and their side of the field shouted their support.

I watched in confusion at what was going on. The team captains met with the referee and did something that looked oddly like a coin toss. *What's that for?* Did they determine who got what by chance? The teams lined up in their formation as the game began. Nothing made much sense to me. I knew it was good when my school had the ball, but they didn't seem to get very far before the other team smashed them to the ground. "Man!" Paul shouted when one of the big guys on the other team plowed over one of ours who held the ball. I looked over at him in surprise at his emotion.

"Did you see that?" he asked me. "Johnson was so close. Just another three feet and touch down!"

I nodded in agreement that it was just too bad, thought I didn't know why. I didn't want to ask Paul the rules of the game. I didn't want him to realize how stupid I was about this whole thing, but at the same time, who cared? My only reason for coming was to be with Paul. Maybe I should do a little cheering by following the mood of the crowd.

It wasn't anywhere near real to me, but Paul didn't seem to notice. When our team scored, he gave me a high five. When their team did something he didn't like, he shouted with all the others around us. I stood and cheered when he did. And sat and muttered my condolences when he booed the other team.

Finally, half time came. I enjoyed watching the marching band and the dancers more than the game. Probably because I could at least follow it. Paul told me he was going to go get more concessions and asked if I wanted to come with.

"No, I'll just stay here and watch the performance."

"Okay," he said, giving my ear a tug.

I watched him as he left and then occupied myself with some people-watching. I had a little bubble of personal space all around me. I hadn't noticed it before because Paul was right next to me, but even in the crowded bleachers, I wasn't touched by anyone on either side. In front and back of me there was enough room that someone else could have sat. Normally that would have bothered me, but now that I knew who and what I was, it no longer seemed so important. I was fine if normal people found me difficult to be around. They had good instincts, I guess.

But if that were the case, then what did that say about Paul? I chose to believe it was because he'd known me for so long. He saw past my oddness and found something interesting about me. My heart warmed at the idea. As I sat there contemplating the reasons why Paul was so perfect for me, a slight commotion caught my attention. Someone moved among the crowd.

The people displaced by the stranger didn't seem to notice him once he'd passed, but when he came close enough for me to see, I sucked in a deep breath. It was the ugly demon boy I'd seen earlier with Quinn. He headed straight for me with a mischievous gleam in his eyes.

He sat next to me, forcing the person to the side of him to slide over more. It was almost like they didn't pay attention to the ugly demon boy, but knew for some reason they should give him more room.

"I know who you are," he spoke in a rough voice.

"Good for you," I said, shrugging. I didn't want to act too suspicious or afraid so I decided to pretend I didn't have a clue to who or what he was … which was actually pretty true.

"I know what you plan to do."

"Really? And what's that?" I asked, looking at him briefly before shifting my gaze back to the performers on the field, trying to act like I didn't care.

"You think you can withstand him, but there is no way." He chuckled as if it were funny. He leaned in closer, his terrible breath making me almost gag, and whispered, "My master has his eyes on you. He has chosen you to be his next *fortunate one*. He knows what you are capable of and wishes to grant you more if you will join him."

I finally looked over at him, stunned. The demon lord wanted me? And what was a fortunate one? Did he know we were preparing to fight him? Did he know about the others? Was Quinn aware of this? This ugly demon boy had been to see her at least twice. Who knows how much contact he'd had with her?

"Who are you?" I asked in a whisper.

"A messenger," he said as if trying to sound important. "I've been authorized to offer you this privilege. There are not many like you, so once my master discovers one, he wants to move in quickly."

"But why me? What's so special about me?" I hoped he'd tell me more without me asking specifically about the others. If he didn't know about them already, I didn't want to give them away. Quinn said there was a change in the balance of power and that's how she came to find us. How much had the balance tipped with multiple supernaturals in the same place?

"You are one of the strongest in ages. Once my master felt the shift in the balance, he knew something important was going on. He sent another to learn about you, even try to turn you. That has not given him the information he desired, so he sent me. From what I can tell, there is at least one other somewhere here, but their abilities are so insignificant that he will be able to sweep them up with no problem."

He didn't know about the five of us? Why not? Hadn't Quinn said that was the reason he'd be aware of us? Was she lying? I didn't know what to believe anymore.

He leaned in closer to me as if wanting to tell me some secret. I leaned back slightly and held my breath.

"For you, though, he wishes to offer you a position of greatness. Once he trains you, you will be more powerful than any other besides himself. If you make an alliance, you'll be unstoppable together. You are even more powerful than his last *fortunate one.*" He looked me over from top to bottom as if appraising me. His expression turned lecherous. My skin crawled.

I was being offered a position of power by a demon. Who was the other fortunate one? What would happen if I became the next highest in power? I shook my head in disgust for even contemplating this. I didn't want to become a demon or the servant of anything, even if he did claim I would be second in power. I didn't want to lose Paul either.

"No."

"No?" he asked, sounding shocked at the simple word. "But you could be so great. You could have everything you wanted."

"No," I said again. He lied. I wouldn't have unlimited power. I'd be a slave to another.

"You will regret this," Ugly Demon Boy said, breathing heavily. He seemed angry, yet almost afraid at the same time.

"Whatever," I said, trying to ignore him.

He huffed and crowded close to me. "You think you can defeat him?" he hissed, spraying me with his spittle. "You may be one of the strongest in ages, but he still has so much more experience than you. You will never be able to withstand him." He stood up and leaned over me to scare me. "I will enjoy watching him destroy your soul. He'll then have you anyway, and you will be nothing. You will be even lower than the lowest. I will enjoy stepping on you."

I'd had enough. I stood up and turned to him, bringing my face close to his. The skin he wore on top of his demon face was horrible to look at, but beneath it his eyes were scared. He might talk tough, but even now I knew I could beat him. Not that I'd try in the center of the bleachers.

"Back off," I said slowly. "Never threaten me again. Go ahead and tell your master that he can try to take me, but I won't come easily."

He tried to cut me off. I grabbed his arm and pressed hard with my fingernails, making them harden and form into claws. He squirmed in pain. I whispered through clenched teeth, "Leave now, and maybe you can survive tonight to tell your master my answer."

I pressed harder with my claws before letting him go. He hunched his head down into the shelter of his shoulders and backed away from me, never breaking eye contact. I stared at him, giving him a look that I hoped was terrifying. He obviously thought I was some huge threat, but now that the moment was over, I began to feel weak and a little frightened.

A touch on my shoulder made me jump. I whipped around, arms up to defend myself. Paul took his hand off my shoulder and stepped back slightly.

"Sorry, I didn't mean to surprise you." He looked down at the stuff in his other arm to make sure he hadn't spilled anything. While he was distracted, I looked back at Ugly Demon Boy. My heart thudded at the look on his face as he stared at Paul. When he caught me looking at him, he grinned an awful grin, stepped into a shadow, and disappeared.

CHAPTER TWENTY-THREE

A cold chill ran down my spine. This was bad. I looked at Paul quickly. His expression turned from amusement to concern in seconds.

"What's wrong?" he asked, sitting down next to me and placing the goodies he bought on the bleachers on his other side.

"Nothing," I said, trying to shake off the feeling I had.

"Was that guy bothering you?"

"No." I didn't realize Paul had seen him. What did he look like to Paul? I couldn't ask him without raising suspicions. "He was just from the other school and came to harass me about our team."

"Do you know him?" Paul asked.

"I've seen him a couple of times before," I answered truthfully. "Guess he thought he'd come here to try to scare me." I looked back to where I last saw him. "Didn't work, though."

"Good," Paul said. "Don't worry, we'll beat those guys. No problem." He looked at the scoreboard. I glanced at the score as well, but didn't have a clue how we'd gotten any of those points. The other team was ahead of us by thirteen.

Paul offered me the nachos and a drink. I took them absently and started munching as I watched the half time performance wrap up. He reached over and took some, then placed his hand on my knee. I put my free hand on top of his and squeezed it softly.

Ugly Demon Boy's strange offer ran through my mind. The demon lord must have confused the power of the five of us with just me. But how did he know about me? Had they been spying on me? Or was his information from that one night outside the school when I first saw Quinn shift into her demon form? I didn't think he saw me then, but it was a possibility. When the game started again, I barely noticed anything. Even when Paul jumped up cheering at a touchdown — I'd finally learned the name of some of the terms — I was distracted.

Eventually he noticed I wasn't into the game at all. He sat next to me and asked, "Aren't you enjoying the game?"

"What?" I asked, coming out of my thoughts of the whole demon issue.

"The game?" he asked.

"Oh, yeah, it's great." I looked up to the scoreboard and noticed we were ahead now. "Oh, when did that happen?"

"Have you even been watching for the last thirty minutes?" He looked at me with concern obvious on his face.

"Off and on," I shrugged.

"Do you even like football?" he asked softly. I looked up at him wondering how to answer that. Would he be bothered if I said no? He wouldn't believe me if I said yes. I decided to walk the middle.

"I don't not like it. I just don't know much about it."

"Why didn't you tell me?" he asked. "I could have explained the whole thing to you."

"I don't know," I said, looking into his eyes, enjoying the concern in them for something so trivial as a football game. "I didn't want to interfere with your fun. I figured I'd just watch and cheer when you did."

"You don't have to like something just because I do. We could have gone somewhere else tonight instead of the game." He took my hand in his.

"It wouldn't really have mattered where we went. I was just excited to do something with you. I could care less on the location." I smiled at him.

He smiled back and put his arm around me. I laid my head on his shoulder. We watched the game like that for a while. Paul whispered some of the rules and basics of the game so I could follow it a little better. I'd never be able to repeat the rules or try to explain how the game was played, but I sure enjoyed the closeness as we sat together.

We eventually jumped up and cheered each time our team scored a touchdown or intercepted the ball. By the time the fourth quarter ended, I was so excited about our team's performance I actually hugged Paul when they made the last touchdown and scored the field goal. I decided if I ever had to watch a football game again, I'd definitely do it if Paul were with me.

***

As Paul drove me home, the excitement of the game was still on his mind. I felt a small thrill, but it was only temporary for me. I probably felt the overflow of his emotions. If this were similar to what Denise felt, no wonder she sucked people's energy.

Paul held my hand as he drove, only letting go long enough to shift gears. I loved how he maintained contact. He pulled up in front of my house and kept my hand in his, effectively keeping me in the car with him. "Thanks for enduring the football game tonight." He smiled, making my heart melt. I had to remind myself why I thought it was important for us to keep our distance. He was so adorable.

I smiled back. "Thanks for putting up with someone as clueless about it as me."

"That wasn't hard to do. You pulled it off beautifully for the first half. I had no idea you didn't really care for the game."

I probably could have kept up the charade if I hadn't been so distracted by Ugly Demon Boy's information. I'd managed to put it mostly out of my head while Paul was right there, leaning close and describing the plays as they occurred. Even now, the stuff Ugly Demon Boy said didn't seem real. Paul was what I wanted to focus on.

I looked at him in the dim light of the street lamp as it lit up the inside of the car. I could just stay here in the car with him. I glanced toward the house and then back at Paul.

He looked at the house as well.

"I really don't want to go in," I admitted.

"You could stay out here with me, but…"

Yeah, that but…

Was I ready to fully commit to a relationship? I wished I were, but it would be best to wait until after I knew what this whole thing with Quinn and that demon lord would end like. With Paul as my reward if I lived, I'd do my best to make it.

"You are so good to me," I whispered. "Thanks for understanding me even though I don't understand myself sometimes."

He sagged slightly. I felt his disappointment. "Oh, I don't understand you at all, but I never expected to. I just tell myself to expect the unexpected."

I raised my eyebrows.

"I've never been disappointed so far."

"So at the dance tomorrow, what are you expecting?" I asked, genuinely curious.

"To have fun and dance every dance with you."

"That sounds doable," I agreed. "I'll try to make sure to not surprise you too much, though I can't make any promises."

"No need to. I'm flexible." He reached over and tugged on my ear. I smiled and kissed my first two fingers, then placed them on his full lips. When I took my hand away, I nearly leaned over and kissed him for real. I forced myself to open the door and step out.

"I'll pick you up at Emily's just before seven, right?"

"Seven." I nodded. That should give me enough time to get home from our last meeting with Quinn and get ready.

I walked to the house, trying not to look back. At the door, I smiled and waved when I saw him still watching me. Good thing he hadn't walked me to the door since I didn't want to deal with the awkwardness of the goodbye there. So much easier in the car.

CHAPTER TWENTY-FOUR

It was hard to focus at first when we met with Quinn on Saturday morning. She said she couldn't stay with us for very long or her master would become suspicious. *If that's true, why did she even make us meet today anyway?*

I tried to get her alone to ask her about the Ugly Demon Boy, but she kept brushing me off. "We've got to get started. There will be time for talking later." She stepped away from me but touched me behind the ear.

The vision hit me fast. This time, I knew what it was the moment it started, but was powerless to break free of the spell. I reached for my core, but it was gone, leaving me empty and helpless. I tried again and again, but she'd put an impenetrable case around it.

I couldn't function knowing my core was inaccessible. Quinn threw fireballs at the others and some at me, but without my core, I was just a normal girl.

Quinn said we could fight off the visions, but how? This time I wasn't even drugged. She'd just touched me behind the ear. I placed a finger there, but found nothing odd. A fireball hit me in my distraction. I screamed in pain. The pain caused me to feel a flicker of my core. It was there. The case surrounding it thinned. I looked up in time to see Quinn throwing fireballs at the others.

I ran toward the other girls, throwing myself in the way of the next fireball. I turned in time to catch it. Grasping it tightly in my hands, the searing pain of the flames shot through me, yet I couldn't let go. My hands clenched reflexively and there was nothing I could do to break my grip. I screamed, unable to stop myself.

The pain flowed up my arms, reaching my elbows. My hands and arms glowed blue. They weren't covered in flames, and I knew my hands would show no blisters or charring, but a painful heat and power radiated up my arms.

Is this real or a vision?

After that first vision I didn't know what to believe. I looked up to see the others staring at me. Quinn stopped throwing her fireballs and allowed the clay demons to crumble to dust.

"What are you doing?" Kat screamed at me.

I looked at her blankly, not quite understanding. I didn't know for sure why I grabbed that fireball. At the time, it seemed like a good idea. I only knew I had to keep a hold of it. The burning disappeared, replaced by comforting warmth.

Quinn approached me slowly, staring at the blue fireball in my hand. It suddenly registered that when I'd caught the ball, it had been orange, but now it was blue. Quinn stepped closer with her hands raised in a defensive posture. Did she think I'd do something to her? I felt no immediate need to do anything. I only wanted to hold the fireball. Let it infuse me with the power it held. I eyed her cautiously as she took another step.

When I realized she was going to try to take the ball from me, I stepped back in anger. The block around my core shattered and embraced me. My teeth grew longer in response to the threat.

"Claire," Quinn said slowly. "You must be careful."

"Why?"

"That fireball is growing in power," she said.

"Oh," I said, taking another look at it. It was slightly larger than when I'd caught it. Its light pulsed in time with my heartbeat.

"What's going on?" Emily asked. She looked between Quinn and me. "How can she be holding that? You said it would burn flesh."

"I don't know," Quinn said, stunned.

Kat spoke up. "That first time you used the fireballs, Claire caught one and threw it back at you. Remember? When I went to heal her, there was nothing wrong with her hand."

Quinn looked at me with renewed interest.

I tried to pay attention to what was going on around me, but the fireball claimed all my focus.

"So what are you going to do?" Denise asked, looking at Quinn. I reluctantly tore my attention away from the fireball.

"She needs to release it before it grows too powerful and ends up destroying her."

I cringed at the idea of releasing all that power. I wanted to keep it. Taking my left hand off the ball slightly, I was relieved when the power didn't change. I placed my hand back on it and stroked the top, enjoying a pleasant shock as I caressed it.

Everyone watched me like they thought I'd lost my mind. Kegan held his hands in the same position he used against Quinn. I grinned, chuckling at their nervousness. What I wouldn't do for a power like this to add to my own.

"Claire," Quinn said firmly. "You must release that."

"No." I spoke quietly, but the sound seemed to reverberate off the walls.

"You must!" she said again, a little more forcefully. The quiver in her voice gave me more courage.

"And how would you like me to do that?" I asked with a sneer.

"Let it go. Throw it at something!" she shouted.

"At you?" I cackled.

Quinn shook her head but didn't say a word. She looked terrified at the possibility. What would that do to her? Would it kill her? It had come from her in the first place, but the longer I held it, the stronger it grew. This could be a wonderful weapon. No wonder demons used them.

I rolled the ball over in my palms and caressed it again. The energy buzzed around me. The others stepped back cautiously. Quinn stood transfixed as she watched me. Her mouth moved silently as she prepared for what I might do next.

I moved suddenly, like I was going to throw the fireball at her but I didn't release it. She screamed and dropped to a crouch, throwing up a shield. The power I had over her was intoxicating. She was terrified. I was ecstatic. If I could frighten her, then we could definitely succeed.

My laughter came unbidden. I examined my core and felt its strength. An idea came to me and knew I could pull it off. I gripped the blue fireball in my hands. Digging my fingers into it, I pulled my hands away from each other, still keeping the fireball within my grip. The further I pulled it, the thinner it got, but the power didn't disappear. Instead, it infused me. The warmth I'd felt before changed to a searing heat and entered every cell in my body. I felt invincible. This extra power would be welcome and useful.

As soon as the fireball was gone, Quinn called an end to our practice and disappeared without a word. The others stared at me, almost as if they were afraid.

"Wow." Kegan looked me over. "You look different now." He held his hand up and motioned around my entire body. "You okay?"

"More than okay. That was amazing."

"How did you do that?" Emily asked. "And why?"

"She stole my core. I wanted it back. The pain helped to shock me back into it. I wasn't expecting the fireball to do that."

They all watched me for a moment, but when I didn't do anything sudden or amazing they seemed to calm down.

"What now?" Kat asked.

"The dance?" Emily said. We looked around at each other. When no one said anything else, we all left the gym almost as fast as Quinn had.

***

"What if I change?" I asked. Kat, Emily, and Kegan stood outside Emily's back porch.

"We'll be here to help you." Kegan had his hands up ready to grab the air and hold me if needed. Kat had a shield ready, and Emily wore her hard outer shell.

"Are you ready?" I wasn't. I didn't want to know for sure. I wanted to just hide in Emily's house and cancel the date with Paul.

"For ten minutes now," Kegan said with a grin. "Just come out already."

I took a deep breath and lifted one foot. I put it down again and shook myself, trying to get the courage to do this.

Emily sighed in exasperation. "Come on. It will be fine. If you change, we'll keep you safe. If you don't, then you get to go to the dance."

"If you don't hurry, none of us will make it. We've got less than an hour to get ready." Kat looked at her watch.

I looked up into the dimming sky. The full moon had crested the mountain about twenty minutes ago. I couldn't believe it was so huge and visible even though the sun hadn't fully set on the other side. It was a strange sight, not something that happened often.

"Today, Claire."

"But what if—"

"You already told us you don't feel any different. You'll be fine. Now get out here." Kegan reached for me.

"No, I'm coming." I closed my eyes and took a step outside into the moonlight. I waited for my body to freak out. Nothing happened. I opened one eye cautiously. The others looked at me with huge grins.

"See, nothing." Emily said patting me on the back. "Now let's go get ready."

***

My dress was unbelievable. It had started out as one of my mother's black cocktail dresses that she no longer wore and put in the back of my closet, telling me someday maybe I'd want to try it out. It was definitely old but with Kat as my own fairy godmother and Emily doing my hair and makeup, they'd managed to transform me into something I never thought possible.

Kat tweaked the dress enough to modernize it for me. She'd even added her own touches to make it sparkle and gleam in the light in a way it would never have done on its own. It fit well, but allowed for good movement.

"Do I have to return home by midnight?" I examined myself in the mirror in Emily's room.

Kat laughed and Emily snorted. I just smiled with pleasure at the idea I was going on a date with Paul to my first real dance. I'd never been to a dance. I hoped I'd be able to pull it off when asked to dance. Kat and Emily assured me there wasn't a whole lot to dancing other than moving around to the music in the way that felt most comfortable. They'd even turned on some music and gave me a demonstration. I eventually joined in and realized it really wouldn't be that hard.

Emily reached up and added a crystal-studded barrette into my short hair. "Perfect," she said with a smile.

Kat nodded in agreement. We all stood in front of the mirror and admired the results. They were both dressed and ready to go, but they took pity on me and fixed me up as fancy as they could. In a rare moment of emotion, I wrapped them both in a hug.

"Thank you."

They turned to look at the real me instead of just my reflection. I smiled and shook my head slightly, trying to make sure no tears would form. How could I tell someone the friendship over the last couple of weeks meant more to me than anything?

"No worries," Emily said, squeezing me back.

"I'm just glad you let me practice my spell-casting on your dress. Hopefully it won't unravel tonight while you're dancing." She said it seriously, but winked at me when I looked at her in fear.

"So they'll be here any second. Do you think we should make them wait, or should we be downstairs ready for them when they come?" Emily asked.

Kat looked at me. At the same time we each said, "Wait." We laughed and sat down on the bed.

Paul found out who Emily and Kat were going with and they all agreed to go in together on the cost of a limo. I didn't think a limo was normally used for Homecoming, but Paul assured me it was. I wasn't going to argue. At least the people he'd chosen to double date with were girls I could tolerate. Denise was still with her newest boyfriend James and would be going with his group of friends.

I heard the limo pull up outside. My enhanced hearing came in handy in everyday situations as well. "They're here," I said. Emily jumped up and rushed over to the window, peeking out through the slit in the curtains.

"They are." She checked herself in the mirror one last time. I resisted the urge, not wanting to jinx it since I didn't quite dare believe it was real.

Emily's mom knocked softly on the door a few moments after we heard the doorbell. "You all look lovely. Have a good time tonight. It's not often you get these types of magical nights."

Emily hugged her mom and moved toward the door. Kat gave her a quick hug as well, and my awkward hug was swallowed up in her mom's warm embrace. "I can't wait to hear all about it tonight."

"Mom, you don't have to wait up for us," Emily protested.

"Of course I do," she said.

Emily shook her head and proceeded to the stairs. I followed behind Kat, feeling the nervousness begin anew. What would Paul think? I regretted not taking advantage of the mirror one more time. Was the dress still okay? The little joke Kat made about it unraveling still made me slightly nervous. If I could face a demon throwing fireballs or attacking me with swords, I could surely handle a dance. Couldn't I?

I almost wished I were heading into battle instead of a dance. I was so nervous about what would happen and how to act with Paul. I stopped at the top of the stairs briefly to catch my breath and calm my nerves. I had nothing to worry about. We'd have a good time. Everything would fall into place just the way it was supposed to.

I closed my eyes and took the first step blindly. I opened them immediately, not wanting to run the risk of falling down the stairs. He looked amazing but the adoration in his eyes was what caught my attention.

My heart was lost. It now belonged completely to him. I was powerless against him and I knew it. My heart clenched in fear when I realized what this could mean.

Chapter Twenty-Five

As we walked into the gym, Paul had my arm in his, and wouldn't let it go as he reached in his pocket for his tickets. He led me over to the corner where the camera was set up. Our time waiting in line allowed me to come to grips with the strange environment I found myself in.

Couples came in and gathered with friends, forming little groups. Some stood in line for pictures right away like we did. Some were already on the dance floor. Some lined the walls looking more awkward than I felt. Vibrations from the music worked their way into my soul. I couldn't wait to get out there and dance, surprised at the feeling of longing that infused me.

Paul must have noticed my distraction with the dance floor. "We don't have to dance much if you don't want to."

"What?" I asked, stunned.

"You seem kind of nervous. We can just hang out and talk. Maybe dance a couple of slow dances," he added hopefully.

"Are you kidding?" I asked, unable to conceal my smile. "I can't wait to get out there."

"Really?" he asked, surprised. "I thought you said you didn't know how."

"It looks so fun. I may look foolish out there, but I don't care."

Paul nodded. "Great. We'll get out there as soon as we're done with the pictures." I squeezed his arm in excitement and looked at the slow-moving line ahead of us.

I tapped my foot to the beat of the music, itching to get out there. It was so unlike me that I wasn't sure what to do with it. Maybe excitement was what the full moon did to me. I was actually happy. When I giggled, Paul looked down at me in surprise.

Finally our turn for pictures came. Paul led me to the backdrop and placed his arms around me. I brought my arms up and placed them softly on his chest, just below the shoulders. He leaned forward and placed his head against mine, smiling at me. I grinned in pleasure at the closeness of him.

The flash of the camera startled me and I looked at the camera guy in confusion.

"That was the best pose I've seen all night." He smiled at us before motioning for the next couple to come forward.

I looked at Paul. He shrugged. "I wouldn't argue.

I've heard he's the best in town and always does the photos for these kinds of things."

"Okay, if you say so." I let Paul pull me onto the dance floor.

As soon as we stepped into the flashing lights, I felt energized. It was different than my core, but it felt amazing. I started bouncing on my toes to the beat. Paul moved smoother than me, so I watched him and tried to match his motions in my own way. I couldn't take my eyes off him as he moved. My body responded to the music unconsciously.

Though most dancers didn't touch their partners during this fast song, Paul managed to grab hold of my hand for a moment or run his fingers over my arm or shoulder as he danced around me. Tingles of pleasure crossed my skin and before I knew it, I found myself face-to-face with Paul as a slow song began.

He moved in closer, placed his left hand in the small of my back as he took my left hand in his right and held it close to his chest. I brought my free hand up to his left arm. A thrill ran up my fingers as I felt his warmth beneath his shirtsleeve. He moved to the rhythm of the music with an ease that melted me. I could stay in his arms forever. Why I'd ever been nervous about this date, I couldn't remember. This felt perfect. We were meant to be together. I looked up into his eyes, ready to admit the way I felt, but I stopped myself.

He looked down at me and smiled softly, placing his forehead against mine and brushed a soft kiss across my brow. Shivers ran down my spine. I was almost sure he could have felt it where his hand rested on my back.

We didn't leave the dance floor for over thirty minutes. Eventually, I felt ready for a break, but only to get a quick drink and sit down with him. I watched others on the dance floor as Paul got us some punch. I noticed Kat and Emily for the first time since we got there. I'd almost forgotten about them. Denise was surrounded by a group of those she fed off of. Her enjoyment was obvious. I smiled at those around her looking tired but happy. They would sure enjoy this evening, but they would be so much more tired than the rest of the room who kept their distance from Denise.

I kinda liked tolerating her.

Just as I grew restless and ready to join the others on the dance floor, Paul stood up and took my hand. I watched as a group of people split off from the main group and started doing some kind of choreographed dance. Paul grinned.

"Want to learn?" he said, leaning in closer so I could hear him over the music.

I nodded, and he pulled me closer to the group. I watched them for a moment, trying to follow the pattern, noticing it eventually repeated itself. Paul stood in front of me and showed me the moves in slow motion a couple of times before he picked up the pace and matched it to the music. I stumbled through the moves, but soon got the hang of it enough to not look too ridiculous.

We'd been at the dance for close to an hour before I began to feel tired, so we went to sit down. I reached for my core, not planning on taking everything. I just wanted to give myself a boost in energy. It infused me with a second wind. Every little ache I'd felt disappeared, and I sat up straighter.

"Wanna go dance again?" I asked Paul, full of excitement and anticipation.

He looked me over quickly and almost sighed. "In a minute. Let's go outside to cool off first." He stood up and took my hand.

I looked longingly over to the dance floor, but he squeezed my hand and pulled me with him. "We'll come back and dance. I just want to catch my breath for a second."

I gave in and followed him outside, cautious when I glanced up at the moon. The moment I took a breath of the fresh air, I immediately knew he was right. It felt wonderful outside. My core allowed me to feel more than I could on my own. I wasn't cold at all. I looked up into the night sky. The moon smiled down on me.

The stars winked as if they knew my secret.

A sense of foreboding came over me. Right now I was happy, but what would happen if I lost my temper during the full moon? I hoped Denise would stay far away from me tonight, just in case. I shivered at the thought of what I might do if I got angry.

Paul put his arm around me, and I calmed down immediately at his touch. We walked down the stairs far enough to lean against the wall I'd seen him lean against in my vision. It shook me up temporarily, but I pushed the thought out of my mind. This was nothing like that.

Paul leaned against the wall and spread his feet apart just enough that I could stand in between them. He took both my hands in his and looked in my eyes. At first I wanted to look away, but I couldn't help myself. I looked deeply into his. They were so beautiful. I longed to lean in closer to him, to reach up and kiss him. Instead I looked away, turning my head to the mountains.

"I just love the night sky," he said, looking in the same direction.

"It is beautiful."

"Yes, it is," he agreed. I could see out of the corner of my eye he wasn't looking at the sky anymore, but at me. I looked back at him, shivering again.

"Are you cold?" he asked, pulling me closer to

him. With my core around me, I felt comfortably warm. Probably even warmer than he was, but with his body against mine, the heat intensified.

"No. I feel wonderful," I whispered into his chest.

When his arms wrapped around me, I felt at peace. Almost as if I were whole and well. I felt more human than I'd felt in a long time. I snuggled in closer and tucked my arms behind his back. His muscles quivered slightly as I placed my palms against his back. Through his shirt, I heard his heartbeat quicken. Mine responded in kind. I was on slightly dangerous ground, but I didn't care. I loved the way I felt with him.

I'd flip-flopped on my resolution to keep away from him too often that now I just wanted to make sure he was mine forever. *But how?* I pulled back gently and looked up at him. His blue eyes looked darker in the late evening light. "Thanks for bringing me tonight," I said quietly.

"Thanks for saying yes." He didn't smile but still looked happy. I picked up on the change in his heartbeat again and felt a thrill. He leaned closer to me again, breathing in the air, making it feel like he was stealing it from me. His eyes never left mine. He was questioning me again. I knew what he wanted this time. I wanted it, too. I looked away from his beautiful eyes and focused instead on his lips. They twitched slightly. I bit my bottom lip in anticipation of what was coming.

I looked back into his eyes, hoping to convey my emotions. It only took him a moment to read my acceptance before he closed the distance. I closed my eyes and parted my lips slightly. The seconds before his lips touched mine were agony, but so worth the wait.

Paul brought his hands up my back, placing one behind my shoulder blades, brushing my bare skin as the other cupped my head. His lips moved over mine gently, as if afraid to startle me and make me back away. I leaned in closer, trying to reach him better, to let him know I wasn't going anywhere. I brought my hands to his sides and gripped his shirt. When that didn't help me, I brought them up to his shoulders and pulled him down closer to me so I didn't have to stand on tiptoes. He moved his arms again and wrapped them tightly around me before crushing me to his chest as he lifted me off my feet.

He spun me around and set me on the top of the wall. The break in the kiss bothered me, but now I was slightly higher than him. I bent down quickly to claim his lips again. I kissed him with a ferocity that almost scared me.

Shivers covered my entire body. It instinctively knew what to do. In the back of my mind, I kept telling myself to calm down a little, to take it slower, but deep within me lay a longing like I'd never known before. This was so much better than the way my core made me feel. It was as if my core were expanding and joining with the power I'd absorbed with that fireball I took from Quinn. Everything felt alive.

I grabbed onto Paul with my hands, digging my nails into his shoulders. I couldn't get close enough. I kissed him harder. He gasped. Realization at what I'd done hit me. I pushed away from him, lifting my fingers off his shoulders while pressing against him with my palms.

He stepped back slightly, looking shocked at my response. I eyed him closely, taking one hand and touching his lips with my fingers. Had I bitten him? His lips looked fuller, but not damaged. I checked his shoulders. Luckily, I'd just been holding on tight. I hadn't actually dug my claws into them. I pulled my hands up to look at them, sighing in relief they were still normal fingernails. The confusion in his eyes brought me back to myself.

"I'm sorry," I whispered. "I think I got a little carried away."

"I'm not sorry," he whispered back, placing his hands around my waist. He lifted me down off the wall and held me close to him, tucking my head underneath his chin.

The euphoric feeling had yet to dissipate. I wished I could go right back to kissing him, but after realizing I'd begun to lose control, I didn't dare. What if I'd actually bitten him? What would happen to someone bitten by a sort of werewolf? I mean, I hadn't ever transformed, but I no longer doubted it was possible. I would have to be very careful.

I felt his intention to move before he pulled back. I relaxed my hold on him but didn't break contact completely. He leaned down and kissed my forehead, breathing in slowly as he brought his lips to my cheeks before he moved carefully back to my lips. This kiss was slower and gentler, but just as intoxicating. I reveled in the feeling of the warmth of his lips and breath. The softness of his skin was incredible, yet he had enough stubble to make the contact on my tender skin tingle. I remained cautious during this kiss, but it was difficult. I wanted to let go completely. I'd never forgive myself if I accidentally bit him.

We stayed in each other's arms for what seemed like ages, but when he let me go it felt too soon.

"We should go back inside," he said eventually.

I could only nod. As much as I hadn't wanted to leave the dance floor, now I didn't want to go back to it. It would seem so different now. He took my hand in his and intertwined his fingers through mine.

We had just gotten to the steps when the doors burst open and Emily rushed out. "Claire! Hurry, we've got a problem."

"What?" I asked.

"Denise."

Chapter Twenty-Six

I stopped dead and looked at Paul with panic all over my face.

"I'll be right back." I bolted toward Emily, but then slowed when I caught him following me. "Uh, Paul, I don't think you should come."

"Why not?" he asked.

I hesitated for a moment till inspiration hit. "Girl thing." He didn't stop completely but slowed down. "I'll meet you in the gym in a few minutes."

He nodded and I ran after Emily, hoping he didn't follow.

"What happened?" I asked as we passed the gym and headed down a hallway leading to the back parking lot.

"Kat had the feeling we should go check on her since we hadn't seen her for a while. We saw her making out with her date, but he was really weak. It didn't seem like she was going to stop."

"Did she bite him?" I asked, picking up the pace, though I didn't know exactly where I was going.

"No. Kat froze her with some sort of spell so she wouldn't keep going or end up biting him. Kat's holding her now." She pushed her way through the doors and led me to Denise.

"Where's Kegan?" I asked. "He could help."

"In there somewhere." She pointed into the building where the dance music was reduced to a deep thumping of the bass. "I thought you'd be more helpful."

I took in the scene. Denise's date James lay across the hood of a car, looking almost dead. His chest rose and fell slowly. Stepping closer to him, I leaned over his chest and heard his heartbeat. It was steady, but slow. Denise looked indignant.

"What are you're doing?" I snapped.

"Just having some fun," she sneered back. "And from the looks of you, I'd say you've been doing the same thing."

I reached up to my lips, wondering how she could possibly know what I'd been doing.

"Nothing compares to it, huh?" She smiled knowingly.

I shook my head.

"It could be better. We could take what we want. Be in charge. We have the power."

"No." I shook my head again. "We have to stay in control."

"Why?" she asked. "No one could stop us. We can easily get rid of Quinn. She's obviously afraid of you. We could even defeat the demon lord. Then the whole world would be ours."

Kat gasped. Emily looked between Denise and me.

"Do you hear yourself?" I asked. "You really want to give it all up?"

"We wouldn't give anything up. We'd gain everything."

"You don't know what you're saying."

"Yes, I do!" Denise shouted and flung her arm out. Kat screamed in shock and fell to the ground, unconscious. Her holding spell on Denise vanished. Denise somehow managed to suck the energy away from Kat.

I automatically accessed my core and wrapped it around me. Denise was unstable. She could do anything in this state. Emily tried to talk to Denise, but before she said more than a few words, Denise backhanded her, knocking her into a car. Emily crumpled to the ground and lay still.

I moved around Denise trying to get into a good position in case she attacked.

"I'm so tired of this," she said, swinging her arms around the parking lot.

"Tired of what?"

"Tired of living this life. I want more. I want it all," she hissed.

"I can't let you do that."

"Yeah, right. And how are you going to stop me?"

"I'll figure something out."

"That's a joke. You can't even transform properly. It's a full moon and you haven't changed at all. You're weak." She reached out and tried to pull energy from me.

I took a tighter hold onto my core and felt immense satisfaction that it didn't change in the slightest.

"No matter. I can still get it from those two." She glanced at Kat and Emily, still lying on the ground.

"After all they did for you? You'd drain them?"

"Survival of the fittest," she shrugged.

I looked around the parking lot. Not a lot of options for weapons, but I ripped a windshield wiper off its hinges and brandished it like a sword. Denise stepped back and ripped a side mirror off a different car. She threw it at me. I ducked easily and lunged forward.

She shrieked in pain and anger as the wiper hit her leg. I smelled the blood immediately, but it didn't call to me.

Denise bent down to inspect the damage to her leg. She looked up with murder in her eyes. "You'll pay for that."

"Whatever." I lifted the wiper blade in front of me.

Denise tore the wiper from the car she'd ripped the mirror from and slashed downward making the air hiss.

"If you do this, you'll be even worse off than Quinn."

"That won't happen. I won't let him control me. I won't fall like she did. I'll only have myself to answer to."

"You are so stupid." I shook my head.

Denise screamed in rage and lunged toward me. She missed me with her wiper blade as I stepped quickly to the side, smacking her across the back with mine. She stumbled forward, hitting a car. She then grabbed onto the bumper to steady herself before she turned to face me again.

I glanced quickly at Kat and Emily to see where they were. Emily still lay on the ground, but Kat stood up slowly. She looked at Denise and back to me.

"What can I do?" she asked.

I didn't want to hurt Denise, which seemed strange to me when I thought about it. We really needed her for our battle when the demon lord came, but she had to be stopped. If she turned evil, then we'd be hard pressed to fight what was coming for us. I needed her to survive, but I needed her to come to her senses first.

"Hold her," I said. "I'll try to distract her."

Kat nodded and started chanting a spell. The air tingled as her spell grew stronger. I stepped forward, hoping to keep Denise's attention on me. I saw from the corner of my eye that Emily was stirring. She looked pissed when she turned her head to Denise. Maybe with the three of us, we could subdue her.

I wiggled my wiper blade in front of me and smiled wickedly at Denise. "Want to try that again? Or should we put these down and just go for a full-on cat-fight?" I lifted my free hand and felt my fingernails shift into claws. Clicking them together, I dragged my hand across the beat-up car I'd stolen the wiper from. The claw marks added a nice touch to it.

Denise glared at me. She raised the wiper blade up and rushed me. I braced myself and raised mine in response. Two feet from me, she slammed into nothing and was knocked backward, hitting her head on the pavement with a sickening thump. She lay still, not moving. The wiper blade fell from her hand before she even hit the ground.

I looked over at Kat, dumbfounded, and saw a satisfied expression warring with concern as she stared at Denise on the ground near her feat.

"What happened?" I asked.

Kat shrugged. "I threw up a barrier so she couldn't get past."

"Nice," Emily said, joining Kat.

I took a moment to catch my breath. I couldn't believe what just happened.

"What should I do with her now?" Kat asked.

"We should see if she got hurt when she hit the ground," Emily said, stepping closer to Denise. Kat moved closer as well, bending down as she approached.

"She looks completely out," I said.

Kat knelt down on the pavement to reach Denise better. She gingerly felt under her head, lifting it carefully to check where she'd hit the ground.

"It's not bleeding," Kat said, "but she's got a huge lump. Should I heal her?"

"You'd probably better," Emily said.

"But be careful," I added. "Who knows what she'll be like if she wakes up."

Kat placed her hands on the back of Denise's neck and muttered her healing charm. Denise's color changed slightly, but she didn't stir.

"She feels off to me," Kat said when she released her hold. "Something's wrong."

"Really?" Emily asked. She leaned forward and looked Denise over carefully. "She looks the same. Do you think it has something to do with her sucking so much energy from James?" Emily glanced toward James, still lying across the hood of the car where Denise had left him. We all followed her gaze.

"Who knows?" Kat said. As soon as she spoke, Denise's eyes flew open. She grabbed Emily around the shoulders and sunk her teeth into Emily's exposed neck.

Emily screamed in pain and Kat grabbed Denise, trying to yank her off. I jumped onto Denise, knocking her and Emily back to the ground. Denise screamed in rage, and I growled at her. I ripped her away from Emily, throwing her into the side of a car.

"Get Emily out of here," I shouted to Kat. I could smell a faint scent of blood, but it wasn't as much as I would have expected from someone who'd been bitten by a vampire.

Denise moved so fast, I almost missed her as she lunged toward Emily again. With my core, my reflexes were barely a match for Denise's blood lust. For a moment, Denise was so focused on reaching Emily again that she didn't try to fight me off. She dragged me forward.

"Move!" I shouted to Kat again. She had placed her hand on Emily's neck, trying to heal it. She let go and they both ran off. Emily seemed dazed, but at least moved by her own power.

As Emily got further away, Denise focused on me instead. I had my hands around her waist, trying to hold her back. She put her hands on my arms, trying to break my grip. I didn't loosen my hold at all. She snarled and gripped both my arms above the wrist. She got her fingertips over my pulse. A sudden drain on my energy reserve nearly knocked me down.

I panicked when I realized if she kept a hold of me, she'd be able to take my strength. I let go, but ripped into the fabric of her dress across her stomach with my claws. I had gotten some flesh, but I didn't know how much.

Denise let go of my wrists as I clawed her. She whipped around so suddenly, she caught me off guard as she struck me across the face and hit me again before I could get my hands up. Denise was in a fury. She moved faster than I thought possible. Her face twisted in an ugly sneer as she hit me again and again. She seemed possessed.

I stopped trying to think, letting my instincts take over. My arm lifted on its own and managed to block her blows without seeming to even try. I grabbed her arms and held her tight so she couldn't keep hitting me. Using all my strength, I forced her to the ground almost losing my balance and fell on top of her. I managed to keep upright and straddled her, making my dress slit up the thigh.

Dang, that sucks. When Denise twisted underneath me, trying to break free, I forgot all about my dress and forced her hands to the pavement. I was way too close to her face for comfort, so I leaned back. That gave her more room to maneuver. She brought her knees up, hitting me in the back. I almost fell on her but kept myself upright, just barely.

I let go of one of her wrists and slammed my fist into her chest. She gasped for breath, bringing her free hand to her chest. My blow didn't do what I'd hoped it would. She wasn't like Quinn. I looked into her eyes as she struggled for breath and saw terror in them. It wasn't a Denise type of terror. It was different somehow.

I brought my hand up again and slammed it into her stomach just below the breastbone. This time, the power from her center knocked me back enough that if I hadn't still been holding onto Denise's other arm, I'd have been thrown off her.

Denise lay still, as if dead. A whiff of sulfur passed my nose as I scrambled quickly to check on her and felt her pulse. She was still alive, but she was out. I cautiously let go and looked around the parking lot.

Kat and Emily were about ten cars away, watching us. I stood up and brushed my dress off, looking around again. What exactly had happened with the power coming off Denise? Did vampires have the same kind of core that demons did? Was my core like that?

I looked down at Denise. She was still out. Should we try to call Quinn? She'd given me her cell phone number after Denise sucked my blood that day with the blades. I found it odd that Quinn wasn't at the dance. Weren't principals supposed to be present at school functions? I didn't know for sure, since I rarely attended them myself. Maybe she'd know what had happened to Denise. I motioned for Kat and Emily to come closer. I'd need their help.

"Stay here. I'm gonna get my phone from Paul." I turned to head back to the school and stopped in my tracks.

Chapter Twenty-Seven

A stronger smell of sulfur in the air made me think Quinn had finally shown up, but it wasn't her. My eyes fell on a deep red demon. The lights from the parking lot made it glow. The figure stood taller than Quinn's demon form, and more muscular. It must be male, I thought absently. I wrapped my core around me tightly, enjoying the sense of strength it brought.

I slipped out of my heels, amazed I still had them on after all that I'd done with Denise. Stooping over quickly, I picked them up and held them as weapons. I didn't know for sure what I could do with them, but I figured the spikes on the heels would be better than just my bare hands.

The demon smiled at me. I grinned back. Though I was nervous, I figured I could handle one demon. The demon stepped forward, and out from behind it, two more arrived. My grin disappeared.

Emily and Kat stepped up beside me. We stood still, watching the demons in front of us. Emily whistled a low tune that reminded me of a death march.

Kat cleared her throat and Emily stopped. I took a second to look back at Denise, still on the ground behind us.

"What do we do?" Emily asked.

"We fight," I said simply.

"Without Denise and Kegan?" Kat asked.

"We have to. I don't dare wake her up."

"When you hit her that last time, something escaped from her," Emily whispered. She had her phone out and was texting furiously. She caught my glance and said, "Kegan."

"I probably just managed to extinguish her power like with Quinn," I said, shaking my head while keeping my attention on the three demons in front of us.

"It looked different than when you hit Quinn," Emily insisted.

"Whatever. We've got to take care of this first," I snapped.

"So do we split up and take them one-on-one? Or do we work together?" Kat asked as she slipped off her heels. Emily saw us both holding them, and did the same with hers.

"Quinn said to do it together," I said. "Let's try that first."

"Right." Emily shivered as she changed the make-up of her skin.

Kat chanted a spell. A slight shimmer surrounded

her as she shielded herself. I wished I had something like that to help me, but knew I was on my own. I couldn't risk weakening Kat. I took another good grip on my core and said, "Now!"

I rushed forward, with them only a second behind. The demons seemed surprised at our attack, probably used to having their victims run the opposite direction, screaming in terror.

Emily reached them first and slapped her shoe on the neck of the one closest to her. It screamed and grabbed at his neck. I jumped up and kicked it in the gut.

"Hit it higher," I shouted at Emily as I turned to the next one. Emily brought her fist back, ready to hit it in the chest when it straightened. She hit is as hard as she could but it didn't damage its core. He looked surprised when Emily went for his legs and knocked him onto his back. She jumped up and slammed her foot into the demon's chest. The blast of power escaping him knocked Emily back. She bounced hard on the ground before jumping back up. The demon disappeared into a pile of dust.

Kat smacked one of the demon's arm with her shoe. It oozed dark blood, but this demon remained upright.

"Help Kat," I shouted at Emily. "I'll take this one." I brought my shoe up and slammed the heel into its face with enough force that it stuck. The demon howled in rage and swiped at me. I was too quick for it. I dodged him as Emily rushed the other demon and knocked into him with her shoulder. They hit the ground, skidding to a stop three feet away. She tackled better than the guys playing football had last night.

Kat dropped to her knees to the side of the demon Emily had tackled and brought her hands up high, intertwining her fingers. She slammed both fists into its chest. She found the center on the first swing. Power exploded from the second demon in a shower of dark sparks.

The third demon must have sensed it was alone with three crazy teenage girls and disappeared into a shadow behind a car.

Emily and Kat looked up in surprise when they saw me standing alone.

"Where did it go?" Kat asked.

"It just disappeared."

"Is it going for backup?"

My eyes widened as her words sank in. "Quick. We need to find whatever weapons we can."

The three of us rushed around the parking lot, trying to find anything to fight with.

"What if they can pull things away from us like Quinn can?"

"We'll have to avoid them, then. I don't know

how much more damage we can do with just these." I picked up my shoe that fell from the demon as he disappeared and cringed at the gore on the heel. Demon flesh was nasty.

We quickly scanned the area and found a tire iron in the back of a truck, an empty gas can, and a tire in the back. An unlocked car had a set of barbells in the back seat. Another car had some baseballs and a bat. Our arsenal wasn't much, but it was better than nothing. We'd have to rely on our skills. We had my speed and strength, Emily's shifting, and Kat's spells. We just had to remember to get them in the chest.

We waited, but nothing happened. I was sure the demon would have gone for back up. But where was he? Now that they knew we were willing to fight back, would the demon lord try for full force now or wait and come for us later?

I looked at the others. They watched the shadows, waiting to see what would come out of them. Emily texted Kegan again. I glanced back at Denise. She still lay without moving. I tapped Kat on the shoulder and asked, "Should we check on Denise?"

"It would be good to have her. If she's on our side."

Emily nodded. "I'm sure she'll be different now. I swear something left her when you blasted her center."

"Do you think she was possessed?" Kat asked.

"Maybe that's where those demons came from."

"I think Emily and I should hold her down while you check her out," I said.

"Agreed." Emily reached up and touched her neck.

"Did she get you very bad?" I couldn't see any bite marks.

"She managed to get me for a second before I shifted my skin. She got a little blood, but nothing from a vein."

"Do you have her venom in you?" I asked. The thought of it made me slightly sick to my stomach.

"I don't think so. I don't feel any different. What did her venom feel like?" Emily asked.

"I didn't know it was venom at first. It tingled and burned, but I thought that was just the cut I got from Quinn's blade. Then it made me feverish and sick. Quinn said it was poisonous to me since I'm a werewolf. I don't know what it would do to you."

"I guess I'll have to wait and see. I don't think I got any venom."

"I hope you're right. I wouldn't want you to become a vampire, too." I paused and looked Emily over. "A shape-shifting vampire would be so unfair."

Emily chuckled and we both bent down Denise. She looked peaceful, almost like she was asleep. Kat waited until Emily and I had a firm hold on

Denise's arms before she knelt down. She ran her hands over Denise's body, hovering just millimeters from touching her. She placed her hands behind Denise's neck again and felt the back of her head.

"That all seems fine. She doesn't feel the same as before. Whatever it was is gone now." Kat removed her hands from Denise's head and placed them gently on her center, where I'd hit her and made the energy explode. "She feels extra warm here, but it's not a terrible heat. It's like a healthy heat."

"So do we wake her up?" Emily asked.

They both looked at me. Why did it have to be my decision? "You guys think she's back to herself. You decide."

"What if we're wrong?" Emily asked.

"Don't be." I looked them both in the eyes.

"We'll need her if they return," Kat said.

I glanced back to where the demon had disappeared, still surprised they hadn't returned.

"I'm sure she'll be back to herself," Kat said.

I nodded and held on tighter to Denise, just in case. Emily did the same. Kat placed her hands on Denise's head while chanting. Denise made no movement at first. "I wish I had my crystal," Kat murmured. She increased her efforts. As Kat's chant got louder, Denise began to stir. Her eyes fluttered before opening. She looked at Kat first, and then at

Emily holding her arm. When she turned to see me, she flinched and tried to pull back. I kept a firm hold but tried to not be threatening about it.

Kat spoke, "Denise, are you okay?"

"What's going on?" she whispered. Her throat sounded dry.

"Do you remember anything?" Emily asked.

She shook her head. "Where are we?" She looked around the parking lot. When she only saw the two cars she lay between, she seemed a little flustered.

"We're in the parking lot at the school," Kat said.

"Why? And why are you holding me down?"

"You attacked James and nearly killed him," Emily said bluntly.

Denise gasped. "No!" She clenched her eyes tight.

"Then, when Kat tried to stop you, you attacked her and knocked me out when I came after you," Emily said.

Denise shook her head as if in denial. "I'm sorry." She looked at me. "What did I do to you?"

"You tried to convince me to join you in taking over the world, thinking we could defeat the demon lord and then be invincible."

Denise's eyes opened wider with each word I said.

"Then we fought. You bit Emily."

"No!" Denise looked over at Emily in panic. "Are you okay?"

"Yeah, I think so." Emily reached up and touched

her neck where Denise got her. "Claire stopped you and then struck you in your center. A burst of light and energy left you. We think you were possessed."

Denise reached up and touched her head.

"Just after she knocked you out, three real demons showed up," Kat said. "Emily and I killed two of the demons, but the third one left. We don't know if he'll be back or not."

Denise looked at each of us with fear and remorse in her eyes.

"If we let you go, are you going to play nice? Or can I just knock you out again?" I asked.

"That wasn't me, I swear. I won't fight you." Denise looked at all of us.

I stared into her eyes, looking for a lie in her words. From watching her reactions to all we'd told her, I believed she was genuinely surprised at what she had done. But what if the demons came back? Could we ever trust her?

"Do you have any idea what happened? Why you started acting the way you did?" I asked. "Were you really possessed?"

Denise shook her head, but then she stopped and widened her eyes. "Wait. I ran into the ugliest kid I've ever seen when I was coming back from the restroom. He started talking to me like he knew me. As if I'd have anything to do with him. Everything from meeting him until now is blank."

"You don't remember bringing James out here?" Kat asked.

Denise shook her head. She wobbled and nearly collapsed when she stood up looking around the parking lot. "Where is he?"

Kat pointed to the car where he lay across the hood. Denise rushed over to him, stumbling in her hurry. I followed right on her tail wanting to be there just in case I needed to help him. Denise grabbed him by his arm and flinched.

She ran her hands over his chest, feeling for his heartbeat. She leaned closer to him. For a moment I worried, until I realized she was listening for his breathing. She touched her lips and leaned toward his neck. I flinched, ready to pull her away from him.

Emily stopped me. "It's okay, she's going to help him," she whispered.

I looked at her in surprise.

Denise kissed James lightly on his neck, just where I expected her to bite. She lingered there for a moment. *Is she really giving him energy back, or trying to keep herself from biting him?* Eventually James's breathing improved. The color returned to his face. Denise moved back, and James opened his eyes.

He looked confused at all of us staring at him. He

glanced at Denise and opened his mouth as if to speak. He shut it again without a word.

Denise cleared her throat. "You know, James, you're going to give me a complex if you pass out when we're making out." She grinned at him, though her eyes were tight.

"I passed out?" he asked. He looked at Kat and Emily as if he recognized them, but seemed surprised to see me.

"Yeah," Denise said. "I guess I'm just a little too much for you. Maybe it's time we went our separate ways."

James nodded slowly, still looking confused.

"I appreciate you bringing me to the dance, but I'll find a ride. You should just head home and get some rest. You'll feel much better tomorrow." Denise said it so smoothly that I could feel the effects of her charm working on him.

James thanked her for such an enjoyable time, as if he'd been trained to be polite, before he slid off the car. He walked away from us, keeping a hand on the cars as he passed them. Kegan rushed toward us and looked at James for a second before joining us.

"Nice timing," Kat said.

"What happened?" he asked.

I just shook my head.

"Do you think it's a good idea to send him home in that state?" Emily asked.

"It's better than letting him stay here. He'll be fine till he gets home. He'll probably sleep for most of the day tomorrow. I took so much from him, and he'd been without it for so long before I gave it back. At least I didn't bite him."

Kat and Emily looked at each other.

"Was I that close?" Denise asked.

Kat nodded. "I bound you with a charm just before you could do it. You'd already had your teeth bared and were leaning toward his neck."

"She attacked him?" Kegan asked. He looked at Denise in horror.

Denise shivered. "Thank you for stopping me." She burst into tears.

Emily held Denise while she sobbed. She was very lucky the other two had stopped her. If she'd actually bitten him and ended up killing James, I don't know if I'd have let her live.

"What the heck did I miss?" Kegan asked.

We filled Kegan in on the details while watching the shadows, waiting for something to come to us. Nothing happened.

"We should go back into the dance. Our dates will be wondering where we are," Kat said.

"Right." I looked at the gym with mixed feelings. I'd been making out with Paul one minute, and the next I was fighting a vampire and then demons after that.

"Do you want to join us now that you sent James

home?" Emily asked Denise. "We should stay close together in case something happens."

"She could be my date," Kegan said. I looked at him in surprise. "Lisa took off with someone else when I told her I had to come see what Emily wanted."

"Ooh, sorry. That sucks." Emily patted him on the back.

"No big deal." He shrugged and adjusted his glasses. "Her friend set us up. It was doomed from the start."

"I don't think we should stay here," Kat said. "What if they come back? We don't want to have the whole school watching us fight the demons. They could get hurt."

"True," Emily agreed. "Maybe we should head home."

"Any idea where Quinn is?" I asked. "Wasn't she supposed to be here tonight?"

"She doesn't have to be since they've got teachers and parents as chaperones," Denise said, "but it is kind of funny that she's not around. Especially with those demons showing up. Wouldn't she have some clue they were coming tonight?"

"Not if they've discovered she's been helping us. They may want to keep her out of the loop. Or they could have captured her." Emily looked worried.

CHAPTER TWENTY-EIGHT

I spotted Paul easily. He stood talking with Kat's date Zach and Emily's date Caleb. They saw us immediately. Paul turned toward me. He watched me cautiously, making me wonder what he thought I'd been doing. Paul eyed Denise and me. He visibly relaxed when he saw us together in such a friendly way.

Denise leaned over. "I need to talk to James' friends and let them know he went home. I'll join you guys in a second."

I hesitated. Kegan and I exchanged looks, and then he joined her as she walked away. *I'll bet everyone will think they're dating now.*

I smiled at Paul as he approached me. He looked full of questions. I shook my head and shrugged. He rolled his eyes and leaned forward to kiss the top of my head. Kat and Emily joined their dates, so I took Paul's hand and led him back to the others. Paul came willingly, but I didn't look at him again until we'd joined our group.

Emily spoke. "How would you guys feel if we left the dance now?"

"But it's still early," Zach protested.

"We could go to my house, have some ice cream, and play some games," Kat offered.

Caleb said, "Why don't we go to my house and watch a movie in the theater room? We've even got a popcorn maker in there." Emily squealed in delight and hugged his arm. Caleb's family was loaded and his house was huge. They lived up on the side of the mountain overlooking the whole town.

Kat looked at Zach hopefully. He seemed more excited about that idea and readily agreed. Paul leaned close to my ear and whispered, "What's going on?"

I looked at him in surprise and sighed when I realized I wouldn't be able to just brush this off. "I can't really tell you, but we should leave the dance. Denise had a problem with her date and sent him home, so now she needs a ride." Maybe that would put enough mystery on the whole thing and he'd be happy with that answer.

Paul nodded thoughtfully. "I think a movie sounds fun." We moved across the gym on the edge of the dance floor. My feet itched to get back out there and dance again, but I knew we had to leave. I'd definitely come back to one of these dances again. As we passed by James's group of friends, I caught Denise's eye and motioned for her to join us.

Kat looked at our dates and asked, "Is it okay with you guys if we give Denise and Kegan a ride home? Her date wasn't feeling good and had to leave, and Kegan's date left him."

"Dude, that sucks," Zach nodded sympathetically.

"Not really. Denise makes a much better date anyway." Kegan put his arm around Denise lightly. I knew he was just being kind, but the look on Denise's face made me think she took his comment much more seriously.

The other two guys nodded eagerly. I realized they had each gone out with her before. They both insisted she join us for the movie. Paul was the only one who seemed uncomfortable, but when I squeezed his hand, he relaxed and put his arm around me as we left the building.

Denise quickly took over the conversation in the limo, but we all enjoyed it. I sat close to Paul, feeling his warmth against me while we watched the others all laugh and joke about the strangest things. I closed my eyes and leaned into Paul, feeling completely at peace. Emily, Kat, and I held our own against three demons and were still alive. I didn't even have to transform.

As the limo turned a corner on the mountain road, it slowed to a stop. Looking out the dark windows, we spotted taillights angled weird compared to the road ahead. The headlights of the wrecked car made the steam rolling from the crumpled hood seem ominous. Paul rolled the window down to get a better look.

Denise leaned over him and gasped. "That's James's car."

Kat's date knocked on the window separating the front from the back and rolled it down. "Stay here. We know this guy."

Once the limo parked, everyone climbed out. Kat rushed forward, beating the rest of us to the wrecked car. She peeked in and leaned back in surprise. "He's not in there."

Blood splattered in the wreckage, but not enough to indicate he was in terrible shape. Denise stepped back to cover her mouth and nose. I looked around the area, looking for any sign of where he'd gone. I could smell the blood easily enough to track it, but what would the others think if I took off sniffing like a dog?

"I think he went that way," I said, pointing into the darkness.

"How do you know?" Emily's date asked. Paul looked at me closely. I floundered for an explanation until I saw a drop of blood on the ground about five feet from the car and showed it to the others.

"Oh, right," Caleb said.

Paul looked at me with even more scrutiny. "How on earth did you see that?"

I shrugged.

"We should follow it, see if we can find him," Kat said. Anxious waves rolled off her. She was really worried for him, and I knew she wanted to heal him.

Denise took a step back when the rest of us stepped forward. "Maybe we should call 911. I'll wait for them here while you guys go look for him," Denise offered.

"Good idea," I said. "I'll stay with you." I didn't want to leave her by herself just in case the blood smell overpowered her senses and she took off in search of him herself.

"That would be a good idea," she whispered as if she had the same concerns.

Kat and Emily led the guys as they went searching for James. Paul seemed a little concerned at leaving us alone, but I told him he'd need to help with James when they found him. When the limo driver pulled out his phone and said he'd stay with us, it seemed to ease Paul's worries slightly.

"No service," the driver said. "I'm going to walk down the road a little and see if I can get some bars."

Denise and I remained silent. She walked around the car examining it. He'd crashed into a tree, but we saw no tire marks. He hadn't used his breaks before hitting it. I was actually surprised he had gotten up and walked away from the wreck. Had he fallen asleep at the wheel? Was he just so exhausted from his run-in with Denise?

"This is my fault," Denise said with a crack in her voice.

I didn't know what to say. I wanted to try to comfort her, but it was true. It was her fault.

"Why am I the way I am?" she asked softly, looking at me.

"Because it's in your nature."

"But why are you able to fight what you are?" she asked.

"I never fought it before. I just let my anger rule everything." I shook my head at my memories. "Now that I know what I am, I'm better able to understand my actions."

"I was doing so well before I knew what I was. Now something deep within me wants to be set free. I want it, yet at the same time I despise it." She sat down on the back bumper of James's car and put her head in her hands. "Even now, it's taking every ounce of control to not go looking for James. And not to help him either."

"Maybe we should move away from his car." I reached for her hand, surprised when she let me take it to lead her to the limo.

Instead of climbing in the back seats to wait, she leaned against the limo and looked in the direction the others had gone. The limo driver stood twenty feet away with one hand tucked into his jacket, the other holding a phone to his ear. I checked the clock on my phone. They'd been gone for five minutes.

Denise shivered and stood up straight. "Something's wrong," she whispered.

I stood up too, scanning the area yet not seeing anything to concern me. "What is it?" Denise's body tensed.

"I feel strange." Denise rubbed her arms.

I accessed my core and allowed my senses to have control. I took a deep breath, tasting it for anything unusual. Nothing seemed abnormal. I could smell James's blood, tangy and salty mixed with the surrounding trees and greenery. While my mind categorized the different smells, my eyes took in the area. With my core, I could see deeper into the trees than without it, yet nothing seemed sinister in there. No unexpected sounds. A few small animals scurried through the fallen leaves while insects went about their lives as if we didn't exist.

I was just about to ask Denise to describe the strange feeling when a whiff of sulfur brushed my nose. A demon must be close. My core infused me more completely. My fingernails hardened and my teeth lengthened.

"Do you sense it?" Denise asked.

"Yes, but I don't know where it is." The trees stood still without even a hint of movement through their branches.

"What do we do with the limo driver?" Denise asked. She gasped.

I looked at where he'd been just moments before. He was gone. I spun around, looking everywhere. He had disappeared.

I turned back to Denise in time to see the limo driver grab her from behind. She screamed and struggled against him, but he had her arms pinned to her sides. She shouted, "Let me go!"

The limo driver cackled, looking crazed. The breeze shifted and the sulfur scent deepened. He was obviously possessed. Denise brought her head back hard and smacked him in the chin. He snorted in pain, but didn't let go. Denise wheezed as he squeezed tighter.

I jumped forward and grabbed one of his arms, trying to pull him away from her. It didn't seem to help. While yanking on his arm, power drained from me. I realized it was Denise as she sucked away his energy. I released him immediately. Soon his grip on her weakened and Denise breathed easier.

A tingle down the back of my neck alerted me to a new danger. I spun around and barely avoided a blow to the head by another attacker. This was a true demon with red skin resembling scales, not a man possessed. As he swung again, I dodged his attacks by instinct mostly while my rational mind tried to figure out what was going on.

Was this planned? Were the others being attacked as well, or just Denise and me?

My stomach clenched as I thought of Paul and the possibility that demons might hurt him. The fear turned to rage, forcing me to just react. I grabbed the attacking demon and smashed him in the face. The move stunned him, allowing a better shot at his center. I hit him three times before finding the right place. He burst into sparks and disintegrated.

I turned toward Denise. She had sucked enough energy from the driver that his hold on her failed. He fell to the ground. She brought her foot up and stomped on his chest, forcing the demon to leave his body in a burst of energy. The driver lay still. Denise jumped over him, running in the direction the energy had gone.

A form began to take shape. Before the energy reformed, Denise rammed her fist into the demon's chest. It disappeared in a burst of sparks. She bent over, placing her hands on her knees as she struggled for breath. A smile escaped me when she looked my way.

"Nice," I said. She nodded and smiled back.

"That's the first time I've been able to get a demon in the core," she said. "Felt good." She suddenly stood up straight again and blurted, "There are more coming."

I whipped around looking for signs of them. A small form stepped out from the trees.

Ugly Demon Boy grinned at me just before he transformed into his true demon self. He almost looked better as a full demon than in his disguise as a human.

"You!" Denise hissed. "You were the one who met me in the hallway."

"So?" Ugly Demon Boy said.

"What did you do to me?" she demanded.

"I weakened your resolve enough to allow those three demons to possess you."

"There were three?" Denise gasped.

"One wouldn't be able to fully control you. You have a strong will, so we needed to make sure we could really get a good hold on you. Too bad the others had to interfere before you had made the final transgression and killed an innocent."

"If I were possessed, it wouldn't have been me killing James."

"Oh, but it would have. The demons only put the idea into your mind. You were the one who felt the desire. They let your natural tendencies override your reason, and you did the rest."

"So while fighting Claire, was that me, or them?"

"Both," Ugly Demon Boy said.

He looked at me and sneered. "You could be so much more than you are. Why fight it? You'll never win."

"Of course we will," I said. "We've beaten off all the demons you've sent."

"You think they were difficult?" Ugly Demon Boy said. "The Master has better in store. You won't defeat them." He stood smugly, trying to stare down at me. Since he was shorter, he looked ridiculous.

"Watch me." I was going for brave, but what he said made me nervous. The demons we'd fought up to now still took a lot of work.

"I'm giving you both one more chance," he said. "You can join the Master now, or be destroyed. Wouldn't you rather be one standing with power than crushed by his power?"

"I will answer to no one," I said.

"Same here," Denise said, standing next to me.

Ugly Demon Boy shook his head and said, "Such a waste," then disappeared into a shadow.

CHAPTER TWENTY-NINE

A burst of light flashed across the sky, lighting up the trees lining the road. Denise gasped. I had to clench my teeth to keep from making the same terrified noise. A huge army of demons appeared out of the shadows. They lumbered forward slowly, as if they were waiting for a signal to attack.

I floundered around for my core, needing its comfort in the face of this enemy. It helped, but didn't take my fear away completely. This was it. If I didn't overcome now, I would be lost forever.

Denise took me by the arm. "We'll do our best. It's all we can do."

"Right." I nodded. "Better to go down fighting than just give up."

Denise grabbed my chin, forcing me to look at her. "Thanks," she said.

"For what?" I asked, confused and a little bothered by her touch.

"For standing by me. For finally believing I'm not as evil as you once thought."

"Oh." I smiled briefly. "I still don't like you all that much."

"Same," she smiled back. Letting go of my face, she turned to face the oncoming army of demons.

"Let's do this," I said.

"Maybe they'll return in time."

I nodded absently, not sure if I wanted them to come back. They would keep Paul and the other guys away.

I flexed my fingers as my claws formed. My teeth grew long again and my core pulsed in anticipation. With some unspoken signal between the two of us, we charged the same demon, front and center. He was huge, and I figured going for him first would put us at an advantage. If the other demons saw we weren't afraid, maybe they would be easier to defeat. It worked earlier.

Denise gripped him by the head and yanked with all her strength. I slammed into his center with my fist. He dropped to the ground, but I hadn't extinguished his core. Denise pushed him onto his back. I tried again. His power burst forth in a shower of dark sparks.

Denise let him go. We both jumped to the next demon, hitting him together and he burst to dust immediately. We downed a third one before the other demons realized we were too powerful working together.

One grabbed Denise from behind, wrapping his arms around her. She sucked his power immediately, but I had no way to hit his core since her body blocked him. I attacked another one. Three more joined him, making it difficult to fight them off. The slashing of my claws forced some of them back a bit, but not much.

A scaly hand covered my mouth and nose to suffocate me. I bit hard. The demon screamed in pain and ripped his hand away from me. I spit out the chunk I'd bitten off and then spit again, trying to get the bitter taste of demon blood out of my mouth. The wounded demon snarled at me and slashed with his good hand. I ducked, grabbing him by the shoulders, and brought my knee up into his chest. He exploded into dust, making me choke.

Man, they're nasty. I was still choking when the next demon attacked. He hit me from behind with a fireball. I'd been wondering when one of those would appear. His didn't hurt nearly as bad as the ones from Quinn, but it stung. I spun and grabbed the next ball he threw at me, returning it. When it smacked him in the face, I laughed at his shocked expression. I rushed him and slammed him in the chest, but didn't get him in the right spot. He produced another fireball and held it against the skin of my neck. The pain caused me to stumble. He snarled in triumph and followed me to the ground, holding the fireball against me. The smell of my own burnt flesh choked me. A howl of pain ripped from my throat.

The howl was primal and came from deep within. His eyes widened in fear, but he didn't retreat. I focused all my attention on the pain and willed it to change me. If my skin was that of a wolf, the fireball wouldn't hurt.

I squirmed under him, trying to get away, but the fireball didn't let up. I reached for it, hoping that using my hands would help stop the burn. I moved it away from my neck. He forced it back down and got my shoulder. I screamed in pain again with the new injury. I searched for Denise but she fought three demons of her own. A couple of demons stood unoccupied, watching my attacker as he held me down. They seemed to be enjoying the sight.

At least I didn't have to fight more than just this one. It was hard enough to keep my wits about me through this pain. I focused on my core, letting it build up my strength. Where was my control? Why couldn't I access the wolf?

And what about that fireball I'd absorbed before? Could I do something with this one now? With my hands on it as I tried to push it away, I fought to grab the fireball instead of wasting my energy trying to escape from it. My hands burned, but it was nothing like the burn on my neck. The demon snarled and I hissed in return.

With both palms around the ball, I struggled to remember how it worked with the other fireball. Soon the familiar warmth and power radiated up my arms. The demon looked stunned. He tried to release the fireball but couldn't. My hold on the power from him forced the energy to leave his body and enter mine. Soon he slumped over and lay still, pinning me underneath him until I pushed him away. He fell off with very little effort on my part.

I looked at the fireball in my hands and then up at the other demons facing me. They looked dumbfounded and a little scared. I ripped the ball in two and threw it at them. The first demon exploded in a shower of dark sparks. The fireball merely bounced off the second one. I charged her. She surprised me by charging forward. I had hoped she'd be scared enough to run, but she met me head on. She dodged my blow at the last second. When she touched me on the neck, an ice-cold tingle shot down my spine.

The vision was one of pitch-blackness. Blindness. I freaked and screamed in panic. How could I hope to fight against something I couldn't see? My core was still there. It flooded my senses, improving my hearing and smell. The darkness still surrounded me, but the worry left. She approached me from behind. The sounds were distinct. I waited until I felt her lined up perfectly behind me, and then I spun around quickly with my elbow held high, hoping it would strike her in her core.

She grunted, and I felt her fall. My vision flickered briefly, giving me a glimpse of her before it went dark again. That tiny moment of clarity allowed me to gauge where her core was. I stomped hard with my foot but didn't kill her. She was wounded though. My vision didn't return immediately. I could see a little, yet something was off. Three demons closed in on me all at once.

I dodged them at first, trying to drop one as he passed, but my timing was off. I missed him as he jumped over me, whirling mid-air to kick me in the back. I fell hard, tasting the dirt as gravel embedded in my hands and forearms.

I rolled onto my back barely in time to kick my feet up. Instead of hitting his core where I'd aimed, I only managed to knock him off balance. One stood over me and threw fireballs. I knocked a couple away, but they came so fast. The third demon pulled debris from the side of the road and showered me with all the objects. I couldn't block them in time.

I felt a kick before seeing the demon even approach me. *I see their movements too late!* I dodged what I thought was coming only to move myself into position for something else unseen.

I slashed out but hit nothing. I closed my eyes, trusting my hearing and sense of smell. My anger rose as I fought with no success. The absence of my sight forced my hearing to work harder. The movements of the demons soon became easier to distinguish.

I punched at the demon closest to me, using only my senses. The heat of the fireballs before they left the hand of the demon allowed me to dodge them once I learned to recognize it.

The objects they threw had their own unique sounds, allowing me to duck when needed. Some hit me, but I felt pretty smug when the flying objects missed me and hit one of the other demons. They growled and cursed in their guttural language. A large branch hit my side, knocking me to the ground. I hissed in pain, feeling the warmth of blood as it oozed from the wound. I gripped the branch in both hands the next time it came, yanking it from my attacker and swung it like a bat. My side hurt as I made contact with the demons.

I opened my eyes then wished I'd kept them closed when I counted seven of them. I recognized the one who'd touched me and rushed her. Three others attacked me and fell before I finally slammed my branch into her chest. The sudden halt of motion and slurping noise jarred me. She was still alive, but couldn't move very quickly with a six-foot branch sticking out of her chest so I attacked again, kicking just under where the branch poked out. She collapsed in a puddle of goo. My vision returned to normal.

More demons joined the fray. Denise held back four of them while I fought eight.

With my core surrounding me, I didn't tire as easy, but fatigue began to catch up. My side felt slick between my skin and the dress when I moved. *Will I die of blood loss, or something else first?*

With each downed demon, two more appeared out from the darkness of the shadows to replace them. If this happened every time, they'd eventually overpower me. The thought of giving up never crossed my mind. I kept fighting them off, feeling like I'd done it all before. They didn't have many new moves.

As a demon disappeared in a shower of sparks, a rock hurled toward me, hitting my leg and knocking me to the ground before I had time to dodge it.

A ragged wolf-like howl of agony tore from my throat. I was still fully human, besides my long teeth and claws used to fight off the ones who got close enough. I struggled to get up, but the muscle was damaged. Torn flesh screamed at me. The bone was whole, but the pain still gripped me like a vice, dragging me back to the ground.

The demons surrounding me snarled with glee and dove at me. Their claws, horns, and spikes ripped my skin and dress. Uncontrollable screams tore from me. I'd never experienced so much pain. I wanted to shut out everything and cease to exist. I dug my mind into my core and let it surround me. It had always given me comfort and strength. Now at least it could give me peace as oblivion enveloped my senses.

CHAPTER THIRTY

Inside my core, every emotion I'd ever had crowded together. Anger surrounded the core as if keeping it all inside. But pushing through it, a warmth radiated. Love and acceptance.

Peace covered me. I could still love myself no matter what form I took. When that realization hit, my core burst and infused every cell with strength. Power surged to my injuries and stopped hurting. The damaged muscle in my thigh no longer throbbed. The oozing on my side stopped. All the little nicks, cuts, and bruises I'd sustained while fighting off those demons were gone.

After healing itself, my body tingled everywhere. My arms burned, then relief came suddenly. More warmth than I felt before surrounded me, but it wasn't heat. My muscles stretched. I opened my eyes to watch myself change but I only saw the fear in the eyes of the demons surrounding me. I laughed something that sounded like a bark. The rapid transformation ripped my dress. It fell off in shreds as I stood up and attacked the demon closest to me.

Instinct told me to bite at him with my teeth and tear his throat. *This isn't hard at all. Quinn was wrong.* Decapitating a demon as a werewolf was easy.

Well, easier. They kept coming, but their fireballs didn't faze me. Demon claws weren't nearly as painful to my wolf fur. I tore into them, enjoying the destruction. They fell before me like flies. New ones kept coming as soon as one succumbed, but this time I welcomed it. I wanted to fight.

Soon, the number of demons surrounding me dwindled, allowing me time to look around. An excited yip came when I saw Kat battling with Denise. Kegan and Emily faced other demons together.

A movement from the trees caught my attention. I turned to confront the new arrival when I realized it was human. It smelled delicious. I rushed forward. After the stench of fighting demons and ripping them apart, I craved this pleasant aroma.

Wide human eyes stared into mine. Recognition hit at once. *Paul.*

I stopped in my tracks, and backed up slightly. Was the good smell coming from him? And in what way did I want that? Searching my intentions, I was relieved to find the craving was for blood. But not his. I scanned the darkness behind him and saw three other bodies standing there watching me. After catching another whiff of the blood that called to me, I held my breath. It helped. A little. They had found James. He stood under his own power, but he looked very confused.

I whimpered, embarrassed and ashamed at my desire to attack James. I turned away quickly and rushed back to the others. At least Paul hadn't seen me transform. He probably didn't know I was the werewolf. *Now, how to keep it that way?*

Barreling forward, I knocked down the demon attacking Emily, giving her a chance to stomp on his core. It took her three tries before she got him in the right spot. As soon as she did, she looked up at me and shouted, "You did it!"

I nodded, unable to speak. I flicked my eyes toward the guys and whined. She looked at me, confused until I nodded my head toward the boys again. When she saw them standing in the shadows, she nodded. "Don't think there's anything we can do about them now. Hopefully, they just stay out of the way."

While distracted with killing another demon, I missed Paul's approach until he shouted, "Where is Claire?"

Kat turned briefly and shouted, "Get back!"

Paul looked angry and shouted again. "Tell me where she is. Is she hurt?" He looked around the area, seeing the remains of the demons that hadn't just exploded to dust. The limo driver was still on the ground near the limo. Paul ran over to him and checked for a pulse.

"Leave him alone," Denise growled as she finished off a demon of her own.

Paul stopped short at her tone. He looked inside the limo, then walked around the area looking for me. My heart thudded at the concern on his face.

"Where is she?" he shouted again.

"She's fine!" Emily screamed. "Now get back."

"Not till I find her!" he screamed, rushing toward the battle. Kat took her attention off the demon she was fighting to throw a spell at Paul. He hit an invisible wall and slammed back onto the ground, the breath knocked out of him.

Kat fell to the ground too, knocked down by the demon she fought. He nearly impaled her with the spikes on the back of his arms, but she rolled away just in time. I growled in irritation at Paul for his interference with the fight and charged the demon attacking Kat. She threw a spell at him and stopped his attack long enough for her to get up. She slammed him in the core before my arrival.

Paul was slower getting up, but when he did, he managed to see the remains of my dress lying near him. He scrambled over and grabbed it, looking freaked as he turned to look at the girls fighting the demons. His eyes fell on me.

Three demons attacked me at once. I yelped in pain when one pierced me with a blade in my hindquarters. I couldn't turn quickly enough to avoid the blow aimed at me from another demon holding a huge branch. It hit me across the back and I stumbled. I gained my footing enough to stop the third one from making his mark.

I ripped his head off quickly before turning to the others. The one with the blade brought it up again, aiming for my head. I ducked and bit at his leg, forcing him to the ground. My pounce missed his core. Not enough force that way. Ripping his head off was the only option. I found myself covered in gore. With his head gone, he crumbled to dust. Two others flanked the one who hit me with the branch. They approached as one.

I glanced at the others, hoping at least one of them would be available to help. They all fought at least two demons each, so I lowered my head and charged, getting thrown back when his core burst in a shower of black sparks.

I gained my balance and jumped at the next demon. I ripped his head off, but the one with the branch struck me again, forcing another yelp of pain out. I was getting really tired of this one. I limped around him, keeping my eyes on his, hoping to see the next decision register before he made his move. He didn't give anything away with his eyes, so I lunged for the branch, longing to get that out of the way.

I gripped it in my teeth and yanked, but didn't get it away from him. Another yank resulted in a crack. On the third yank, it broke in half. He still held the longer piece, but now he'd have to get much closer to use it. I spit out my half and snarled. A slight tremor of fear rolled through him, giving me courage to pounce. He raised the branch up to stop me. It hit me where my front leg met my chest and went in. My weight knocked the demon to the ground and jarred the stake deep, forcing out a gasp of pain. I quickly ended this demon's existence and limped away. I shook myself, but I couldn't get the offending wood out. It was too deep to dislodge.

I limped toward the others, hoping one of them could help me. Each step caused a whine of pain. I collapsed ten feet from the others and whimpered when the wood dug into the ground and forced its way deeper into my chest.

Kat heard me and ran toward me, throwing lightning bolts at the demon closest to her. Where had she learned to conjure lightning? The others joined together to fight off the remaining demons. It didn't seem like there were as many as before. Maybe they could keep them occupied while Kat helped me.

"Claire, are you okay?" When she looked me over and saw the wood sticking out, she turned pale.

I looked back to my injury and then back at her. I tried not to whine again, but I had no other way to express the pain.

"It will be okay. I'll take care of it." She placed her hands gently on the offending wood and pulled carefully. When it didn't move easily, she frowned and looked into my eyes. "This will probably hurt."

I blinked at her, trying to convey my understanding. She sighed and said, "On three?"

I closed my eyes and nodded. She counted evenly and at three yanked hard. I flinched and howled in agony. As the shock of the pain lessened, I felt her hands on me again as she tried to heal me. It wasn't working like the other times.

"I can't do this if you aren't human." She sounded worried.

I looked down at my injury, surprised at the amount of blood pouring from me. Kat pressed hard on the wound, trying to stop the flow, but it still oozed out between her fingers. I had to get healed as soon as possible, but I had no idea how to return to myself. I looked at her in panic.

"Can you change back?" she whispered.

I shook my head. I had no idea how to try. If I released my core, I'd pass out from the pain. I hesitantly tried to let it go. It refused to budge. It was so entwined with everything about me.

Kat looked around frantically as if trying to find something to help. When she saw Paul looking confused with the remains of my dress still in his hands, she shouted to him, "Bring me that!"

Paul hesitated. When she shouted again, he scurried over. Kat ripped the fabric from his hands and wadded it up to put pressure on my wound. "Hold this." She yanked him to the ground next to me. Paul fell awkwardly and adjusted himself so he could hold the cloth. He looked uncomfortable. Longing for him filled my soul. I wished he wasn't here to see this, but I was so glad to see him.

"Push hard, and don't let go or she'll bleed to death," Kat snapped. She ran toward the limo.

Paul looked at me in panic and pushed hard. A whine escaped me and he lessened the pressure. He pushed hard again when the bleeding increased. This time I clenched my jaw, refusing to make a sound. His presence soothed me enough to close my eyes. I ignored the pain and the weakness that crept up on me. I sensed Kat's return, opening my eyes to see what she was up to.

She'd retrieved her purse from the car and had a crystal of some sort in her hand. She took Paul's hand away from the wound and held the crystal over my wound as she began chanting. It seemed to help, but not enough.

"The healing won't work. I don't understand this

body." She looked into my eyes. "You've got to shift back or you won't make it."

I sighed and closed my eyes, trying to focus. This attempt to release my core was just as difficult. It felt like it was the only thing keeping me alive. As much as I desired to become human again, it felt just as unreachable as becoming wolf had been before.

"Paul, can you help her change back?" Kat asked as she tried another thing with a different colored crystal.

"What?" he asked, looking at my wolf body.

"This is Claire. She has to return to her human form." Kat's head was still down as she looked at my wound, but it popped up immediately when Paul fell on his butt and he scooted away from me.

"No. It can't be." He shook his head, staring at me.

"Of course it can," Kat huffed. "We're in the middle of a battle with demons. I've thrown lightning bolts! Why can't Claire be a werewolf?"

Paul backed farther away, forcing a moan of anguish to escape me. I couldn't stand the look in his eyes so I turned my head and tried again to let go of my core. If it didn't kill me, then Kat could heal what was left. Though if Paul would never come near me again, did I even want to be healed? I still couldn't let it go, but it was becoming weaker. Maybe I'd lost my battle.

Kat stopped her chant and looked at him in disgust. "If you can't handle this, then you don't deserve her." I glanced at him as he stood and backed away. She bent back down to me and muttered. "Go cower in the safety of the trees with those other losers."

I closed my eyes again and tried to help her by shifting back. My mind was still my own; my body was not. I couldn't even find the control to move my legs. I focused my thoughts on the core and felt around it, trying to see any difference in it through this wolf form compared to when I'd accessed it as a human. Something seemed different, but through the haze of my approaching unconsciousness, I couldn't decide what it was.

An overwhelming feeling of peace once again enveloped me. I was done. I'd fought well, but had been overcome. I turned my head enough to reach Kat's hands as she worked on my injury. I longed to speak to her, but did the only thing I could think of. I licked her hand in the same way Max always licked me to show his love.

Kat choked back some of her words and she began sobbing. I felt bad for putting her through this, but it really was better this way. We'd defeated most of the demons. They could stop the rest.

My head fell back to the ground. Kat's chants got more intense, comforting me with the tone of her voice, and the up and down cadence. I felt myself slipping away into a deepness more enjoyable than sleep and prepared to let go. The strength of my core slipped, sending a tingle across my arms.

"No!" Kat's shout shocked me to consciousness. The pain returned. "Stay with me. You can't die. We need you to help us finish this!"

I looked at her in sadness.

"Fight! You have to come through this. Don't give up. Give me a little more time. I can figure this out." She shouted as she frantically tried to heal my wound. She was making progress since the blood flowing had slowed. Or was I running out of blood?

Kat's head jerked up quickly and she stared at something behind me. A presence approached, but it didn't feel evil. I tried to look behind me, but felt too weak to manage it. Paul's cologne and his own personal scent made my senses reel. He had returned.

He knelt behind me and placed his hands on my head. My head relaxed under his touch. This felt better than the place I'd been slipping away to.

Paul leaned toward me and whispered in my ear. "I'm sorry. I didn't mean to freak out. It just shocked me to find you this way." He stopped talking for a moment and Kat's chants took over everything again.

"I don't know what I can do, but Kat thinks me being here could help." He paused. Kat looked at him again. I wished he'd move to a place where I could see him better. My head was too weak to turn.

He spoke again. "I don't want to lose you. I just got you back. If you slipped away from me again because of something I did, or didn't do, I don't think I could handle it." My heartbeat fluttered at his words.

Kat nodded and Paul continued. "So you have to get better. Understand? You do what you need to. I'll always be here for you."

My breathing changed slightly, not hurting as much as it had before. Paul leaned in closer and whispered more. "I don't care if you are a werewolf. I'll stand by you." His strong hands stroked the fur on my head. He let one hand move to my ear and tugged it like he always did. It felt wonderful. He still thought of me as me.

"What do you need me to do?" he asked Kat.

"She's got to hold on and not die before I can finish it," Kat said. "I need her in her human form. I don't understand wolf flesh."

Paul shifted around to face me and held my head in his hands. He leaned closer and looked me in the eyes. He looked at me like he had at the dance. He didn't see my yellow eyes. He didn't see the fur all over me. He didn't see the wolf.

He saw me.

My core softened. The tingles on my extremities got stronger.

"Claire, come back to me," he pleaded.

CHAPTER THIRTY-ONE

I tried, but it didn't come fast enough. I focused again on the core and began peeling it away gently. The more it slipped away, the more the pain built. Wolf fur gave way to skin as my body shifted back. The hairs on my head where Paul continued to stroke returned to my own. A cry of pain as the core slipped away completely escaped my lips.

Kat frantically chanted. The intense pain in my shoulder decreased as her words took effect. I shivered with the cold, suddenly aware of my nakedness. Paul's hands left my hair and he moved back. I tried to bend over to cover myself with my hands. I felt so exposed.

Warmth suddenly surrounded me as a white shirt covered me. Paul's scent was strong on it. I looked up in gratitude. He'd taken his shirt off and given it to me.

Kat's amazing healing powers completely fixed the damage to my shoulder from the branch. I still felt woozy and weak, knowing she couldn't give me back the blood I'd lost, but now at least I'd have a fighting chance at recovery.

She took the white crystal and hung it around my neck. "Keep this on. It will help you still. I've got to go to the others." She looked at Paul. "Watch her."

Paul helped me to sit up and wrapped his arms around me, holding me against his chest. "I thought for sure I'd lost you."

"Me too," I said, thinking of the way he'd retreated from me when he realized I was the wolf.

"Don't ever leave me," he whispered fiercely. "I couldn't survive without you."

I snuggled deeper into his chest. How could he still feel that way after knowing what I was? It was a miracle that he still thought of me as Claire and not wolf.

My body felt better, but was too exhausted to even think of standing. I wished I could get up to help the others as they fought the dwindling number of demons surrounding them. Emily and Denise finished off the last one together in a strange and beautiful dance. I longed to be there with them. As soon as he was destroyed, they paused. Nothing else came. They all looked as confused as I felt about the end. Where was the demon lord? Would he really let his demons be destroyed by five teenagers without coming to lend a hand? He hadn't bothered to come terrify us. If he were so powerful, where was he?

Kat began healing the others' minor wounds when the answer to my question appeared. Quinn and Ugly Demon Boy, one on each side, accompanied him with a guard of four more demons. These demons looked even more muscular and evil than the others had. Quinn appeared in her demon form, looking strong and menacing. The demon lord looked five times as powerful as his guards. No wonder Quinn seemed so afraid of him. He emanated power and authority.

Paul's grip on me tightened when he saw them. I tried to break free of his hold, but couldn't do anything against his strength. "You have to help me up."

"No. You can't do anything. You're still too weak."

"If I don't, we'll all be dead." I grabbed his hands and he reluctantly put his hands under my arms to lift me up. Only with his help did I manage to stand, and stay standing. Weakness flooded every part of me. I reached for my core. I found it pulsing softly deep within. It strengthened me, but nowhere near enough to fight another demon.

Quinn looked at me. Concern flashed across her eyes before she wiped any expression from her face. She must still want us to help her. Seeing me like this must have blown her hopes.

Kegan, Emily, Kat, and Denise rushed over to stand next to Paul and me. Kat looked at me with concern. Emily asked in a whisper, "Can you fight?"

I shook my head imperceptibly.

Denise traded places with Emily and stood close to me. "Will you let me share some of the energy I stole from the demons? It feels odd, but it could help you."

I agreed and stiffened slightly when she leaned close to my neck and placed her lips on my skin. First a shiver followed by tainted energy infused me, making me hot all over. Denise sagged briefly for a second and said, "Sorry, I know it's gross, but it's energy."

I checked the hold on my core, comforted that it was still how it should be. The energy Denise gave me felt strange, but it stayed away from my core. I was grateful for it anyway, because otherwise, I'd have no chance at all.

Paul stepped back but didn't let go of my arm. I turned to look at him.

"I'm not leaving you," he said when my eyes met his.

"You have to. I can't worry about you and fight them at the same time."

Emily leaned over. "We need you to go calm down those pansies over there huddling under that tree." She pointed to their dates hiding from what we faced.

"If you don't leave, I'll turn you into a toad." Kat winked at me.

"Right," Paul said as if he didn't quite believe her. Kat raised her hand and wiggled her fingers quickly.

Some sort of power passed me. My skin tingled. It was probably a little spell to make the skin react, but Paul backed away. "Okay, I'll go check on the others."

"Smart man you've got there, Claire." Kat winked again.

I smiled and said, "Don't worry. We'll be fine." *Hopefully.* I looked back at the demons facing us. They hadn't attacked yet. Maybe they wouldn't. Since they'd seen what we could do, I hoped they wouldn't be too eager to fight right away. I wanted as much distance between Paul and them as possible.

As Paul retreated, Ugly Demon Boy sneered, "What, you gonna let a bunch of girls fight for you?" Kegan huffed but Ugly Demon Boy didn't notice.

Paul turned around briefly. When Kat sent another spell at him, he continued on.

"Weakling!" Ugly Demon Boy shouted at him.

"Shut up!" I shouted back at him. "Let's end this."

He bristled and stepped forward but the motion from a finger of the demon lord stopped him immediately.

The demon lord looked me over and nodded. "She is spectacular." His voice was deep and smooth. It sounded more enticing than it should. Almost something to be desired more than despised. He looked at Quinn first, and then at Ugly Demon Boy. Quinn didn't look at me, nodding instead at her master. Ugly Demon Boy scowled at me.

"I have come to take you with me, Claire. I haven't seen such potential in one since Quinn here." He reached over and patted her on the head like a pet. "You will be my new fortunate one." Quinn's shoulders came up as she ducked her head in submission. She looked pissed but didn't react more.

"If you decide to fight me, you will all perish. If you come with me now, I'll let these others go without harming them. You can trust me. I have so much to offer you." His voice called to me, making me want to agree to anything he asked. It was intoxicating.

Of course I wanted to join him. He was amazing. I looked at his form; his body was huge, strong, and perfect. He didn't have any of the ugliness of the other demons. He needed no second skin like the form Quinn used to fool the world. I stepped forward, longing to join him. Two hands took hold of my arms on both sides. I turned to look at who had touched me, seeing fear in the eyes of Emily and Denise. Someone whispered, "Don't move."

Who had spoken, and why I shouldn't move? He called to me. Desire for him pulled at me more than anything else I'd ever wanted.

My eyes feasted on the magnificent creature in front of me. He was gorgeous with all the desirable physical traits I'd ever thought were important in any male, all wrapped up in one perfect being. He smiled at me and nodded, encouraging me to come to him. The hands on my arms tightened. I tried to shrug them off. They held firm.

I looked back at the girls holding me again and pleaded, "Let me go to him. He's magnificent."

The shocked look on their faces made me pause. Kat said, "See him," as if it were a command. I looked back, seeing something else entirely where the gorgeous being had been. Hard, dark scales covered his muscular chest. His arms were still huge, but they were covered in spikes and calluses. His chin split down the center, ending in two sharp points. His teeth were too large for his mouth. Saliva dripped from them. His once enticing eyes burned into mine. He'd fooled me. I had longed to join him based on the beauty I'd seen. Seeing him for what he really was made my stomach turn.

He scowled when he realized I was no longer mesmerized by his image. "Come to me!" he demanded. The boom of his voice dug deep into my ears, piercing my mind. I wanted to obey him but fought against the desire.

"Very well. You have made your choice. You will all die." He looked to his four guards and nodded. They stepped forward as one and advanced on us. Those around me prepared themselves.

I checked my core, smiling when it completely surrounded me. It infused everything. I could transform into a wolf at any time. *Should I do it now, or wait to see if I can handle them in this form first?*

Kat conjured a shield that stopped them momentarily. A counter spell opened it, and they continued their march toward us. Denise raised her arms and pulled the energy from them. After a few seconds, something cut off her supply as if it had been severed by a knife. Denise wobbled a little before regaining her footing. Emily transformed her body into something hard, reminding me of metal, and ran forward. She hit the first one in the core. He swiped at her, knocking her into a tree fifteen feet away. She hit hard and took a moment to get back up.

Kat cast a spell. A large rock hurled toward another demon, hitting him in the chest. It didn't faze him either. She threw another one at a slightly different spot. It didn't access the core.

Kegan blasted them with air and earth. They walked through it without any apparent trouble.

We looked at each other, worried we'd never be able to do it against these larger, more powerful demons. Hitting them in the core didn't seem to make any difference. Could I even decapitate them? I felt for my core once again and began to transform. It came so much easier this time. I let it happen.

The demon right in front of me looked at me oddly when I stood as a wolf in the shirt. A low rumble rolled from my throat. He pulled back in surprise. I took advantage of that and jumped at him. As a full wolf, I was larger than my girl form. My weight knocked him back, but he wasn't as easy to overcome as most of the other demons. He started to rise before I could get a good hold on his neck. I slashed at him and tore a piece of his nasty flesh but couldn't get a grip tight enough to rip his head off.

While he was down, Kegan rushed forward to help me. The demon stood up and threw his hand at Kegan. He fell hard as if he'd been hit and took a while to get back up. Emily made it back to us and lunged at the demon, grabbing him around the waist and knocking him back to the ground. She raised her hands and brought them down to his chest. He grunted but didn't lose his power. I took advantage of his loss of breath and tore at his neck. Long moments later, I finally got him good and decapitated.

I quickly tried to assess who would need my help the most. Kegan and Kat fought one together. Denise and Emily each fought a demon alone. Denise was holding up pretty good. Emily had shifted into a wolf form and snapped at the demon before her. She was quick, but not quick enough. He kicked her in the stomach. She jumped away with a yelp. I lunged for his throat. He pivoted, causing me to miss. I took a chunk out of his shoulder, but he didn't seem to feel any pain from it. Regaining my footing, I tried again. He dodged me with no problem. Emily shifted back to herself with her hardened skin and assaulted him again. He tossed Emily away like she weighed nothing and came at me.

His speed was impressive, as if he could move from shadow to shadow like Quinn, but he didn't disappear. It was all his own power. I had a fraction of a second to decide whether to dodge him or meet his attack. The tilt of his head gave me an idea. I ducked as if trying to avoid him, but at the last second jumped at his throat.

Just as I clamped my powerful jaws, extreme pressure around my chest forced the air out of me. He tried to pull me away, but with my teeth securely in his neck, he soon stopped. Instead he squeezed harder, trying to crush me. I shook my head back and forth, trying to get it to dislodge. I didn't have a deep enough bite to make it to his spine. If I let go, I'd never have another chance to reattach myself before he thrust me away from him.

The demon's blood oozed from my mouth. I refused to swallow it. He slowly lost some of his strength as he continued to crush me. Or was I feeling a loss of sensation?

I hope he's dying and not me.

From the corner of my eye, I saw the other four working together to fight off the two remaining demons. I wanted to finish this one off soon and join them.

Frustrated and amazed that the demon was still standing upright as we struggled, I tried to reach him with my paws. My front legs were bound tightly as the demon crushed me to him, but my hind legs were accessible. I dug in, trying to find a good purchase. My claws slipped off his scaly body. The blood dripping from his neck wound made it even harder to find a good grip.

I squirmed, trying to get my teeth in deeper and find a good spot to rip at him with my claws. The demon teetered slightly but held his ground. I bucked harder. He didn't seem as sure on his feet this time. His neck gave way. I couldn't tear the head completely from the body with this bite.

The demon attempted a scream, but I'd torn out his windpipe. It gurgled and hissed. I took another bite, feeling the bones of his spine this time. I yanked quickly and felt it break. The demon collapsed forward, falling onto me.

My head hit the ground and it took me a few moments to realize he'd pinned me beneath him. It took me too long to free myself from his dead weight.

Ugly Demon Boy looked at me with a mix of hatred and fear. I almost jumped at him, but Kat's scream made me change my mind and charge toward her. A demon raised a wicked blade and was just about to bring it down on Kat. Kegan redirected the blade with a blast of air just as I slammed into the demon from the side. I didn't quite knock him down, but he stumbled. Emily ripped the blade from him.

I tore at his legs, trying to keep him from moving away as Emily lifted the blade up and swung it fiercely at him. She didn't get a clean shot but managed to imbed the blade into his shoulder. He roared in pain, striking Emily with his good arm. He tried to take the blade out of his shoulder. Kat hexed him and he was immobilized. Kegan threw more blasts of air at him, making him jerk and twitch. His knees buckled and he fell hard.

Emily regained her feet and took hold of the knife again. She tore it from his shoulder and swung a second time. This time she succeeded. His head fell from his shoulders and he crumpled to the ground.

All of us turned to the demon fighting Denise. She looked tired, offering a weak smile when we joined her. Her lips were covered with blood. Her eyes looked different. She'd bitten him — whether to drain him of his powers or poison him, I wasn't sure. He lunged for Denise, but Kegan forced him back with air.

"Hold him!" Denise shouted.

Emily grabbed onto him with her metal-like arms. I slashed at his legs to drop him. Kat immobilized him. Denise stepped forward, placing her hands on his chin and around the back of his head. She took one deep breath with her eyes closed, and yanked. A crunchy snap followed by a slight hiss cut off his scream. Denise threw the head away and jumped back to avoid the blood spurting from him. Emily hurried and threw the body away from her, joining Denise in her retreat. *How did Denise get that strong?*

We heaved a sigh of relief when it was finished, but it didn't last long. The demon lord clapped his hands as if he had enjoyed our performance.

"You are all brilliant," he said with a huge grin, making his face almost disappear with the size of his mouth. Quinn glanced at him briefly but maintained a cool control over her features. Ugly Demon Boy, on the other hand, stared at him with his mouth wide open.

"I must have you all," he said. "What must I offer to have you accept me?"

Quinn twitched slightly, but didn't betray anything. Ugly Demon Boy nearly choked on his words. "You aren't seriously considering giving them a second chance to join you?"

The demon lord looked at him, making Ugly

Demon Boy cringe and bow his apologies. Then he focused his attention on us again. "I will make you more powerful than any other. You will only be under me, and none other."

Quinn looked up with a flash of anger in her eyes.

I shook my head in disbelief. Growling at him, I tried to convey how unacceptable his offer was. I really wished I could speak in this form.

Emily looked the demon lord up and down. "We wouldn't want to look as ugly as you all do."

"No way," Kegan said. The others nodded in agreement.

I raised my head high and bared my teeth.

The demon lord's grin disappeared and he frowned at us. "So be it." Lightning quick, he threw a black fireball, hitting Emily squarely in the chest. She collapsed. Kat dropped to her knees and felt Emily's neck. Denise, Kegan, and I looked at her, fearful of her response.

"I can't find a pulse."

I growled in rage and charged him.

CHAPTER THIRTY-TWO

"Destroy the others. This one is mine," the demon lord commanded as he stepped forward to meet me.

Quinn hesitated. Ugly Demon Boy roared with glee and attacked. Denise and Kegan met Ugly Demon Boy while Kat took Quinn. Kat threw a hex at Quinn just before the demon lord took all my attention.

He threw a black fireball at me. I ducked just in time to avoid it. The scorching heat as it passed felt much worse than Quinn's fireballs. If it could take out Emily in her iron skin, it could kill me as well.

I searched inside myself, checking my core's power. The wonderful sensation of all my energy easily accessible made me feel faster, stronger, and more confident than a moment ago. I hoped it would be enough to stop the demon lord. I had always assumed we'd to fight him off together.

The demon lord sent fireballs at and debris me. I used my instincts to avoid most but couldn't dodge everything. Since the fireballs were more important to avoid, a few rocks and branches hit me hard enough to make me lose my footing. Bruises formed, but no broken bones. Yet.

He was toying with me. I snarled and attacked, biting his leg. His tough, spiked skin prevented any damage. I lunged at him again, using my claws. It was more like the scratch on the car at school than on skin. He was impenetrable. Would his neck be the same? Could I bite him there at all? If not, then how could I decapitate him? His core wouldn't be something we could touch easily. Over and over again I rushed past him, looking for a weak spot to bite or claw. Nothing.

His chest was covered with thick plates of dark scales. I jumped and scratched his face. He growled in anger but his wound closed almost immediately, leaving only a greasy smear behind. At least he wasn't completely invincible. If I could hold on long enough, maybe eventually I could stop him.

I glanced at the others. Kegan and Denise looked almost ready to finish Ugly Demon Boy off. He slumped over as if too exhausted to keep going. Kat struggled. Quinn had been commanded to fight, but it didn't look like her heart was in it.

A fireball slammed into me. Black spots clouded my vision as a ragged howl burst from my throat. It burned even worse than the ones during practice, and this was through my wolf skin. My fur burned away, leaving a scorched circle the size of a salad plate on my hindquarters.

I moved forward, limping slowly in agony. I wouldn't survive many hits like that. With each movement, I gasped in pain. The demon lord eyed me narrowly, seeming surprised again that it hadn't done as much damage as he expected. I stood up and faced him again, ignoring the pain. Sending extra amounts of my core energy to the wound helped mask the pain. It wasn't healed, but I could move more easily now.

A fireball formed in his hand. I lunged for him, jumping high at his face. He stepped easily to the side, avoiding me completely. He threw the black fireball at me, a glancing blow instead of straight on. The burn ran down the same side, but it only burnt off the fur, not getting deep into the tissue beneath.

Jumping again, I managed to take him in the chest with my full weight. It felt like hitting a wall, but he stepped back, stumbling to regain his footing. I grunted in satisfaction. I could at least make him move if I hit hard enough. I aimed my next jump at his neck. My teeth hit two separate areas. The back of his neck was covered in hard scales that didn't give way at all to my jaw pressure, but a couple of teeth sank into the flesh under his jaw line.

He hollered in pain again and grabbed at me. He pulled me off easily and threw me hard. My back leg cracked against a tree. I whimpered in pain and tried to stand on it. It luckily wasn't broken clean through, but putting any weight on it was excruciating.

Good thing I have three other legs to stand on. I wheezed out a laugh. That was something I never would have thought as a bonus to being a wolf.

Anger at this demon lord rose my hackles. How could he think that just by telling us to join him, we'd be all over it?

The demon lord looked at the others. He threw a black fireball at Denise. I yipped in alarm, trying to alert her to what was coming. She saw it too late to move and I braced myself to watch her death. Suddenly, a blast from Kegan knocked her to the ground. Ugly Demon Boy wasn't as lucky. The fireball hit him squarely in the chest and Ugly Demon Boy dissolved in a slimy puddle at Denise's feet. She squealed and scrambled back in disgust.

The demon lord growled a curse. He turned to me in anger, apparently thinking it was my fault it had happened. I ducked in time to avoid the volley of fireballs. I crawled away quickly, mentally preparing myself for the expected pain.

When it didn't come and the fireballs ceased, I looked up in shock to see Kegan and Denise facing him. Kegan gathered the elements he had control over, air and earth, using them to distract the demon lord.

He brushed the rocks and dirt away like they were flies. Denise tried pulling energy from him. A black snakelike beam left the demon lord and flowed into Denise. She gasped when it hit her and stumbled. The demon lord waved his hand and cut the flow from Denise. She staggered and fell to the ground, looking sick, as if she couldn't handle his energy.

He threw another fireball at her. It wasn't black this time, but red like the ones Quinn had thrown. He growled, and threw another one at Kegan. He easily brushed it aside with his air. Another fireball hit Denise in the shoulder, knocking her to the ground. She gasped in pain, but managed to get up. She wasn't steady on her feet, but was upright.

Quinn shrieked in pain. I whipped around, stumbling as my leg gave out. Quinn was no longer a demon. She looked human and weak. Kat looked stunned at the change. Quinn screamed again. The sound penetrated deep within me. I recognized it as a scream of joy. She was free. The hold of the demon lord was gone. We were close. He'd been weakened enough that she was free of him.

"Come to me!" Quinn shouted. She looked at each of us still standing.

"You dare betray me?" the demon lord said, his voice dripping with hatred.

"You are no longer my master." Quinn reached

353

for a fireball, but found nothing.

"You will not use my gifts against me."

Quinn looked terrified for a moment, but then she shouted to us. "The pentagram!" She reached toward Kat, closest to her, and a white light connected them. Her other arm pointed at Kegan. Another beam of light shot out. "Connect with the others!" she shouted.

Kegan and Kat looked terrified.

"Do it!" Quinn shrieked.

Kat reached toward Denise at the same time Kegan reached toward me. I felt the jolt as the beam of light entered me. Without conscious thought, another light left me and connected itself to Denise. Our bodies linked through this inner web of power. I felt invincible. My soul was complete. I had more power than I ever thought possible.

"Never!" the demon lord shouted. A ball of power slammed into Quinn's chest. He yanked on the energy still connected to him. Quinn collapsed, and the web of light vanished. I dropped to the ground as my own weakness caught up with me.

Struggling to stand, I caught sight of Quinn. Was she dead? The demon lord threw more fireballs at her, but Kat deflected them and sent spells at him. It only distracted him slightly. He continued his attack.

I approached him slowly, not wanting to alert him

to my presence. He was occupied with fighting the others. With the demon lord distracted, I made my move. I lunged at him from the side. I knocked him down, but couldn't get a good hold on his throat. When he placed his hands on my chest, my core began to dissipate. Was he draining me of energy? I abandoned my attack and moved away as quickly as my damaged leg would allow.

"You are becoming very annoying," he muttered as he stood up. "If you won't accept me as your master now, then you must be destroyed."

I growled at him, trying to convey how much I'd rather die than join him. He seemed to understand me anyway.

"Very well. I'll destroy your mind before your body. And then your soul will be trapped forever in my portion of Hell."

Fear gripped me, but I was completely stunned when he disappeared into the shadows. I looked around for him, but couldn't see anything.

Denise stepped closer to me, and we readied ourselves for the attack. The trees showed no signs of more demons. Nothing. Silence permeated the air. Not even a slight breeze disturbed the leaves or branches.

A terrified, pain-filled scream ripped through the air, shocking me into motion. *Paul.* I had never heard him scream before. I charged as fast as possible with a broken hind leg, ignoring the pain shooting through me with every step. Three other screams joined the next one. The demon lord was torturing the guys.

We burst through the trees to meet a horrifying scene. The demon lord had three of them floating in the air in various positions. Zach hung upside down while Caleb floated on his back in the air, flailing his arms. Paul was upright and bent in half. And James lay unconscious on the ground as if he'd been dropped.

Denise stretched her arm forward and pulled energy from the demon lord. It snaked away from him again. He snarled at her and cut the flow off. He let go of his hold on Zach, who plummeted toward the ground. My attempt to help was too slow. Kat threw a spell out and stopped him just before he hit the ground. She slowly let him down the rest of the way. Zach scrambled to his feet and took off running through the forest.

The demon lord swung Caleb around, letting him drop at the same time he dropped Paul. Kat was so focused on Caleb she didn't see Paul. I hurled myself toward him, sliding through the thick leaves. The weight of him landing on my back knocked all the air out of me. I couldn't move. Paul moaned and rolled over. When he saw me lying there, he shouted in surprise and jumped up.

I struggled to get enough air in me to breathe. Paul grabbed me by my ears and turned my face to his.

"Claire," he gasped. "Are you okay? I'm so sorry." He put his face next to mine and kissed me on the nose. I blinked in surprise. I'd seen him do that to Max. He leaned back and lifted my head to get a better look at me.

"Did I—" He started to speak but was cut off when the demon lord materialized behind him and grabbed him by the head with one hand, as if he were nothing more than a doll.

"Shall I dispose of him before your eyes?"

Paul's own eyes widened in fear as mine narrowed in anger. My core sent a burst of power through me. I was up and tearing into the demon lord before conscious thought caught up with me. Paul dropped to the ground.

I sank my teeth in the demon lord's neck. I would rip his throat open. I felt flesh, softer than the hard scales on the back of his neck, but I couldn't penetrate it. My bite didn't break the surface. I growled in frustration with my mouth still full of impenetrable flesh. If I couldn't decapitate him, how could we defeat him? His core wasn't accessible at all.

The only thing that damaged him in anyway was when Denise sucked his energy. She was our only chance. I had to talk to her. I cringed at the idea of letting go of my wolf form. I was so much stronger and faster this way.

Diving off the demon lord's back, I shifted as

soon as I let go of his neck. Hitting the ground on my feet, my cracked leg gave way. I fell forward, using my hands to catch myself. I turned to Denise and shouted, "Drain him! He's still too strong."

Denise nodded and tried pulling from him. He chuckled at her as he cut the flow again and again, each time she tried. Kegan sent blasts of air and rock at him. He deflected them, sending fireballs in return. I picked up a rock and threw it at him with all my human strength. The rock bounced off without bothering him. He turned back and hurled a fireball. I grabbed it with both hands and gritted my teeth through the pain of the burn. It was hotter than the one from Quinn, but I forced myself to hold it.

The energy consumed me. It flowed up my arms, changing the fireball from its red to a light blue that got brighter the longer I held it. My head jerked back, yet no screams could relieve my agony. The demon lord growled and threw more and more fireballs at me. I used the one in my hand to block them, stunned when the blue fireball absorbed the red ones.

Denise pulled more of his energy away from him. I distracted him so he didn't cut the flow as he'd done before. Denise panted with the exertion, but kept pulling from him. The fireballs grew less frequent. Powerful vibrations rocked my arms and body as the energy ball grew.

Chapter Thirty-Three

Kat shouted, "Claire, be careful! You're glowing!"

A pulsing orb surrounded me. A prickling sensation covered every inch of my skin. It hurt. I drew in ragged breaths, feeling myself struggling to contain all this energy. Any attempts to pull the fireball apart were stopped in order to block the fireballs the demon lord kept throwing at me.

"I can't stop!" I screamed in panic.

Denise moved closer to the demon lord as he focused his attention on me. As she pulled more energy from him, the black snake of power thickened. Kat tried casting more spells at him, but they either didn't make contact or they didn't bother him. Kegan lay on the ground, unmoving. *When did that happen?*

The demon lord noticed Denise as she crept closer and cut off her attempts at draining him. She staggered slightly but didn't fall. Kat held a shield up in front of her and Denise as they walked closer to him. The fireballs he threw bounced off the invisible shield. He disappeared for a second, and then reappeared closer to me.

I turned to keep him face to face with me, holding the glowing fireball between us. He stepped carefully around me, trying to get a better angle. He watched the fireball cautiously as if he didn't know what to expect from it.

The power it emitted nearly overwhelmed me. Desire to absorb it battled with fear that it would destroy me if I took that much at once. I extended my arms as far as possible, pulling my arms apart in hopes of defusing some of the power. It entered my palms and flowed up my arms. I screamed at the fire in my veins. My skin appeared translucent, showing me the energy as it flowed into every cell. My vision was more enhanced now than it had ever been with my core.

Everything around me became clearer. The demon lord's breaths as he circled me were steady and even. Denise and Kat's feet crunched on the soil as they approached us. James's slow breathing as he lay unconscious on the ground twenty feet away. Paul's heartbeat as he watched us. Caleb's sobs as he cowered under a bush. I could even hear Zach as he ran blindly through the forest.

My attention focused on the demon lord. It was time. Either I'd destroy him or myself, but it would finally be over.

I gripped the blue fireball tighter, stopping it from completely entering my body. I dug my fingers into the center of it, feeling it split in half as it tore apart. The demon lord gasped and stepped back from me slightly, but then he stopped and stood his ground.

I advanced slowly, keeping my eyes on him. The glimmer of fear in his eyes made me smile. I caressed the fireball in my right hand while holding the one in my left close to me. It felt good. I didn't want to let it go, but something inside me feared it at the same time.

With each of my steps toward him, the demon lord took a step back.

"What's the matter?" I sneered. "Are you afraid of a little girl?"

He scowled and took a step forward to meet me. "I fear nothing. Especially something as insignificant as you."

I cocked my head to the side. I tossed the fireball into the air and caught it. His eyes never left the blue orb. "Of course you aren't. You're the big bad guy, and I'm just … how did you say it? Magnificent? No, that's not right. You said amazing. No, that's still not right. Oh. now I remember. You called me spectacular. You wanted me on your side enough that you offered me everything. If I'm so spectacular and you must have me, don't you think I could beat you?"

"You are nothing without my influence." His nervous tone betrayed his confident words. "I would have given you more power than you can imagine, but in your current state, you are nothing."

I shrugged. "So I shouldn't bother doing this?" I leapt at him and slammed the blue orb into his chest.

He screamed in agony as the fireball entered him. His darkness changed. His scale-plated chest grew transparent. I could see deep within him and almost lost myself in the chasm that appeared before me. I held the fireball against him until it nearly flickered out, and then I brought the second one down to replace it. He screamed again, much more guttural as every inch of him shimmered as if he were disappearing.

The blue fireballs didn't last long enough. I reached toward my belly, hoping to pull something from me to finish him off. I felt extra energy in me, but I couldn't produce a fireball. My hands tingled. I put them together and willed a fireball to appear. A flicker of light appeared between my fingers just as the demon lord regained some strength and thrust me away from him.

He disappeared and materialized next to Paul, grabbing him by the throat. Paul struggled against him, using his hands to try to claw his way free. The demon lord chuckled and shook him. Paul stopped moving and fell limply to the ground.

Seeing Paul as he fell made something click within me. A combination of a howl and a cry of anger shattered the night. I transformed again. But this time it was different. I remained mostly human, yet my arms lengthened and my muscles increased. Hair covered my body, replacing my bare skin, yet the glow around me never disappeared. Every ache or pain was gone. I only felt rage.

I charged forward and slammed into the demon lord. I hit him repeatedly in the chest, one fist at a time. Blue fireballs continued to materialize through my fingers as I hit him over and over. Each strike caused him to diminish in size and form. His energy dissipated into the air in bursts of black sparks. The blue bursts of light coming from my hands devoured them.

I met his eyes for one final time, the fear and disbelief in them apparent. A grim satisfaction engulfed me. He'd messed with the wrong girl.

I raised both arms high and brought them down together in one last, power-infused strike. The final blast burst from him. He disintegrated in a shower of sparkling dust that disappeared before they hit the ground. I melted back into my true human form and found myself kneeling on the ground with my hands buried in the leaves. I raised myself up and immediately turned to Paul.

He lay still on the ground. I crawled over to him and placed my hands on him, searching for any sign of life. I tenderly touched his neck, feeling for a pulse, but my hands still tingled too much to feel anything.

"Kat!" I screamed. Paul had bruises all over his

chest and shoulders. His neck was swollen. I didn't dare move him to find any other damage. I was terrified he was gone.

Kat joined me in my inspection, feeling his neck. She gave it up and moved to his wrist to find a pulse. While she did that, I leaned in close to listen for a breath. A slight whisper of movement against my tear-stained cheek sent relief through me. *He's alive!* I pulled back in excitement and examined his face. Nothing had changed, but I had hope now.

"I feel a very faint pulse," Kat said, placing her hands on his neck. I watched her closely, swallowing the lump forming in my throat. Her face fell as she slowly moved her hands to the back of his neck. "I think it's broken," she whispered.

"No." I shook my head, not willing to accept it. "Check again."

She closed her eyes, and felt with whatever powers she had. "There is something very different here compared to right above and below."

"Can you heal it?" I asked. My heart clenched as I waited for her answer.

"I'll try." She reached into the bag that she somehow managed to keep a hold of and pulled out her other crystal. She placed it against his skin on the back of his neck next to his spine. I closed my eyes and begged. As she began chanting, the crystal changed from clear to a glowing red. She maintained it for a few minutes. Paul's breathing became more apparent.

"It's working!" I gasped.

Kat leaned closer and spoke more quickly. I felt an urgency with her words and willed her to heal him. Paul's eyelashes fluttered faintly, but his eyes remained closed. I grabbed his hands and squeezed them between mine. He felt cold. I wished I could make him warmer. An idea struck and I rubbed my hands together. They still tingled with the energy I'd absorbed so I touched them together lightly, hoping to make a small fireball. One just big enough to help warm him up. It fizzled out when I tried to contain the power to a minimum. I tried again and failed to hold it.

Kat's chanting became frantic. My gut clenched when the crystal cracked, then shattered, under the strain of her spell. "No!" Kat screamed. "I was so close, but I've lost it."

She put her hands under his neck again as a tear fell from her eye. "Claire, I'm so sorry."

I stared at her in shock. "Try again!" I demanded when her words finally sank in.

"It won't work without the crystal. I can't concentrate the power enough."

"What about the one you used on me?" I asked, looking around for it. She had tied it around my neck when she'd first healed me, but now it was gone. I had no idea when I'd lost it. I sagged down in defeat.

"The pentagram!" The power contained in that had been amazing.

"There aren't five of us anymore." Kat choked on the words.

I leaned over Paul and felt my heart break.

"He's still alive," she whispered.

"But he's paralyzed!" I shouted. "He can't be hurt. I've got to do something. He'd be fine if it weren't for me. I should never have gotten close to him. I knew something would happen if he were with me."

"This isn't your fault," Kat said softly.

"It is!" I screamed at her. "I should have stayed away from him. I could have just joined the demon lord and saved everyone. He'd have left you all alone. But now Emily is dead. Kegan probably is, too. Paul is paralyzed. It is my fault." I collapsed and rested my head on Paul's chest. His heart beat strong and steady. His breathing was good. But without his spine complete, he'd never move again. I couldn't let that happen.

"I have to do something," I searched Kat's eyes for any sign of hope. "Will you try again? Please."

Kat nodded, though she didn't look hopeful. She placed her hands under his neck on his spine and chanted again. I reached deep within myself, searching for that spark of power I'd absorbed. I would give that to Kat, to help her in her healing. She said she needed a more concentrated form of power. The blue orb I'd held in my hands was the most powerful thing I'd ever seen. If I could bring it out and share it with her, would it be enough to heal a broken spine?

Kat seemed weary as she chanted, so I whispered, "Keep going. You can do it. I'll help you." She closed her eyes as she continued.

I placed my hands over my heart and felt the glow form beneath my breastbone. I willed it forth. My hands tingled and then burned. I pulled them away from me. My core lightened as I drew the energy from myself. The ball glowed red at first, but after holding it between my palms and focusing on it, it turned blue. I concentrated on it and forced it to obey. I didn't want it too powerful where it would hurt Kat or Paul, but the power had to enter them in the perfect amounts. Small tendrils of power flowed from it as if blown by a breeze. I concentrated on one and linked my mind to it, willing it to move toward Kat.

It inched slowly. I rushed it, making it slip away from me. I snarled in frustration and started over, hoping Kat could keep it up as I tried again. I moved it more carefully this time and sighed in relief when it made contact with Kat's fingers. She opened her eyes in surprise at its touch. I whispered, "Keep going."

She nodded. The tendril of power increased

slightly as it left me and moved into her. She spoke more clearly now, as if she were totally refreshed. The blue orb in my hand pulsed, wanting to blend with her. I didn't dare let more join the power I was already giving her. Another tendril formed and reached for something to come in contact with.

I pulled it tight and made it as thin as possible while still trying to keep the one flowing steadily to Kat. Once sure I could maintain two separate threads, I allowed the new one to enter Paul. It touched his chest first, burrowing deep within his breastbone. I focused hard, determined to give him power and strength. He needed to have energy to help heal himself. Too much would hurt him.

From the corner of my eyes, I saw Denise approach. I focused my attention back to Paul and Kat, determined not to get distracted. When she knelt down next to us, I glanced quickly to see her laying Emily down softly next to Paul.

"Paul's not dead!" I shouted, angry that she'd brought Emily's dead body.

"Neither is she!" Denise snarled. She stood up and left again.

My joy at the news sent a burst of energy out. Kat gasped. I quickly smoothed it out and thought about helping Emily, but decided against it. She would have to wait. Right now, Paul was more important. Kat glowed with the extra power she received from the fireball. It made her dazzling. I couldn't look at her long. I looked at Paul instead and prayed that she could heal him. Kat radiated confidence. She was doing something good. But would it be enough?

I moved closer to Paul. My leg brushed against the bare skin of his arm. Power flowed through him from Kat and the tendril of energy from my hand. Soon the flow returned to him through my own leg, as if we were sharing our energy. I concentrated hard, focusing all my thoughts and consciousness on him being whole.

As Denise approached carrying Kegan, something in Paul shifted. The flow of energy through him didn't seem as halted. It flowed free and unrestrained. Kat removed her hands from him and the tendril of energy I'd been feeding her disappeared. I released the energy ball, feeling it return to my core, but the sharing of energy between Paul and myself took longer to fade.

I touched Paul's face, caressing him as my fingers moved to his neck. It was no longer swollen. The bruises that covered his body moments before were now gone. His pale skin glowed softly in the moonlight. He looked relaxed and comfortable lying in the leaves on the forest floor. I leaned forward and kissed him gently on the lips, feeling more emotions in that simple act than when we'd kissed at the dance.

He had entered my soul so completely in the last

few hours that I wondered how I could even maintain any sort of normal relationship with him. He was my other half. He brought me back to myself.

I looked at Kat and whispered, "Thank you."

She smiled softly. "You did most of it. I just directed where it should go. He'd never have made it without you."

I looked back down at him, still unconscious, and snuggled against him, laying my head on his shoulder. I shivered when the heat of his healed body touched my cool skin. My core was gone, released with the blue energy ball. Lying next to him, I didn't care whether I'd ever wake up again. I was exactly where I wanted to be.

Chapter Thirty-Four

I woke up in Emily's guest bed to the smell of bacon and eggs. Rising slowly, I felt strange aches and pains. Taking a moment to examine myself didn't reveal any visible damage. Even the shoulder where I'd been stabbed by the branch was smooth and perfect.

My stomach growled, encouraging me to venture down the stairs. A huge grin spread across my face when I saw Emily. She seemed no different than before. Apparently her run-in with the demon lord last night hadn't damaged her too much. If her mother hadn't been standing right there with a plate of bacon, I'd have drilled her about what happened after I passed out.

"So did you girls have fun last night?" her mom asked.

"Yeah, Mom, it was great." Emily winked at me. I tried unsuccessfully to cover a giggle.

"Where did you go after the dance again?"

"Caleb's house to watch a movie," Emily said.

"What kind of movie?"

"Oh, it was one with witches, werewolves, shape-shifters, vampires, and demons."

"Sounds scary," her mom said shaking her head.

"Yeah, in parts, but we handled it like big girls," Emily said, grinning wickedly. "We weren't nearly as terrified as the guys."

I barked a laugh at that. My hands clamped across my mouth at the sound. Emily just laughed, making me laugh harder.

Emily's mom smiled. "Yeah, guys like to act tough, but it isn't always so."

We nodded vigorously and piled our plates full to avoid further discussion.

When we had time alone, I asked, "What happened? I thought you were dead."

She shook her head. "I almost was. I managed to shift just before the black ball hit me. I think that's what saved me. I wish I'd been more helpful during your battle against the demon lord."

"I'm sorry he got you. You should have seen what happened when he hit Ugly Demon Boy with his black fireball." I shuddered at the way he'd melted, glad it hadn't been that way with Emily.

"What about Kegan? Was he hurt?"

"They said he was hit by a fireball, too, but it had less energy so it just knocked him out. It took them longer to wake him up." Emily leaned forward and rested her elbows on the counter. "I think Denise was really freaked about it."

Denise was crushing on him for sure. I just didn't know what Kegan thought of her after all this.

"Kat and Denise debated on trying to wake you up, but Kat insisted you be left alone. Then they argued about what to do with Quinn. Kat wanted to revive her, but Denise wasn't sure. We didn't know what she'd do now that she was free of the demon lord." Emily moved forward on her chair and continued, "When they finally decided to wake her up, Denise and I held her down while Kegan stayed poised to strike her in her center again if it seemed she would turn against us."

"What did she do?" I asked.

Emily smiled. "At first, she looked at us in fear, and then she asked what happened to the demon lord. When Kat and Denise described how you'd defeated him — very impressive by the way — she sighed in relief and lay back down in the dirt just looking up at the sky."

I raised my eyebrows in wonder. "So where is she now?"

"I'm not sure," Emily admitted. "She helped Kat wipe the memories of Caleb, James, and Zach, but Kat wouldn't let her do it to Paul. She thought Paul would be better off keeping his memory intact. Then she and

Kat worked together to heal you completely as well as Denise and Kegan. They also got rid of my headache. Once we'd taken care of everyone, including the limo driver, we tried to clean you up. All that blood and gore all over you was pretty gross." Emily shuddered. "You were passable — in the dark — but when we got to Caleb's house we found you something to wear instead."

"We really went to Caleb's?" I asked, confused at the purpose of still going there.

"Yeah, had to give the guys something to remember so they wouldn't wonder about what happened to their night after the dance. We couldn't wake you or Paul up so we took him home and decided to bring you here to sleep over so Kat and I could watch you. Kat went home a couple hours ago."

"How did you convince my parents to let me stay?"

"Imitated your voice and called your parents. Figured you wouldn't care. And then you wouldn't have to try to explain anything to them."

"Before we left though, Quinn thanked us all. She even came over to you and touched your head gently."

"So she's really free from the demon lord?"

"She must be. You apparently put an end to his existence. Quinn felt pretty sure he was completely gone, not just back to his realm in hell. She didn't feel his pull or his control on her anymore. She said she felt free."

"But is she still a demon?" While I was pretty sure we could stop her, I didn't really want to go through anything like that again.

"No, she's no longer a demon. She said she is now mortal again, though still a supernatural." Emily leaned closer. "Apparently, she was once a powerful witch. That's why she could teach Kat all those spells and stuff."

"I wondered about that." I nodded, trying to take it all in.

Emily watched me silently for a moment. As she got up to leave, she patted me on the shoulder.

"I wish I'd been able to see you defeat him."

I looked up at her and tried to smile, but I couldn't quite muster a convincing one.

"What's wrong?" Emily asked.

"I'm not sure. I just can't believe it's all over. Are we really going to be able to go back to being normal teenagers?"

"Who knows, but would you want to go back to how things were before?"

I thought about that and shrugged. "In some ways yes, but in others, no."

"We'll just take things one day at a time. We are different now. Probably more weird crap will happen to us, but look at what we survived."

I smiled at her enthusiasm, feeling much better about things.

"I'll let you be alone for a bit." She walked quietly from the room.

I felt strange. It was almost surreal. Emily's kitchen was clean and tidy. Little specks of dust floated in the air in front of me. The way they moved in the air looked so calm and peaceful. Nothing like the way the demons had burst into sparks or dust last night. Had we really done it? Would I ever have to do it again?

The doorbell rang, pulling me back to the moment. The door opened and Emily burst into giggles. She leaned back from the door and hollered to me. "I hope you don't mind some company."

I stood up and walked to the front room in time to see Paul step in the doorway.

A grin spread across my face. Paul's answering smile made my heart flutter. He lifted his arm and showed me a black leash. "Wanna go for a walk?"

I narrowed my eyes and asked, "Is that for Max, or did you have someone else in mind?"

Paul's eyes widened in panic when my words sunk in. He sputtered and said, "Max, of course ... He's in the car ... I'd never ... I mean…" Paul looked at Emily for support. She just shook her head.

I giggled and ran to Paul, wrapping my arms

around him. He hugged me tightly, making it hard for me to breathe. Eventually he let me go and pulled back enough that he could look me in the eyes.

"You will always be Claire to me. No matter what." He reached up and tugged my ear.

I smiled at him. "And you will always be mine." I stood on tiptoes and pulled his head lower. I kissed him in a way that didn't leave any room for argument.

Authors Note

Thank you so much for reading CLAIRE: Daimon High Book One

I hoped you enjoyed it.

Please consider posting a review or rating on Amazon or Goodreads. Reviews help spread the word. It's the best way to say "thank you" to any author.

If you have questions or comments, please feel free to contact me at laura@lauradbastian.com

Thanks for reading.

L.K. Bastian

Acknowledgements

I have been working on this series for so long, it would be impossible to name all the people who have had a part of this. My writing group in Tooele was key to getting me to keep working on this. Thanks everyone.

Facebook sparked the idea with a silly quiz to find out if I would be a witch, a vampire, a werewolf, or a shapeshifter. (I can't even remember what my results were) Thanks FB. You really are helpful to a writer.

My sister Angela has been awesome at helping me with issues I had with this story and being my cheerleader.

Lindy D was my go to beta reader for the whole series to make sure all the stories worked together and to ask questions about football.

Cindy has been my constant chat room buddy to commiserate with me when it seemed too overwhelming.

Jaclyn helped brainstorm so many of the magical and mythical things.

Juli, you rocked at all the edits on this monster project. Couldn't have done it without you.

And my own friends from High School that came to mind so often when I wrote this book. Thanks for making my High School experience so much better than what any of my characters have experienced.

Daimon High Series

About the Author

L.K Bastian is also known as Laura D. Bastian, depending on which genre she's writing.

This urban fantasy series started from an idea sparked on Facebook. (See, FB is totally helpful in writing.) It is slightly darker than her usual contemporary romance so she took her initials as her pen name.

Laura grew up in a small town in central Utah and now lives in another small town in northern Utah. She wishes she was daring enough to travel widely and go to all kinds of places, but because of fear and lack of funds, she writes of things she'd like to do, places she'd like to go, and people she'd like to meet. Or magic and powers she wishes she had.

She met her husband in college and together they are raising 5 children, a few pets, and a garden when the weeds don't overtake it all.